Eden-459

Eden-459

Martin J. Stab

GMA Publishing
Newburgh, Indiana

Copyright © 2002 Eden-459, Martin J. Stab, all rights reserved.

E-Mail Address: GMAPublishing@aol.com

ISBN: 1-59268-007-0

All rights reserved. No portion of this book may be reproduced, stored in a retrieval system, or transmitted in any form or by any other means- electronic, mechanical, photocopy, recording or any other- except for brief quotations in printed reviews, without the prior permission of the publisher.

This is a work of fiction. The characters are drawn from the author's imagination and any resemblance to any organization or person, living or dead is purely coincidental.

Credits: NASA, ESA, and The Hubble Heritage Team
         (STScI/AURA)

Acknowledgement: C. R. O'Dell (Vanderbilt University) and
                 L. Bianchi (Johns Hopkins University and
                 Osservatorio Astronomico, Torinse, Italy)

Cover By: Christina Gubbins
Manuscript Assistant: John Beanblossom

Printed in the United States of America

Dedication

To my wife Elaine, who became part of this novel through her love, support, sacrifice, patience and skillful editing.

FOREWORD

Naha Air Base, Okinawa, Japan.

It was a clear, warm mid-June night when my buddy Frank Fackler and I were standing on the upper sun deck of our barracks watching for aircraft. From that vantage point, we had an unobstructed view of the runway and the skies over the base.

At about ten o'clock, it happened. We experienced a *UFO* sighting.

"Look...what the heck is that...? Frank said. "Marty...do you see that?"

"Yeah Frank, I see it...holy mackerel...what is it?"

I was scared, grateful for Frank's presence. Despite borderline panic, I had a strong compulsion to keep on watching, but at the same time, I was prepared to bolt for safety. It was like nothing we had ever seen. I positioned my binoculars for a better look. We did not use the term "UFO," but we knew that we had witnessed something strange: A large, slow—moving, circular disk traveling in a northward direction over the base.

These were no distant blinking aircraft lights. Neither was it an unusual cloud formation or weather balloon. As communications specialists in the Air Force, we were exposed to many different types of aircraft, so we knew right away that something unique had traveled through the island's airspace.

It moved at an approximate speed of one hundred miles-per-hour at an altitude of three to four thousand feet. Its diameter appeared to be about one hundred fifty feet. No flashing lights, no antennae, no dome, no windows. The craft made no noise. Its surface appeared metallic.

While the object moved northward, we scaled a fire ladder to gain access to the roof which afforded a wide-open view. Since the craft was moving away from us, we had no fear of being detected by scanners or even *alien* beings.

It was thin and had a noticeable degree of reflectivity as it passed over the lights of Naha City. The height of the craft seemed to be less than five feet. We kept it in sight for about two and one-half minutes.

As the strange craft faded into the distance our adrenaline peaked. We hurried down a fire ladder to a staircase leading to the first floor where we found the barracks office phone. We had to tell someone in charge. We called the base control tower operator, Airman Bernard. I identified myself and reported what we had just witnessed.

"I didn't see anything," Bernard said, "but hold on while I check with our radar center." I expected to hear our fighter jets scrambling into action, or maybe the Base Commander's voice coming on the line. Or at any second, sirens blaring mobilizing frenzied troops to their battle stations.

Instead, Air Controller Bernard had only this to say, "Airmen, I hate to tell you, but the radar people have had no contacts at all for over an hour."

We were shocked and dismayed to say the least. Airman Bernard suggested we file an Unidentified Aircraft Report at Base Operations.

"Thanks anyway," we told him. How could we file a report on something we couldn't substantiate with physical evidence? We needed at least a radar report, a photo, or more witnesses.

We never did file the report, hoping to hear others talking about seeing the same thing, but no one ever came forward.

For weeks I spent my free time watching the night sky waiting for another sighting. I even purchased an 8mm camera just in case.

As time passed, my hopes began to fade. But then one night, there it was.

I had just returned to the barracks from a second shift tour at the Communications Center, and decided to relax in a chair on the second floor outside landing. I propped up my feet on the railing and reminisced about the first sighting. Since I was alone, I found the thought frightening.

Just before 1:00 a.m. I was about to call it a night when it reappeared: The same type of craft Frank and I had seen a month earlier.

In an instant the sighting catapulted my mind from a relaxed state to one of "fight or flight." My adrenaline level skyrocketed, my hair hackled, and my heart raced. Then my body froze as my mind calculated the best course of action.

There I was, sitting alone in the dark outside a building with no one else around, except...*what*?

Common sense asserted itself. No beams of light emanated toward me from the craft. It became apparent that the object took no notice of me and moved northward away from my position. Thank God.

After a few seconds, I stood up. My brain regained control of my body and my legs could again move at will.

Then I took the next logical step: I ran. Racing down the hallway, I thought it best not to look back. After reaching the stairway, I made it to the first floor in three or four leaps. Then I sprinted to the barracks office for the phone.

The Charge of Quarters was dozing off at his desk when I grabbed the phone to report my sighting to the control tower operator. Airman Bernard answered on the first ring. He sensed I was nervous and could hear my heavy breathing. He told me to relax and to tell him what I had seen.

I recounted the event as it happened. He put me on hold while he checked with three different radar systems protecting the air base.

"What's the matter?" the CQ said. "You look
like you saw a ghost."

After what seemed like hours, Controller Bernard said, "We've had no radar contacts for two hours."

Again, he advised that I could fill out an Unidentified Aircraft Report at Base Operations. I did not bother. Not without proof.

If only I had had my camera with me!

It escapes me 'till today how something so visible to the naked eye could avoid detection by modern aircraft radar.

During the sixties we never even heard of the word '*Stealth.*' Could it have been our military? Could it have been from another country? Could it have been extraterrestrial?

Since then, our space technology has carried men to the moon, sent robotic probes into the far reaches of the solar system, and launched sophisticated satellites into orbit around the Earth. During one Mars mission, we even scanned the planet and landed a remote-controlled Rover vehicle, which traversed the terrain and sent live video feeds of the Martian surface back to Earth.

It provided spectacular images of the surface to millions of people around the world.

Today, our Hubble Telescope provides us with spectacular and breathtaking images of celestial bodies throughout the Universe.

One of our latest projects under construction is a two hundred billion dollar international orbiting space station. Countries from around the globe are contributing scientific equipment, propulsion technology, environmental systems, and medical knowledge. Astronaut trainees are now preparing for the station's manpower needs which call for an outstanding team of well qualified, trained, and dedicated men and women.

In the future, we will undertake missions to faraway planets outside of our own solar system. These missions will embrace the next logical step in the evolution of science and mankind. Given the great distances to be covered, the rate of speed required will be phenomenal. The duration of these voyages will take many decades.

Can we accomplish this within the normal human life span? My answer is *yes*.

Chapter 1

At long last, the world united in a common goal.

Cooperation among the United States, Russia, and many other technologically advanced nations gave rise to the formation of a new International Space Agency. Its purpose—to use the world's combined resources to pave the way for superior achievements in space for the benefit of all mankind.

At the International Summit Meeting held in Geneva, Switzerland in the fall of 2009, heads of state from many countries met to discuss important worldwide issues. Among them: Nuclear arms, world hunger, global warming, space exploration and asteroid defense.

Attendees made significant progress on many of the scheduled topics—asteroid defense and space exploration chief among them.

This temporary brotherhood of nations resulted in a treaty, which formed a new space agency—the World Aeronautics and Space Administration—WASA. Its charter: To build an elaborate new International Space Station, prepare for deep-space missions, and develop an asteroid defense system, representing man's greatest effort in scientific inquiry and exploration of space.

* * *

In 2002, the United States Government sold New York's Governors Island, situated off the southern tip of Manhattan, to the State of New York for a nominal fee. A former military installation, it would now serve as a City University of New York Training and Education Center.

Following years of debate over what should be done with parts of the island unoccupied by the University System, in 2005 state and city officials agreed to make it the site of the city's New World International Convention Center. In addition, future plans for the island included the construction of a leading edge Global Science and Technology Museum.

In four years the design, development and construction of the island-bound convention center had been completed. Architects called it "a 21st Century marvel of innovative design."

The ballroom sized reception area carpeted in deep plush throughout held a large circular settee in the center. Smaller couches and chairs lined the perimeter of the room. Gilt-framed oil paintings depicting the Seven Natural and Man Made Wonders of the World hung on the silk covered walls.

An illuminated globe, eighteen feet in diameter hung suspended from its dome-shaped ceiling.

The main convention hall, awesome in its beauty and size could accommodate forty-two hundred guests. Offering state-of-the-art tiered seating—every soft cushioned red velvet seat had telephone and laptop computer line jacks available. Also provided were listening headsets adaptable to both interpreters and the hearing impaired. In addition, each seat had a small but practical fold-down tray, similar to those found on commercial airliners, which provided a convenient utility surface.

The immense stage was wired electrically as befitting the finest Broadway playhouse. The entire backdrop and ceiling converted to a large video screen for use with presentations and special effects. Acoustic specialists had been brought in to ensure balanced superior quality sound.

In addition to the main convention hall the center boasted two hotel towers equipped with world-class amenities and a luxurious, relaxed atmosphere.

A unique mini monorail transportation system had been built to provide fast and quiet all-weather movement between the island's many locations.

Spectacular views of the Manhattan skyline, the Statue of Liberty, and New York Harbor entailed but a few of the scenic perks.

The proposed future Global Science and Technology Museum was expected to highlight the world's richest display of man's scientific and technological achievements. Slated for completion in 2014 it would provide a valuable source of educational and historical enrichment for peoples the world over.

Chapter 2

11 January 2010
New York, New York
Front-page headlines blazoned:
The WORLD AERONAUTICS and SPACE
AGENCY—WASA—
To hold first official meeting today at the New World Convention Center, Governors Island, New York.

Incoming guests faced the city's full brunt of the winter's thirteen-inch snowfall, blustery howling winds and bone chilling temperatures.

On arrival at the Governors Island ferry terminal, adjacent to the Staten Island Ferry, guests encountered a small army of three hundred young, cold, shivering, but determined environmental and anti-space protesters. They climbed atop snow banks and shook anti-space placards with vigor bearing slogans from: "Save the Planet" to "Dollars for Education." Their loud chants, "Earth yes! Space no!" echoed as they attempted to obstruct the passageway into the terminal.

To keep the entrance clear a large contingent of NYPD officers had been deployed. Two dozen mounted police along with at least two hundred fifty police officers on foot maintained order. Sporadic pushing and shoving added to the palpable tension felt by the arriving guests.

Some protestors found themselves handcuffed and escorted to a nearby precinct house. As tensions peaked, police officers wearing riot gear used brute physical force to open a safe passageway to the entrance.

Meanwhile on Governors Island, the Main Convention Hall buzzed with activity in preparation for WASA's 9:00 a.m. meeting. Sound, lighting, and movie projection technicians performed last minute fine-tuning, as TV crews, media newscasters, cameramen and international press reporters took up their positions to capture the important historic event.

Piano-wire tight security by presidential-grade armed security forces had been established. Their alert eyes scanning the area—they remained poised and ready to react at the subtlest sign of trouble.

For months prior to the meeting, the FBI had been receiving credible warnings of anti-WASA activities. A number of environmental and anti-space activists sent letters and e-mail messages to WASA officials voicing their strong objections to the budgeting of billions of dollars toward space programs. Some of them contained wording so strong that violence could not be ruled out.

The ferry provided the only means to cross the harbor to the island with the exception of authorized helicopters. A temporary restriction applied to watercraft, which prohibited travel within one thousand meters of the site. The Coast Guard patrolled the island's perimeter and remained on high alert.

A final security checkpoint had been set up at the Governors Island Ferry terminal requiring guests to pass through metal detectors. All packages, luggage, handbags, personal belongings, and computers received thorough inspection. As a further precaution, trained security dogs checked every person and hand-held item.

One protester masquerading as a visitor might have made his way through security if not for a one hundred pound Black Labrador Retriever named Damien. The dog's incessant barking at the intruder's thick briefcase alerted security personnel. They pounced on him forcing him to the ground, kicked open his legs, pulled his arms behind his back and seized his case. Inside, authorities found a stash of tear gas canisters and smoke bombs.

The perpetrator screamed and spat while being shoved into a patrol car.

"Shut up and sit still, or you're going to need an ambulance," said one of New York's finest.

At 8:00 a.m., despite the discouraging reception at the terminal and the bad weather, invited guests filed into the Main Meeting Hall gazing in awe at the building's sheer physical splendor. Flags representing every WASA member nation were situated up stage.

The air throbbed with excitement as eager attendees awaited WASA's first public appearance, heralding man's quest for advancement in space travel and technology.

Space scientists declared, "the new organization was poised to serve as man's footpath to the universe."

At 8:50 a.m., the full assemblage took their seats. At 9:00 a.m., a hush came over the hall when a tall figure in a dark, fine tailored suit approached center stage.

The emcee Richard Martin took the podium. Illuminated by a soft spotlight he unfolded a large bright blue banner revealing the new WASA logo.

"Good morning ladies and gentlemen," he said opening his arms. "Welcome to our New World Convention Center."

Following enthusiastic applause he introduced the first speaker, Director of NASA, Henry Corbin.

The fifty-nine year old Corbin made a brisk entry to center stage in his motorized wheelchair.

The unexpected handicap quieted the entire audience.

Chapter 3

Corbin, an Air Force pilot during the Vietnam War, received the Purple Heart for injuries sustained during an attack on a North Vietnamese ammunition supply depot. His F4 Phantom fighter jet was hit by a surface-to-air missile forcing him to eject from his plane and parachute into the Gulf of Tonkin.

Hitting the water, he realized he had sustained severe injuries to both of his legs. His flotation gear prevented his drowning until a Navy Rescue helicopter scooped him from the water and took him to a hospital ship.

The swift rescue saved his life despite a heavy loss of blood, but could not do the same for his legs. They had to be amputated at the knees.

Following a long and painful recovery he returned to the States and was placed on medical leave giving him the time he needed to reach an important decision. He would never allow his handicap to become an obstacle to his ambitions. He convinced his commanding officer he could still be valuable in a non-flying assignment and was reassigned to an administrative post at McCord Air Force Base in Washington State.

He earned his MBA from Washington State University while completing his military commitment. The Air Force took notice of his keen intellect and interest in space sciences. Following a promotion to Colonel, he became the Director of the Air Force's Strategic Air Command's Missile Testing and Development Center at Vandenberg Air Force Base, California.

Corbin was a key player in the successful development and testing of the Air Force's first anti-missile defense system. His superb and outstanding organizational and business acumen later earned him a presidential nomination to the position of NASA Director. During his first three years, it became the epicenter of his world.

The most serious demands he made on his subordinates were efficiency and a solid work ethic—nothing he did not expect of himself.

He had an overpowering demeanor. His "what's next" attitude imparted a sense of urgency to every task at hand. To him, a *professional* was someone who had a true passion for his or her work. When issues arose, his was the first word and the last as well.

His aggressive personality thinned his patience with subordinates whenever they bucked his directives. He had been known to re-assign or terminate personnel on impulse in an effort to assemble the best mix of people to get a job done right.

His ironhandedness intimidated some, but garnered him a great deal of respect from his superiors. He could be relied on to get things done, but on occasion at the expense of another's hypertension.

Corbin's tough management style labeled him a bully. Not only did he fill his position at NASA, he wielded it. Whenever he visited project sites, his people organized their desks, hid their coffee cups, and spruced up their personal appearance. He was quick to criticize, but slow to praise.

Corbin's position as NASA's Director gave him the awesome responsibility of overseeing every facet of the agency's wide array of space projects.

He had a fervent interest in space and space flight. His strong curiosity in UFOs compelled him to keep abreast of sightings with inside Pentagon officials.

One of a small group with inside knowledge of the whole truth about the Roswell Incident of 1947, he knew Earth was not alone in holding intelligent life.

Seldom an easy person to get along with, the handicap built such deep resentment in him it caused a negative alteration to his personality. His family and close friends tolerated the change, they understood. But, on the job, it was a different matter.

When he first came home from rehabilitation he found his dependency on others a tremendous burden to bear. Always a fierce independent, now the simplest physical tasks became a challenge.

Corbin's adjustment came slow and hard with one serious backlash. He developed an ulcer. After counseling and much soul searching, he realized he had to make a choice. Keep his ulcer—or give it to others. He chose the latter. He became a master of the art of delegation. For those subordinate to him it was unfortunate because he also mastered the art of severe criticism, even for the slightest of transgressions.

He and his wife Madeline and their two children lived outside Houston, Texas his hometown, since completing his Directorship at Vandenberg. His religion and family meant as much to him as his job, and he seldom missed Sunday morning church services.

Madeline, the manager of a successful interior-decorating firm in Houston, adjusted her workload to her husband's and often joined him when he traveled. The Corbins cherished their time at home. Frequent family gatherings and Texas-style barbecues gave them a feeling of closeness and strength. It was during such private times that Henry might light up one of his favorite eight-inch cigars.

* * *

Approaching the podium Corbin gave a gentle nod to his wife sitting in the first row. He pulled himself up onto his artificial limbs sporting his ubiquitous cowboy boots, to stand at his full six-foot height, shook hands with emcee Martin, and assumed a commanding presence as he steadied himself with one hand.

He looked around and surveyed the impressive hall. Unabashed he presented the audience with his balding, two hundred-twenty-pound, broad-shouldered, Orson Wellesian visage. He tugged at his string tie adorned with a Silver Star medallion.

Corbin spoke in stentorian tones that riveted everyone and his Southern drawl pleased the ear. "Welcome, special guests, colleagues, and friends. I am honored to be here. I must say this place has everything I had hoped for...well, almost, since it was seventy degrees when I left Houston and I'm not at all fond of cold and snow."

A chuckle rippled through the hall.

"This new convention center is the biggest one I've ever seen. And now y'all know that's saying something, coming from a Texan."

Amidst the laughter, American voices could be heard as they explained his pun to foreigners.

"Back to business ladies and gentlemen, I am pleased to be here in New York for this special occasion. A lot of *folks* worked hard to get today's meeting organized. I want to thank every one of them for helping to make it possible.

"For starters, please direct your attention to the ceiling."

Projected high above the audience was a live video feed of the on-board shuttle astronauts orbiting one hundred sixty miles above the Pacific.

"Please wave to them so they know you can see them. I wanted them to participate in our conference," said Corbin, indicating the video projection on the ceiling. "How y'all doing?"

The astronauts responded with a thumbs-up, "Good morning to all."

"Ladies and gentlemen," said Corbin, "as of today we are all part of the New World Aeronautics and Space Agency—WASA."

Corbin exuded the self-confidence of someone dedicated to compensating for his disability by focusing on the positive attributes of a dominating intelligence and keen foresight. He could manipulate people with a charisma which both charmed and entrusted. At once, he commanded the assemblage's undivided attention.

"The cooperation to date by a multitude of countries in space technology has given us a great enhancement toward our resources for space science and exploration. We must continue these joint ventures not only with the Russian contingent, but also with many other member countries.

"We do not need competition. Instead, we need cooperation."

His address was interrupted by applause.

"To be effective we must combine our resources so that we do not waste or duplicate our efforts.

"With the formation of WASA, we have a powerful new tool for man's quest for intergalactic travel. I am pleased to announce that from today forward we will be capable of achieving unimaginable objectives in these areas.

"The benefits of our association are limitless. We will be able to make great strides in fields from medicine to metallurgy. Our new International Orbiting Space Laboratory, when complete, will hold as much promise for those on Earth as for those destined for interstellar travel. We now understand that the key to achieving man's full potential as a species is international cooperation."

Corbin took a sip of water and nudged his glasses up the bridge of his nose. "Allow me to give you a brief outline of WASA's plans for both our space station and future missions to the stars.

"First, we will build and launch into orbit all segments for our new space station. We will then utilize the latest innovation in shuttle design, the X55 shuttlecraft, which will carry our astronauts and equipment to and from the station. After the station's construction has been completed, it will begin its operation as a laboratory and spaceport. The full crew will be made up of fifteen astronauts and scientists.

"Second, we will construct a large and technologically superior spacecraft named the '*E-One*,' which will represent man's first serious attempt to travel to interstellar space with the ultimate goal of finding other planets suitable for human existence.

"Last but not least, we will deploy a crucial asteroid detection network at various locations in our solar system and beyond.

"We have taken our first step with the creation of WASA. It will no longer be a matter of a single country's accomplishment. From now on, it will be the people of Earth who share in the credit.

"And now, ladies and gentlemen," Corbin said, extending his free hand to the audience, "I will be happy to answer some questions."

A tall man in African attire stood up and adjusted his cloak.

"Yes, sir," Corbin said smiling and nodding his head.

"Mr. Corbin, what are we talking about here with regard to cost? And who is going to pay the bills?"

"The projected cost of the space station," Corbin said glancing at his notes, "is about two hundred billion dollars. Cost over-runs are not unusual, however.

"As for your second question, one of the benefits of organizing WASA comes from the even spread of expenses for the projects across the membership. That way we can reduce the financial burden of individual members.

"Smaller and less affluent nations would not be expected to fund WASA at the levels of the United States, Russia, Great Britain, China, Germany, France, and Japan. Nevertheless, their participation remains crucial to the big picture."

"May I ask one more question?"

"Yes go ahead," said Corbin.

"Why do we need an elaborate asteroid defense system?"

"I'm glad you asked that. At present, we lack the infrastructure and capability to protect ourselves from the potential of a catastrophic asteroid strike. Hundreds of asteroids, some of them quite large, cross Earth's orbit around the Sun each year. At present, we are powerless to detect or deter most of them.

"The United States, in fact, has an annual budget of only two million dollars for asteroid detection. This is not enough. It's sad that here and in other countries, we spend more money on syringes for drug users and condoms for teenagers than we spend on asteroid defense programs. We are pressing very hard for new legislation that will provide us with a great increase in the asteroid defense budget.

"Even if we detected a large threatening asteroid our chances of diverting it in time are quite remote. It is clear: We need a significant increase in funding for these programs.

"It is my hope in the near future we will be able to place early-warning detection devices on our moon and on other planets in our solar system. I trust that answers your question.

"I see another hand right here in front. Yes. Madam?" Corbin acknowledged a gaunt, pale-blond-haired woman in a severe business suit.

"Mr. Corbin, my name is Adele Roberts of *The Times London*. Sir, I have heard that controversial human experiments are planned once the space station becomes operational. Is there any truth to that rumor?"

"Ma'am," he said with a chuckle, "I haven't heard that one myself, maybe it just hasn't reached Houston yet."

The audience tittered.

"Allow me to answer your question in a no and yes fashion. No, we are not planning any experimentation with humans as specimens.

"For the yes, some human experiments are included in the overall mission plans.

"Nevertheless," Corbin continued, "it wouldn't be prudent or useful at this point to elaborate other than to say there is important medical research planned. Programs crucial to guaranteeing certain vital phases for future missions are also on the agenda."

Corbin wondered when the time came for complete revelation of the mission charter, who in the audience might remember the evasion.

Ms. Roberts had another question. "Sir, may I ask if what you are referring to may be related to future deep-space travel and possible use of cryogenics?"

Corbin smiled. "Ms. Roberts," he said, "we have nothing to hide." He choked on that one..."Our reasons for work in these areas do point to future space travel, but when you ask about cryogenics, well, the only frozen specimens we plan on having on board are peas and carrots."

A loud giggle erupted from the audience while Ms. Roberts wasted no time sitting down, castigated.

Corbin wrapped things up before he was confronted with questions that might ask confidential details about sensitive experiments.

"Ladies and gentlemen, again, thank you."

Chapter 4

Corbin then turned and sat back in his wheelchair. He waved as he rolled off stage.

Emcee Martin approached the podium again, put on his glasses, looked over his notes and began, "Ladies and gentlemen, it gives me great pleasure to introduce someone who is no stranger to most of you at NASA and other space agencies around the world. He is the director of the Rocket Propulsion Research Unit at the German Space Research Center in Munich, Germany, and has taken personal responsibility for the research, development, design and construction of many of our present-day technological innovations in the area of rocket propulsion.

"He will be working with WASA to overcome some of the great challenges that are sure to lie ahead. Ladies and gentlemen please give a warm welcome to Dr. Oswald Werner."

Werner, an average five-foot, eight-inch balding gentleman with a middle-aged spread, made his slow walk to center stage to ample applause. He placed his notes on the podium and tapped on the microphone as he looked up and gave the audience a slight, but confident smile.

"It is wonderful to be here in New York for this special beginning and I thank Mr. Corbin for inviting me," he said with a heavy accent.

"When we made travel arrangements, my wife Ursula reminded me of her fear of flying. I told her not to worry. I have booked us on the Concorde. That will reduce your suffering by three hours."

An impressive picture of the Concorde soaring above the clouds appeared on the expansive backdrop at the rear of the stage.

"What you are seeing," he said, turning and pointing to the screen, "is an example of a machine which produces great levels of power and speed. That is what we will need for future deep space missions."

Werner then displayed a diagram of a typical current-day rocket engine.

"The engine design shown on our screen has been employed for many missions in recent years. It uses liquid fuels combined with liquid oxygen. It provides a thrust range into the tens of millions of pounds and has fulfilled our power needs to date. However, it will not be adequate to power the space vehicles we plan to build in the near future.

"We could make them larger and more powerful, *ja*, but to do so could exacerbate the pragmatic concerns of weight and spacecraft control. That is the problem we have been working on at our research unit in Munich.

"Our engineers have designed a rocket motor which is quite different from what you observed here," Werner said pointing to the visual. "In fact, different from anything ever seen before."

He then projected a diagram of a new engine alongside the current design on the backdrop screen. "What you are viewing for the first time is an innovative rocket motor we call the *Synchronous Ion Nuclear Exchange Reaction Engine*, or *SINERE* for short. You can see by comparison, the SINERE engine is about half the size of the conventional rocket motor and in fact, weighs less than half of the present design. The most exciting aspects however, are its power output and the type of fuel used."

Dr. Werner used his laser pointer to demonstrate.

"The top portion houses the electronics that control the engine as well as the electrical power schemes. The second portion, or mid-section, holds expendable fuel which represents one component needed for the engine's burn phase. Ah...this will surprise you. The expendable fuel is water. Yes, water."

The audience could be heard murmuring in disbelief.

"I understand your amazement," said Werner, "but allow me to explain further. Water, or H_2O can now be broken down into pure hydrogen and oxygen using our new and innovative molecule-separation system. The hydrogen and oxygen components are divided and then each stored under pressure in ballast tanks. The hydrogen is used as fuel for the motor, and the

Eden-459

oxygen provides replenishment of the main storage reserve for the ship's crew.

As you know, water is plentiful, safe, and even more important, it can be found in many places throughout the galaxy. This gives us a great advantage during long-term voyages.

"The third section contains a small, but powerful nuclear reactor. Because of security restrictions, I cannot give you specifics about the reactor, but I can tell you it is quite safe and represents a total revolution when we consider its innovative design."

At the mention of a nuclear reactor, the audience became animated. Whispering could be heard which reflected their trepidation at the thought of such immense power and destructive potential being implemented for rocket power.

Dr. Werner gave them firm reassurances of the design's safety and asked for their continued attention. They acquiesced.

"The fourth, or nozzle section," he continued, "works in conjunction *mit* the third. Hydrogen gas is fed into an ionization chamber and exposed to laser beams, which causes the hydrogen molecules to become agitated. The molecules are then bombarded with high levels of gamma rays from the nuclear reactor in unit three.

"The resulting ignition when the ionized hydrogen molecules ignite causes an extreme high-energy burn. The reaction generates an incredible amount of thrust. In fact, a SINERE engine the size of the one described here is capable of producing well over one hundred million pounds of thrust.

"So far, noise is the biggest problem we have encountered. The noise level emitted by the engine in a burn mode can be deafening." Werner broke into a small smile as he pointed upward and said, "That, however, will not be a problem in space."

The next large-screen image showed a SINERE engine in full-burn mode evidencing its long, colorful and brilliant exhaust trail.

Dr. Werner took a sip of water. "I must tell you I am very pleased with our progress to date. We have prototypes in testing as I speak, and the reports are promising.

"Well, there you have it. Our new technology, when developed will enable us to lift much heavier loads into orbit, and when the time comes, give us the power levels needed for travel into deep space at ultra-high speeds.

"I hope you have found my presentation exciting. And now I open the floor to a few questions."

A gentleman close to the stage raised his hand straight up and looked around before standing. "Dr. Werner, I am impressed with your presentation. Can you please tell me how long we could expect the SINERE motor to be able to provide power with a full fuel load?"

"*Ja,* this is a good question. We have estimated a full burn with a maximum fuel load will last for over three months, even longer at lower power settings."

The same gentleman continued. "With such unbelievable power and reserve, wouldn't the ship's attainable speeds be quite high?"

"Yes," Werner said. "And ultra-high speeds will be needed for long missions. We have calculated the optimum safe velocity in space to be about five hundred thousand miles-per-hour.

This may sound quite fast, but it does not even come close to the speed of light, which is about six hundred seventy—one million miles-per-hour. *Und,* oh, excuse me—*and,* don't forget we will need to slow the ship down when the time is right, which will again require large amounts of power." Werner asked, "Does that answer your question?"

"Yes," the gentleman responded—but not at all sure.

Dr. Werner called on a woman toward the rear of the hall who gave a brisk wave of her hand. "Yes madam, you have a question?"

"Dr. Werner, will we ever be able to travel at the speed of light? Also, compared with the price of current rocket engines, will the new design cost more?"

"To answer your first question Madam, I do not see that happening in our lifetime. It may be a theoretical possibility, but please understand that we are far from certain what will happen to a crew and its ship at *light speed.*

"In answer to your second question, we have calculated that the initial funding requirements for the SINERE engine will be somewhat higher, however, that will be offset by its versatility and much lower operating costs.

"In addition, we will have continuous long-term reliable use from our new design. So, yes, the initial expenditures are higher, but over the long run, they will in reality be less. And remember, the expendable fuel used—water—has a far lower cost and will be safer to handle than the rocket fuels used today."

"Thank you, Dr. Werner," the young woman said and took her seat.

Dr. Werner removed his eyeglasses, straightened his papers, and closed his notebook.

"I think that is all I can say at the present time and I thank all of you for your attention."

Werner then nodded to the audience, turned, and walked away from the podium as emcee Martin again moved toward center stage to announce the final speaker.

Chapter 5

"Ladies and gentlemen," Martin began, "our next guest has some exciting things to share with us. In all probability, most of you have never heard of him, but his work in the new field of Astro-Engineering and Design has become well known in the space industry. His renowned knowledge and skills have been used during many NASA design projects to date. His superb achievements have earned him a strong reputation in his field. Let us all give a warm welcome to Dr. Rutger Bogort of Denmark."

Bogort, a small man dressed in an ill-fitting gray suit, took rapid little steps to the podium.

"I am happy to be here in New York," he said, "and hope to be able to stimulate even more excitement about our projects today."

He broadcast a wide smile as he ran his fingers through his tousled hair, then wasted no time and began.

Bogort signaled to the technicians to turn the lighting down. The meeting hall became enveloped in eerie darkness.

He clutched his remote controller causing the hall's immense ceiling to burst into a radiant backdrop of spectacular images of bright stars and colorful celestial bodies, which left the audience breathless as they experienced the illusion of being in outer space.

Conference attendees reacted with delight at the sensation of "being there." Bogort manipulated the controls and caused the image to move about, which added a sense of disorientation and even dizziness.

"Above," he continued, "we see what is called outer space. We can observe millions upon millions of stars.

"Out there we don't have a north or south, east or west, and there's no up or down. No gravity can be felt, leaving the human body in microgravity—a weightless state. Space provides no breathable air, so we must bring our own.

"As you can see, beauty abounds, but let me warn you, unless you have the proper equipment you will not survive."

With that sobering thought, the audience became still and quiet.

"Survival is the primary challenge of being in space. If just one small baseball-sized meteor traveling many thousands of miles-per-hour struck your ship, your voyage would end in disaster."

Just as he said that, several bright flashes of light streaked across the entire ceiling's starry scene. The audience winced from the unexpected visual-effect as it took them by complete surprise.

"Ah," Bogort said, "you see what I mean? That one just missed."

The startled audience regained their composure as they listened to the soothing strains of *The Blue Danube Waltz*. Then from the rear of the hall a large spectacular object began to appear among the myriad stars above.

It had eight round modules connected by what appeared to be spokes to a larger center module in the middle. Underneath the center module an attractive light blue *WASA* logo could be seen.

Dr. Bogort activated a sound track. A multitude of on-board activities could be heard taking place inside the craft.

"Ladies and gentlemen," Bogort said raising both hands over his head toward the visual, allow me to present to you for the first time, our New International Space Station."

The riveted audience murmured with conversation and then a tremendous applause broke out.

"You are now observing what the new International Space Station will look like once orbited and assembled above the Earth."

Aiming a laser pointer, Bogort said, "Allow me to demonstrate the various parts of the station and identify each of its components in the order they will be lifted into orbit and assembled."

He began a lengthy explanation of the workings of the space station, the size and function of each module, and how and when each segment would be lifted into orbit and connected like an immense jigsaw puzzle.

"Now that I have described the new station, allow me to begin its rotation."

The overhead image began to rotate.

Oohs and ahs emanated from the audience.

"Ladies and gentlemen, I have given you a rudimentary description of how the station will be built. The countless technical issues are too numerous and tedious to mention." It was then Dr. Bogort asked that the lighting be turned back on as he adjusted his glasses.

"I welcome any questions you have."

Several sets of hands went up.

Bogort surveyed the group, "You there, on the aisle," he said pointing to a woman in a red dress.

"Doctor," she said, "it appears to me the station is designed more for future space missions than for current scientific and experimental needs. Is that true, sir?"

"Yes it is, but that does not mean future voyages are the station's only charter. It will have an elaborate onboard experimental curriculum to follow for several years before being used for pure space efforts.

"We have a lot to learn before we can travel aboard a spaceship deep into our galaxy. Most of the learning required will take place aboard our orbiting laboratory."

Bogort looked around for additional questions. He nodded his head toward a woman in the fourth row with her hand raised.

"Doctor, are there any plans to include weapons of any kind aboard the station, and if you are at liberty to tell us, will there be a military dimension to the mission?"

"Weapons? Let me start by saying at the present time we see no need for on-board weapons. However, I cannot say that will hold true for ships engaged in deep-space voyages.

"Second, there are no military objectives for the orbiting space laboratory. In fact, there are no military plans attached to the entire space program, now or in the future. Any weapons included in a future space mission would be included for defensive purposes alone."

"Defense? From whom or what?" asked the woman.

"Madam, we have no specific threat in mind," said Bogort. "We will be traveling into unknown space and to carry armaments would be a practical and prudent consideration."

Bogort's remarks constituted blatant deception, but he hoped the audience would never know.

"I will take one more question," Bogort said, with the expectation he could answer it with complete truthfulness. "I see a hand right here in front of me. Yes, sir?"

"Dr. Bogort, various parts of the space station are quite large. How will we be able to lift them considering their weight?"

"Sir, the thrust level needed to lift the parts into orbit will be acquired by using the new SINERE rocket motor presented to you this morning by Dr. Werner. We will also employ the method similar to that used during the launch of the present day space shuttles—by attaching the parts to the sides of a rocket.

These initial launches will be unmanned. The rockets will carry the segments up and insert them into a preplanned orbital position and by remote Earth Base commands, will be released. A short time later, we will launch a crew using our new X55 shuttle to rendezvous with the segments for their attachment.

"The X55 has the unique ability to liftoff from traditional aircraft runways. It too will be outfitted with the new and powerful SINERE rocket motor. In addition, the new shuttle will be capable of carrying heavy payloads of equipment and supplies.

"I hope I have answered your questions." Bogort said.

"Yes, thank you," the gentleman said.

"Ladies and gentleman," Bogort said turning toward emcee Martin acknowledging the end of his presentation, "I have concluded for today. I am confident you have found it both interesting and informative. Thank you very much for your kind attention."

Chapter 6

The emcee took the microphone and invited the guest speaker panel to center stage for one final appearance. The audience stood and gave a hearty applause.

Martin then gave the microphone to Director Corbin who offered a few parting words from his wheelchair.

"Ladies and gentlemen, we have had an exciting and informative discussion, haven't we?"

The audience applauded.

"Now my friends and colleagues, I have the honor of presenting to you what we call back in Houston, our Top One Hundred Team."

Outfitted in bright blue WASA jumpsuits, the entire astronaut candidate training class for the New International Space Station proceeded to line up behind the guest speakers.

"Our team represents what an international team should be," said Corbin. "I have come to know each and every member on a personal level. They are the best of the best and we should all feel proud and privileged to have them as our astronauts and future space travelers. They are a diverse group. Yet despite their differences, here they are all the same."

"*What would they say if they knew the real ancestry of two of our Top One Hundred?*" Corbin thought to himself.

"I believe them to be the finest, best-qualified, most dedicated and bravest group of professionals we could ever hope to find for the manned-space missions to come. Each of them is critical to the successful attainment of our goals.

"As our space station takes shape, these are the people you will observe assembling it.

"Working with Earth Base at Houston, you'll hear their voices as they perform their day to day assignments. Soon you will have the capability to chat with each of them via the Internet from anywhere in the world by connecting to our WASA web site."

Corbin raised his hands, palms outward, and waved to the assemblage.

"That's all for today's meeting. I look forward to others like it in the months to come. Thank you."

Chapter 7

Following the meeting, WASA Director Corbin and Doctors Werner and Bogort held a special press briefing in a private conference room. In attendance were twenty-two major domestic and foreign reporters.

Introductions and a light lunch having finished, Corbin poured a glass of water, sat erect in his wheelchair and asked for their attention.

"My friends, these are exciting times. Our undertaking though expensive, no longer exceeds our realm of capabilities. Our panel shared new concepts with us today. Some that I am sure both intrigued and even startled us. I want to make it clear, however, that we believe we can and will achieve our goals. We now have the superb machinery and manpower in place to accomplish them.

"Although rather sensitive issues exist at times, we feel confident we can put forth the information you are seeking in a reasonable fashion. Our sincere hope is that it will enable you and the people of the world to comprehend the urgency of our timeframes and implementations.

"I'm sure y'all have things on your minds, so I'd like to begin by saying that we look forward to answering your questions with complete candor. "Who's first?" he asked smiling.

A tall, austere reporter stood up in the back and introduced himself.

"I am Bertrand Leroux of the Paris News Syndicate," he said, "I have interviewed many officials from my country and learned they have serious concerns about the billions of dollars the international community is planning to spend on space exploration."

Corbin and the other panel members raised their eyebrows in anticipation.

"Several polls taken by my country's media," Leroux continued, "indicate that over seventy-percent of French citizens are not ardent supporters of WASA's plans.

"The polls also reflect popular doubt as to what good can come from deep space missions. Last, they show the French people feel it is more important to have WASA's proposed billions of dollars used to clean up the environment, research cures for diseases and stop global warming."

Corbin sat rigid in his wheelchair and rolled his eyes upward. "Do we have a volunteer to address the gentleman's comments?" he said.

Leroux's commentary caught the panel off guard since they had just left an enthusiastic meeting attended by pro-space representatives from all over the world. And the last thing they expected was a dissenter.

No one came forward. Corbin decided to take it himself. He maneuvered his wheelchair close to the microphone, hovered over it and spoke straight into it.

"Mr. Leroux, before I respond, may I ask a question of my own."

"Yes," Leroux said with obvious impatience.

"Sir," Corbin said, "what is your personal opinion regarding WASA's plans?"

Leroux fidgeted, gesturing to the audience in an attempt to elicit sympathy. His face turned a bright red. "Gentlemen, I think that spending so much money on space programs is ridiculous.

"We have countless meaningful projects here on Earth that need our money. I have already mentioned them. But isn't it my time to ask the questions?"

Leroux's attitude irked Corbin. "It's apparent you came to our briefing with your own personal opinions," Corbin said.

He stared into Leroux's eyes. His first instinctive reaction was to blast Leroux with both barrels, telling him what he thought of his self-serving statement. But realizing that the Press wielded extreme power, Corbin knew he had to tone down his response. He tried to reign in his anger along with his impulse to lash out.

Eden-459

"I'm certain that your political friends in France would have used normal diplomatic channels instead of this occasion to express any unpopular sentiments."

"Forgive me," Leroux said, "but isn't this an open Press briefing, *Mister* Corbin?"

"*Mister* Leroux," Corbin said, "let me put it to you this way, if your government had serious objections to WASA's agenda, they wouldn't have needed *you* to tell us. We have an embassy in Paris which forwards communications of this nature to our Department of State."

The other reporters stared at Leroux, expecting a response. But instead, Leroux grew even more red-faced as he slammed his briefcase shut, knocked his coffee cup to the floor, and stormed out of the conference room.

Corbin, unfazed by the discourse, leaned back in his wheelchair and continued without pause. "May I have the next question, the gentleman waving his hand, there in the back row?"

"Mr. Corbin, my name is Kiomasa of the *Japan Times*. How do we know that using a rocket engine with a nuclear component will not pose any danger?"

"I'll give that one to Dr. Werner," Corbin said. "Dr. Werner?"

"Mr. Kiomasa," Werner said, "the designers of the new SINERE rocket engine have done scrupulous testing using a full array of scenarios. We have also built a fail-safe system into the engine. No release of radiation can take place without activating a unique shutter feature.

"The shutter has electro-mechanical mechanisms that are controlled by the engine's main logic circuitry. In addition, there are radiation-monitoring devices built into the reactor section. In the event of a crash either on land or water, the shutter will automatically close and lock. Once the shutter enters into a safe-lock mode, no radioactive release of any kind can occur.

"Also, it cannot be reactivated without trained personnel and case-specific equipment. They alone would have the knowledge and tools required to deal with the procedures involved.

"Our laboratory tests to date have resulted in a one hundred percent acceptability rating. So, please rest assured it is safe."

"Thank you," Kiomasa said, "but I remain skeptical about using nuclear fuels in our atmosphere. I hope we can develop less dangerous high energy propulsion engines without the use of nuclear reactors."

"I understand your concerns, but let me assure you Mr. Kiomasa, it is safe."

Mr. Corbin then acknowledged Sam Blatenberg of the *Chicago Sun Times.*

"These missions will take decades to complete," Blatenberg said. "How do we solve the problems of an aging and dying crew?"

"Okay," said Corbin, "that *is* a tough one. So far, we have not been able to resolve it. It is a serious concern, which has many implications. If you ask me whether it is achievable, I say yes, but when you ask how, that is something we have yet to work out.

"You see, even if we find a way to get a crew to their destination, we will never be able to get them back within a normal human life span."

"Mr. Corbin," Blatenberg asked, "are you telling us our astronauts will be taking a one-way journey?"

"Yes, without a doubt."

"Why would anyone want to volunteer?"

"That would be a difficult decision for anyone to make," said Corbin. "However, we already have a number of qualified personnel who have shown a sincere interest, and I'm hopeful we can obtain the number needed for our mission.

"There *are* some alternatives. For example, in the beginning we could use robots and remote controlled spaceships as a way of testing deep space and planetary environments as we have been doing with the Mars and Venus probes. We can also build stepping-stone colonies at various places in the galaxy.

"We have no simple answer for this challenge at present, but we are working on it."

"Thank you, Mr. Corbin," Blatenberg said.

"Who's next?" Corbin asked.

A reporter in the middle of the room spoke up. "Gentlemen, I am Natasha Kruchenska of *Itar-Tass* in Moscow. I am interested in knowing how much control over WASA the United States and other governments might have."

Corbin accepted the question. "Ms. Kruchenska, as you know several major governments are participating by budgeting public funds for our programs. These funds are crucial to WASA. We, therefore, have an obligation to account to these governments. They have a sincere interest in our work, and the bottom line is— those folks are paying for it.

"They do not, however, tell us in any direct fashion what to plan or do. We have to be realistic here. If we decide to engage in a program found unacceptable and therefore unsupportable, the issue would be reviewed and finally settled to mutual satisfaction.

"We must avoid the possibility of any participating government withdrawing its financial backing. To date, that has not happened and we are sincere when we say that we hope it never will. Oh, by the way Ms. Kruchenska, are you aware that Russia has supplied us with twenty percent of the manpower needs for our program?"

"Oh...I *see* Mr. Corbin," Kruchenska said, "I was not aware the number was that high." She sat down with a smile. It was obvious she felt happy over that revelation, and began jotting a few notes on her pad.

"I regret that now we have to draw our briefing to a conclusion," said Corbin. "But before you go I want to thank you for your questions and enthusiasm. It is too bad that Mr. Leroux left early. Had he stayed he would have learned our intent was to inform the public—not debate WASA's motives or merits. We shouldn't have had to defend it here."

Corbin thought he handled Leroux in an effective way, but a fist to the jaw might have been more satisfying.

"I look forward to seeing all of you again."

Martin J. Stab

When the last of the reporters made their way out of the briefing room, Corbin and his panel of speakers were relieved that it went well. Just enough information had been disseminated without exposing the entire mission plan.

Chapter 8

May 2012

Excitement ran high at Kennedy Space Center, Florida. The scheduled launch of the first two segments for the space station would take place in two months.

Engineers, technicians, and support personnel performed numerous final equipment inspections in preparation for the launch.

3 July 2012

Director Corbin arrived at Kennedy Space Center to oversee each and every project detail.

By mid July following the successful lifting of all needed segments, the new X55 shuttle would make its first scheduled launch into orbit. Seven special astronauts had already been selected for the mission. They would rendezvous with the launched segments and begin the station's construction.

* * *

The astronaut chosen as Mission Commander was thirty-nine year old Colonel Phillip Bennett of Stockton, California. His trip into orbit would be his fourth. In the past, he served as a crewmember and co-pilot aboard three shuttle missions. Prior to his astronaut training, he completed a stint in the Air Force as a test pilot.

Bennett's wife Eva, also a former military pilot, entered the Astronaut Training Program entertaining the idea of accompanying her husband on a space mission in the future.

* * *

They met at a football game at UCLA while attending college, and hit it off right from the start. Eva found his warm personality, blue eyes and good looks irresistible.

Phil's five foot seven inch frame prevented his making the school's football team, but he did manage to qualify for soccer. He developed strong playing skills, but there too his relatively small physique placed him as a lightweight. He did get some field experience on occasion as a seldom-played substitute, however. Despite his lack of playing time, he worked hard at the sport, and was liked by his coach and most of his teammates.

During the final match in the fall of his senior year, Phil managed to get into the game as a substitute for an injured player. The game was tied when his shining moment arose. With skill, he tackled the ball away from an opponent and headed straight for the goal. It looked as though his effort would decide the nail-biting game as the clock ticked away the last minute. He moved the ball down the left touchline at full speed when he met a six foot one defenseman who did not just spoil his attempt, but gave him a broken leg as well.

Of more concern, was the concussion he suffered the previous year when he slammed heads with another player. That injury had caused the chronic migraines that would remain with him for many years to come. The fact he had to lie on his Air Force medical questionnaire regarding his migraine problem disturbed him, but he did it anyway. He believed his condition to be temporary.

Eva, a transplant from Oregon, could not think about entering a beauty contest, but she was cute, smart and had a quick wit.

Phil and Eva had a strong relationship, but for one thing. Phil's pre-college life posed something of a mystery to Eva. He became secretive when she questioned him about it, as though there was something sinister in his past.

He acted that way toward everyone, not just Eva. Whenever she brought up the subject of his childhood, he made tactful moves onto something else. When she asked about his parents and suggested she meet them, he would drum up excuses as to why that could not happen.

She feared that for some reason he did not want her to meet his parents, but was afraid of hurting her feelings by saying so. For two years, all kinds of negative thoughts entered her mind and festered.

They did, however, want the same things in life, shared similar values and discussed marriage and having children someday. They spent hours talking about their careers and their life together.

Eva and Phil planned to marry soon after he graduated from college and joined the Air Force. Despite her happiness about their promising future, he refused to discuss his earlier years, which left her perplexed. She told Phil it was not fair for him to have secrets. She believed she deserved to know everything about him no matter what it was, and that she loved him enough to overcome any problem.

One night in Eva's apartment after finishing dinner, they firmed up last-minute wedding details. Eva hated harping on the same old issue, but with reluctance, she brought it up again.

"Phil, are your parents at least coming to our wedding?" she said trying to be firm, but instead cried out of frustration.

"I'm sorry," Phil said, "I am, but it doesn't look like they'll be there."

"If I don't get an explanation as to why," Eva said, standing up with her hands planted on her hips, "then there might not be a wedding."

Chapter 9

As Phil agonized over telling Eva with openness who he was, he shared his predicament with another.

A similar scenario played itself out in Rochester, New York—the finale to something that took place years before at Roswell, New Mexico.

* * *

The 1947 Roswell, New Mexico crash of an alien space ship, which became the U.S. Government's highest-profile UFO cover-up, faced complete unveiling.

The military had downplayed details of the incident and made public statements offering "weather balloons" as their official explanation. Just as in a murder, however, where just the victim and the perpetrator know the whole truth, here the military and two lone alien *survivors* of the crash shared the secret.

In July of that year, residents close to the crash site along with hordes of news-hungry reporters had their doubts concerning the government's balloon story. Witnesses observed many speeding military vehicles and personnel converge and cordon off a wide area around the site.

Why did they stop visitors from entering the zone? Why did soldiers point weapons at anyone who tried to gain access to the area? Why all the fuss and feathers for mere *weather balloons*?

The military could not prevent all the binocular-holding outsiders from spying on their mysterious activities. Army soldiers outfitted with biological hazard gear and carrying Geiger counters, arrived at the site. They rummaged through and collected crash debris—bits and pieces of unknown material, and incredibly two *alien* bodies. They wasted no time transporting everything aboard canvas-covered trucks to a hanger at what was to become known as *Area 51*.

Eden-459

Despite the military's efforts to shroud their activities, the following day workers at Area 51 leaked information to family and friends. They told about how the government recovered parts of a crashed space ship and the bodies of two alien travelers.

A special team including medical doctors and scientists placed the deceased aliens into an isolation chamber for study. After determining there were no known hazards associated with handling the bodies, they performed extensive autopsies. More than three hundred photographs of the aliens' external features and internal organs were taken.

One deceased alien, a pregnant female, offered scientists a unique opportunity for anatomical and physiological study.

The beings from outer space appeared human. They measured about five feet tall and had large, dark brown eyes. Their ears and noses looked similar to those of humans, but a little smaller.

They had dark hair and opaque fair skin while their oral cavities were identical to those of humans. The aliens' muscle tone seemed somewhat atrophied. Their external physiology and sexual organs also appeared similar. Tests revealed their blood chemistry to be comparable to humans, though lighter in color.

A surprising discovery showed the pregnant alien's fetus had neural pathways to its mother's brain via a second umbilical cord.

Another important revelation had been made when they measured the density of the aliens' brains. The findings revealed them one-third greater than that of humans.

The most striking external oddity observed—they had six fingers on each hand.

The overall opinion of the expert medical and scientific teams was unanimous. The aliens did not seem to possess any significant differences from humans, other than their appearance of slight malnutrition.

After autopsies had been completed and tissue samples taken, the military transported the alien remains to Wright-

Patterson Air Force Base in Ohio. There under heavy guard, they placed the bodies into top-secret cryogenic storage for future study.

The Army Air Force Command at Fort Worth, Texas feared the incident had the potential to cause mass nationwide panic. Also, there would have been hordes of curiosity seekers and Press attempting to enter Area 51. Security would have become a major nightmare to handle.

It became clear that secrecy would have to be maintained at all costs. Top military authorities gave urgent orders to quell Roswell's Public Information Officer's statement, which disclosed, "A space ship had crashed in the desert." Under strict orders from Washington, they concocted their fallen weather balloon theory.

A short time after the crash, something startling came to light. A local rancher who lived ten miles from the crash site found two strange balloon-like parachutes on his property. He called the Army base to report his discovery.

The military dispatched a special team of personnel accompanied by trained bloodhounds to establish a perimeter around the landing site. They soon discovered tracks that led them to believe two additional alien travelers had managed to eject from their ill-fated ship and land safe, or at least alive—on Earth. The tracks led away from the ranch into an area of small hills.

Evening had fallen when search dogs at last led the military squad to a tiny natural cave formed in the side of one of the hills. Their searchlights scanned the cave's damp and darkened rocky interior just as faint guttural sounds and rustling could be heard.

All of a sudden, they came face to face with two huddled, injured alien creatures. The hounds began barking and in an instant three of the soldiers raised their weapons and prepared to fire, and would have, had not their lieutenant intervened. "Hold your fire men!" he ordered, "they're unarmed!"

The wounded and weary travelers sat with their knees under their chins, arms wrapped around their legs. Their unusual large dark eyes stared up at their captors. The aliens, who appeared paler than human Caucasians seemed calm, even curious.

They looked to be in pain, judging from the rips in their tight-fitting, one-piece spacesuits. The search party could see exposed flesh wounds drenched in what looked like reddish-pink blood.

The aliens did not speak. They started to stand up at a slow pace and held out their hands, palms upward in a universal gesture of peace. When they stood to their full height of about five feet, they just barely reached their captors' shoulders. Their bodies appeared thin and six graceful fingers tipped their long and slender hands. Their oval faces had high, chiseled cheekbones, small noses and thin lips.

The soldiers lowered their weapons as their fear level subsided. They just stood shaking their heads in awe.

"We will not hurt you," the commanding officer said. "Do you understand?" he asked, signaling a universal sign of peace with open and extended hands.

The captives looked at each other and bowed their heads to the squad. In perfect English, they introduced themselves as interplanetary travelers, and added they had been well versed in many Earth languages on their home planet.

All sense of threat and fear left the soldiers as they beheld with wonder the diminutive visitors. They lowered their weapons.

Four soldiers wearing protective biohazard gear assisted the two aliens out of the cave. Unable to walk steadily, the aliens were helped into an Army vehicle, which took them to an isolation chamber at the Army Air Force base near Roswell.

The military used the Area 51 publicity to disguise their true mission: Interrogating the two survivors.

After being examined by medical experts and scientists, the two were judged to pose no physical threat to Earth or its populace.

They gave their names as Luxor and Antar and went on to explain that they came here as explorers from a planet at the near side of the galaxy to gather information about Earth and its nuclear technology. Luxor explained that the recent nuclear explosions they detected in Nevada sparked their leader's desire to investigate the area.

They made assurances of their peaceful motives and that they had been participating in a scouting mission, one of many that had been occurring for over fifty years.

Luxor and Antar knew a return to their planet was impossible. The bulk of Earth's technologies had not yet evolved to a level comparable to theirs. Stranded, they came to the inevitable realization that assimilation into Earth life was their single option.

The United States government realized something also: The future of Earth could be assured technological and militaristic superiority with the help of these two amenable aliens.

An urgent strategy had been developed and a conclusion reached. Luxor and Antar would be given human identities and backgrounds, placed with surrogate families hand-picked by the government, schooled, and allowed to live and flourish as earthlings. The plan was discussed in detail with the aliens, who having no other options, accepted.

Luxor had been placed with the Bennett family in Stockton, California and Antar with the Andersons in Rochester, New York. Separation of the two aliens added to their security and that of their host families.

For some reason they had no objections to being apart.

Chapter 10

Antar's surrogate family, Robert Anderson, a physics professor at the University of Rochester and his wife Mary Ann, also pursued an interest in textbook writing.

Some of Professor Anderson's projects involved consulting work for the Pentagon in the development of military weapons.

The government knew they could be trusted to take adequate care of Antar and assist him to complete assimilation into Earth's society.

On the day of Antar's arrival, Professor Anderson went to the airport and waited for him at the arrival gate. He looked for a man wearing bandages on both hands, concealing Antar's extra appendages.

When Antar met his guardian, Anderson did not find his appearance unusual. In fact, other than the bandages and a facial scar on his right cheek from a deep cut he suffered bailing out of his ship at Roswell, he looked like any other passenger.

After greetings, they drove from the airport to Anderson's affluent home in the suburbs where Antar was introduced to Mary Ann. He was then shown his room and new surroundings.

Antar spoke perfect English and Anderson felt confident introducing him to friends and neighbors as his nephew from Maryland who had come to Rochester to attend college.

When dinner was over Professor Anderson took Antar to his study where they could speak privately. Antar found himself quite at ease with the professor. They sipped wine, a new and pleasant experience for the little alien, and discussed their lives and what the future might hold. Their conversation shed light on Antar's reasons for coming to Earth. He held nothing back from his guardian, or so it seemed.

Professor Anderson brought the conversation around to Antar's home planet.

"The people of Sadarem are peace loving and happy," Antar said, "you could call it Utopia. Long ago they exhibited great bravery and risking their lives, volunteered to travel from my companion Luxor's planet to Sadarem in the hope of beginning a new life."

"What compelled you to go back to Luxor's planet?" Anderson asked.

"In a routine manner, we exchanged our knowledge and culture," Antar explained—but lied. "The leaders of Sadarem wanted to be as cordial as possible toward Luxor's people because of their strong desire to build a more *galactic society*."

"I see," Anderson said. "What can you tell me about Luxor's home?"

"They are unusual but good people," Antar said without much conviction. "Maybe when we work things out I will feel better about them."

"Work things out?" Anderson said a little mystified. "What do you mean by that?"

"It is a long story. Do you mind if we discuss it another time?" Antar asked, evading Anderson's question.

"By all means," Anderson responded, backing off for the time being.

Despite Antar's evasiveness, Anderson felt comfortable with his alien guest. He had no doubt the next few months, until Antar left for college, offered one of the most exciting experiences of his life.

Meanwhile, Luxor's surrogate family, Dr. Thomas Bennett and his wife Lucy in Stockton, California, provided him with a rich cultural environment. Dr. Bennett was a former scientist in government service at Roswell and still took on an occasional consulting assignment.

He had been a Pentagon insider and held the highest-level security clearance. He understood what the government wanted him to accomplish as a surrogate and had agreed to accept Luxor into his home.

Eden-459

Luxor was flown from Washington D.C. to Travis Air Force Base near San Francisco, California. Upon arrival, a government vehicle drove him to Stockton to meet the Bennetts.

When Luxor got out of the car at his new home, he saw the Bennetts, broad smiles on their faces, standing on the porch of their opulent ranch house, accompanied by their two Chocolate Labs.

The sight of the dogs delighted Luxor and he stopped his approach to the house just long enough to drop to one knee and summon the dogs. They bolted to his side, tails wagging, and then proceeded to lick his face with joy. The Bennetts enjoyed watching the romp and to no surprise, became captivated by their new arrival.

The preliminary greetings finished, Dr. Bennett asked Luxor to join him for a walk. He felt a pleasant stroll might afford a good opportunity to share information in a relaxed atmosphere. Luxor revealed his purpose for traveling to Earth to his guardian and surrogate father.

"Antar and I traveled as students learning about the galaxy," Luxor said. "When we departed on our journey to your planet we were not told by our superiors the true purpose of the mission, which failed at Roswell. It was later during our voyage to Earth that we learned its true purpose was to gain information regarding the nuclear capabilities your government possessed."

Dr. Bennett became engrossed in the conversation.

"My leaders were desperate for that information," Luxor continued. "As a non-aggressive civilization living a peaceful existence, we needed a way to defend ourselves against planetary outsiders threatening my planet, Xeron. We had no experience with weapons of mass destruction and planned to glean knowledge from Earth in that capacity."

Luxor paused for a response from Dr. Bennett.

"We are a peace loving people also," said Dr. Bennett, "despite the wars and hostile actions, but why didn't your leaders communicate with our government and just ask for help?"

"That sounds straightforward," said Luxor, "but think about what you are asking. How do you suppose they might have treated us? We did not want to risk exposing ourselves to probable harm, even elimination. Do not forget, we needed information about nuclear weapons, not human lifestyle."

Bennett was consumed with questions, but felt he had to go slow. He did not want his guest to feel pressured or interrogated. He thought perhaps a query about Luxor's companion Antar might seem less intimidating.

"Tell me something about Antar," Bennett said, "I'm curious about your co-traveler as well."

"Antar didn't come from Xeron," Luxor said. "There is something about him I have always been suspicious about."

"Suspicious?" Bennett said.

Luxor did not want to prejudice his host, but did feel at ease with him and decided to explain as much as he could without compromising his integrity.

"Perhaps I am wrong, but I feel he may have a mission of his own," Luxor said.

"Why?" Bennett asked. "What makes you think such a thing?"

"If you knew anything at all about his planet, Sadarem you would understand," said Luxor. "Their people are heartless, evil, and destructive. They are capable of anything. Even though Antar told me he left Sadarem because of his people's hostile tendencies, I always feared his allegiance was split between the two worlds."

"Can you elaborate?" Bennett asked. "For instance, where is the planet located?"

"Sadarem's position in my solar system is similar to Mars's position in yours," Luxor said, as he looked up to the heavens. "It was the first planet colonized by my people. However, we made a mistake when we sent our worst people there."

"Your worst people?" Bennett asked.

"Yes," Luxor explained, they were sent there because of their crimes and lack of morals. My leaders never expected them to survive, but they managed to flourish and multiplied their kind at a phenomenal rate. Unfortunately, their evil proclivities increased as well."

Bennett listened with intent. Australia's Botany Bay came to mind.

"After the Sadaremians developed a strong military they planned to return to destroy Xeron's population and take control of the entire planet."

"That explains why your people wanted our nuclear technology," Bennett said. "Do the Sadaremians have nuclear capabilities?"

"No, just like Xeron, they do not have the raw elements needed for nuclear weapons. But they do have something just as destructive," Luxor said. "They became masters of many hideous types of biological weapons. Some of them have the power to wipe out an entire world in fewer than two weeks."

That revelation both intrigued and frightened Dr. Bennett, but he realized there was nothing he could do about it at that juncture, if indeed anything could be done. His only recourse was to sit tight on the information.

He was most curious about one obvious fact however. "How are your people able to travel such great distances from one planet to another?" Bennett asked.

"We have advanced our technologies in that area quantum leaps further than you have. I am not an expert in all the scientific principles we employ to travel about the galaxy, but I do know we have developed anti-gravity machines. When we synchronize them with the gravitational properties of other celestial bodies, it gives us the capability of attaining a velocity close to the speed of light."

"Luxor, are you aware of how valuable this information could be to my country?" asked Dr. Bennett. "Has the government attempted to ascertain whether or not it would be possible to build an alliance with your planet?"

"Yes I am aware of the possibilities," Luxor said. "When I was debriefed at the Pentagon, I was asked many questions of that nature."

"Did they signal a desire to try to help you get back to your home planet?" Bennett asked. "Perhaps even to attempt to communicate with your people?"

"Yes," Luxor said, "officials proposed that idea, but you must understand my leaders believe our ship was attacked and destroyed by a hostile and fearful military at Roswell. So far, I have not been able to communicate with my home planet to explain it was just an accident."

"I understand," Bennett said. "So what do you think they'll do next?"

"Sooner or later my people will send search and recovery ships to Earth to check for survivors."

"That's logical," said Dr. Bennett. "But wouldn't they expect us to try to destroy those ships as well?"

"No, because they have the ability to cloak their ships in a force field rendering them invisible to your detection techniques. In addition, if they decided to land they would appear human enough, enabling them to blend into your society undetected."

Bennett came to understand that his guest was more than a casual visitor. "Imagine cloaking devices, force fields," he thought. He knew the Earth would be in severe trouble given the wrong set of circumstances.

More to calm his own nerves than information gathering, he soon changed the subject. "I see," Bennett said. "Tell me Luxor, how do your people know so much about our civilization?"

"Besides visiting your planet for many years," Luxor said, "we have been listening to your radio signals. That is how we learned your languages."

"Luxor," said Bennett, "I hope you don't think everything you heard on the radio was real."

"Of course not," Luxor said. "But we did find those programs amusing."

Bennett chuckled. "Oh, do you mean *The Lone Ranger*?"

"Yes, and *Tom Mix* too," Luxor said, as he laughed—a warm and gentle sound.

"Luxor," said Dr. Bennett, "what do people look like back on your home planet?"

"Look like?" Luxor asked. "Can you be more specific? I am an example, am I not?"

"I'm aware your people appear similar to humans except for minor differences. You are evidence of that, but do you have people of color and different physical features?"

Luxor smiled. "I think I see what you are asking," he said. "You want to know whether or not we have people with different colored skin like you do here on Earth. Is that it?"

"Well, I guess...yes."

"I find it peculiar when I see how much you Earth people dwell on things like that. But, in answer to your question, we do have people of different color. Some have pigmentation matching yours—some dark, some yellowish and some even have a green tint to their skin. But unlike you people of Earth, we ignore such differences. In our society it is mental stature and moral backbone that elevates someone, not physical things like color of skin or other meaningless characteristics."

Luxor stopped to take a closer look at a salmon-colored rose growing on a bush next to a fence, and then turned back to Dr. Bennett.

"I want to talk to you Dr. Bennett," Luxor said, "about something the people of my world found most curious." He had Dr. Bennett's full attention.

"One of your scientists put forth a theory and attempted to convince your inhabitants that an evolutionary process took place which caused humanoids to appear on your planet. If I am correct his name was Charles Darwin."

"Why yes, Luxor," Bennett said. "There is such a theory. Don't tell me it's wrong?"

"Do you believe in that theory?" Luxor asked.

"No, not as it's put forth, but it would be enlightening to know how Homo sapiens came to be."

"I can assure you the theory is incorrect."

Bennett was thunderstruck. The Theory of Evolution: Refuted. He could not contain the flurry of thoughts and questions that swirled through his mind.

"Go on Luxor, tell me more," Bennett said. "I want to know everything you know." Bennett stood riveted to the spot. He wondered how many other beliefs Luxor could debunk?

"What happened in actuality was that our planet, and others, sent your so-called *Homo sapiens* to Earth," Luxor said turning to face Bennett. "That is why you have differences in skin color and physical characteristics."

"That's astounding," Bennett said. "I've heard that hypothesis before, but not from an alien," he chuckled. "What was the real purpose for the migration?"

"That is simple to answer Dr. Bennett," Luxor said. "At that time the Earth was unspoiled and held many possibilities for successful colonization."

"I can believe that, but who on Earth now are linked the closest to the people of your planet?" Bennett asked.

"What is unfortunate for the world," Luxor said, "is not many of them are still living."

"But who are they?" Bennett pressed.

"They are your *American Indians*."

"You must be joking," Bennett said. "Aren't you?"

"No, I am not," Luxor said with finality.

Bennett wanted to hear more, but they had reached the house, and just then, Lucy opened the front door. Bennett would have to save any further inquiries for a later time.

Lucy smiled, waved to them and said, "Dinner is ready." They entered the dining room where she had laid out a beautiful spread.

"My wife baked homemade bread and chicken pot pie for dinner." Bennett said. "Are you able to digest these things?"

"Oh, without a doubt," Luxor said, "we have fowl on my planet as well. In fact, there are few differences in our diets. The atmosphere and soil on Xeron are much like yours and yield similar plants and animals. Besides, I am hungry."

Bennett and Lucy both laughed. They invited Luxor to sit down, then bowed their heads and said a prayer of thanks. Luxor followed their example.

"Let's eat!" Bennett suggested.

Luxor had a good appetite. He did not speak as he ate and on occasion, smiled at Lucy to show his appreciation for the meal. Following dinner, she offered them an ice cream dessert topped with chocolate syrup. Luxor enjoyed it so much, he asked for a second helping.

As the months and years passed, Luxor and Antar adapted well to their new environment. It was not always easy for them, but despite their separation anxiety from leaving their home planet, they assimilated into Earth society. They even learned to understand human emotions. What later proved unfortunate, however, was Antar embraced the negative ones.

The single constraint they faced was implemented by the authorities—the truth of who they were, where they came from, and for what purpose, had to remain secret for the present.

Before disclosing their true identities to anyone, Luxor and Antar's motives had to be evaluated, and deemed necessary by the U.S. Government. If they gave permission, it would be government personnel responsible for the secrecy and management of the aliens' files who could make the disclosure at a location designated by that agency.

In time, both Luxor and Antar married and each fathered a son. Luxor's son was named Phillip Bennett and Antar's son, William Anderson. The boys appeared quite human except for the scars left from the surgical removal of the small nubs that were once the sixth fingers on each hand.

When Phillip Bennett announced his plans to marry and William Anderson neared graduation from college, their fathers requested permission from the government to reveal their origins to them.

After much deliberation, the government assented. Their alien military advisor at the Pentagon, General Peter Williams, coordinated the time and place of disclosure, which took place two weeks later.

    General Williams ordered special agents to visit the aliens, at which time they received instructions to be passed on to their sons Phillip and William.
    The young men would travel to the Pentagon to meet General Williams for strict controlled access to top-secret files. There they would be told the complete details of their fathers' extraterrestrial origins.
    Phil Bennett had at last received the support he needed to unravel the mystery for Eva.

Chapter 11

Phil and Eva planned a Memorial Day outing at Avila Beach on the California coast. The day provided the perfect opportunity to prepare Eva for a revelation, which could alter her life forever.

During the preceding week, he rehearsed what he had to say, but it never seemed to come out right. However, that was not what he feared. He knew he could get the words out, but it was the thought of her reaction that brought sweat to his brow.

As the two walked hand in hand along the surf, Phil took Eva by her shoulders and turned her to face him.

"I spoke to my father. He understands how we feel about each other and about our plans to marry." Phil saw uncertainty in Eva's face, and understood her dilemma.

"And what else, Phil? The suspense is killing me," Eva said. She could feel her pulse race.

Phil knew what he was about to say had elements of mystery as well as a frightening aspect. He needed to assure Eva without adding untoward stress.

"He knows how difficult it's been for you not meeting him and my mother. But, he plans to change that soon."

"Oh...Phil," Eva said, "does that mean I'm going to meet them once and for all?"

Phil explained there was a prerequisite. "Yes," Phil said, "we can visit them soon, but first we have to go to Washington to be briefed." He expected an explosion.

It came. "Briefed? Washington? That's outragcous! Is he in some kind of trouble with the government," Eva quite excited, asked, "or in a witness protection program or something? Why can't we just go straight to Stockton?"

"No darling," Phil said taking her face in his hands. "It's nothing like that. In a way, he is something of a hero. You came pretty close when you mentioned the witness protection program, but not because he's a witness to a crime, it's because he received an identity change from the government."

"The whole thing sounds weird, Phil," Eva said, moving a foot or so away from him. "But I suppose if I'm going to get the whole story I'll have to go with you, right?"

"I am afraid so," Phil said. "I've already taken the liberty of setting up the appointment with my father's contact at the Pentagon." Again, Phil awaited the outburst. He was not disappointed.

"The Pentagon? Are you serious? That's crazy," Eva said. "What's going on here? Everything you said is beginning to frighten me." She shook her head in bewilderment. "I guess I'm just afraid of what I might hear."

"It's not that bad Eva, I promise."

"I do trust you Phil, but you have to give me some time to think about it."

"Of course, that's natural, I can imagine what you're going through." Phil stood and watched as Eva turned away and walked along the beach, her hands shoved into her pockets as she kicked at the water. An onshore breeze billowed her hair, adding to her allure.

In a sudden movement, she stopped dead in her tracks and turned around to look at Phil. He was standing with his head hung, looking at the sand. When he turned and looked up, Eva started sprinting toward him. He opened his arms wide, and when Eva wrapped her arms around his neck, he enfolded her in a bear hug, which almost knocked the wind out of her. That moment was the beginning of his life, he knew she was ready to accept the truth, whatever it turned out to be.

"Do you mean you *will* go?" Phil asked, both relieved and happy.

"You're damn right I'm going," Eva said. "When do we leave?"

"We're scheduled for a military flight from Vandenberg next Tuesday morning at ten o'clock," Phil said. "We should arrive at Andrews Air Force Base by four in the afternoon. And Eva, all I can say is please stop worrying. You might be shocked, and you will need some time to digest it, but we will get through it, okay?

"My parents told me about the Washington meeting when I broke the news to them about our marriage. Believe me, I understand how you feel. And I must confess, I do know a little more than I've been at liberty to say, but I couldn't go into it with you because of my father's promise not to reveal details about himself to anyone, even to me.

"If the government ever found out he had, it would have been a serious breach of trust. I'm sorry darling. Please try to accept it—as far as you are concerned, I know nothing. I'll have to be a good pretender when we get there though, and play dumb."

"All right, Phil," Eva said. "All I know is, I love you..."

The following Tuesday, Phil and Eva boarded a military charter from Vandenberg Air Force Base to Washington, D.C.

The smooth flight lulled them into a restful two-hour nap.

Phil awoke from a change in the plane's speed. He heard the pilot announce they would be landing in a few minutes. He leaned over and kissed Eva on the forehead and her eyes fluttered open.

"Are we landing now?" she asked.

"Yes, in about fifteen minutes."

Refreshed from their nap, they gathered up their personal belongings. A car awaited their arrival.

Upon deplaning at Andrews, an Air Force sergeant greeted them. "Good afternoon, I am Sergeant Kuhn. Did you have a good flight?" he asked showing no emotion whatsoever.

"Yes, very nice," Phil said.

"I have been instructed to take you to dinner before you visit the Pentagon," the sergeant said.

"Great, that's fine with us," Phil said.

The driver never asked where they wanted to eat, but after a short time, pulled up to a fine looking steakhouse.

"Here," said the sergeant, handing them an envelope, "please use these courtesy meal vouchers and I'll be out in front when you're through."

"Do we have to be at the Pentagon at a certain time?" Eva asked.

"Take all the time you need," he said. "They expect you there at your convenience."

"Don't worry, Eva," Phil said, "we're not going to miss the meeting. They can't start without us."

After dinner, Phil and Eva got into the car and headed to the Pentagon.

"Washington looks so exciting," Eva said, as she gazed out of the car's windows. "Can we stay for a few days? I'd like to see some of the sights."

"That's okay with me, honey," Phil answered. "I don't have to be back right away."

"Look! There's the Capitol, Phil."

When they crossed the Arlington Memorial Bridge and the Pentagon came into view, it looked as though every light in the huge complex was lit.

"Don't those people ever go home?" Eva asked.

"It is a busy place, ma'am," the sergeant said. "It never sleeps."

"I see," Eva said. The butterflies in her stomach started to bat their wings.

They pulled up to the security gate and their driver handed the sentry a pass.

Sergeant Kuhn escorted the couple to the reception lobby where a seated lieutenant asked Phil the name of the party he intended to visit. Phil complied.

Within moments, a military officer outfitted in an impeccable Air Force uniform, approached from a door near the lobby.

"Good evening, Mr. Bennett," he said with little warmth. "You and your companion please come with me."

Eden-459

They followed him to a small room where they were fingerprinted and photographed. After processing, the officer led them into an elevator and pressed the button for L-4. He did not speak a word and just focused on the elevator door as they descended several levels. At their destination, two security guards met them and led them to a conference room. An oval walnut conference table was equipped with microphones, and a video camera's activity light blinked above.

An aid offered them beverages, which they declined, when a two-star general walked in and gave an order to the aid, "Bring file A-51-USAF-001947 to me."

The aid snapped to attention and in a crisp voice said, "Yes sir," as he exited the room.

The officer gave them instructions. "My name is General Williams and I have been given the authority to allow you the liberty of viewing a top secret military file concerning Mr. Bennett's father."

He positioned a microphone in front of them and continued.

"You will be given twenty minutes to review the file, at which point you must close it and leave the room with my aid as your escort. No notes or picture taking will be allowed. Do you both agree to never divulge any of the information you are about to learn?"

"Yes," Phil and Eva said in unison.

Just as he finished delivering the instructions, the door opened. The aid carried in a file folder labeled 'TOP SECRET' in large bright red letters.

"Phil," Eva whispered, "he's just a barrel of laughs."

He handed the folder to the General, who thumbed through it to make sure it was complete. Williams then handed it to Phil whose face grew pale as he read all fifteen pages. He closed it, and handed it to Eva.

She breathed heavy with anticipation, took a few deep slow breaths, her fingers trembling as she perused the first pages, and paused to look at Phil for just a moment.

Tears ran down her cheeks. At last, she came to understand why Phil could not talk about his family's lineage.

The information contained in the file gave rise to more questions than answers, however, and she became one of just a handful of people who knew the real truth about the Roswell Incident. Stunned, Eva closed the folder.

Displaying cool detachment, the officer said, "Thank you for coming. Please follow your escort. He will show you out to your vehicle."

Still numb, Eva showed no visible reaction to what she had just learned. Words escaped her. All she knew was that she loved Phil Bennett, a half-alien descendant of the famous Roswell Incident.

They left the room with the escort. When they arrived at the elevator Phil looked at Eva and said, "Are you okay?"

"Yes, I'm okay...I have to tell you though, I don't believe what I just found out. I never could have *dreamed* of any of this," Eva said. "When you told me you were born in California I just assumed it was in an ordinary hospital. But Travis Air Force Base?"

Phil leaned in close to Eva's face and whispered out of earshot of their escort. "Didn't you take a good look at the photos that were taken of me at birth?" he asked.

"Yes, why?" Eva asked with a slight frown. "Did I miss something?"

"It's obvious you did," Phil said out of the corner of his mouth. "Several of them showed an umbilical cord connected to the back of my head. Did you think that was normal?"

"My God, what was wrong with my eyes?" Eva said, a little shaken. "I don't know what I saw now...I'm so confused. Listen Phil, I admit I was thrown for a loop back there, but I guess I was more shocked than I thought."

"Eva," Phil said, "just think what the nurses at any other hospital in the world would have thought. Can you just imagine...here is this newborn with a hose sticking out of his head? Oh yeah, they'd say, just another day at Maternity."

Eva had to laugh and was glad for the levity. She wrapped her arm around his waist and little by little raised her hand so that the tips of her fingers brushed the back of his head. Phil turned toward her, laughed out loud and held her in his arms.

"I don't give a damn," Eva said. Breathless. "I still love you."

For the first time since he fell in love with Eva, he was able to relax.

The elevator doors opened. Another escort exited with a young gentleman wearing a business suit accompanied by a colonel. Something about the man caught Phil's eye, but he could not put his finger on it. Entering the elevator, Phil turned and took a second impulsive look down the hall noticing that the men entered the same conference room he and Eva just exited.

Chapter 12

Kennedy Space Center, Florida
Launch Day, 7 July 2012, 08:00 hours

The sun rose above the misty Atlantic and shone on launch pad number seven. From miles away, the towering new *Osiris* rocket could be seen with two Mod One segments attached to its sides.

Perfect weather greeted the scheduled 10:37 hour's launch. The skies were clear with a few white billowing clouds. A steady five-mile-per-hour offshore breeze fell well within acceptable launch parameters.

Swirling white vapors from liquid oxygen vents could be observed as they spewed out and encircled the entire base of the rocket.

As the launch sequence progressed, the control center was busy checking all vital systems' functions.

The slightest glitch would trigger a *hold*, and stop the launch clock. Depending on the nature of the hold, the clock could be restarted where it left off once the situation had been rectified. Any serious technical holds could result in a *scrub*. In that scenario, the rocket's fuel would be pumped out precipitating a long delay lasting for days or weeks. Several alternate launch-time windows had been pre-calculated to allow for delays.

The Launch Pad 10:17 hours

Twenty minutes until launch—T minus 20, the launch control center monitored all systems indicators with caution for a *go* status. An ominous loud siren blared alerting all personnel to leave the pad area at once. The launch service platform then made its slow trek to a parked position away from the rocket. The range safety officer gave an all-clear status as the final moments of the launch sequence countdown approached.

Eden-459

Television news crews readied their cameras and uncovered their lenses as hundreds of viewers watched from observation decks miles away from the launch pad. At the five minutes and counting mark—T minus 5, a loudspeaker carried the audible countdown adding to their excitement. All launch monitoring systems gave a green light. Corbin and his staff removed the red metal safety cover shielding the rocket's ignition start control button.

The first launch would set the pace for the others needed to build the space station. Any serious failure during this launch would be a great disappointment and could set the program back for many months.

At the one-minute mark—T minus 1, the senior control officer gave Corbin a confident look as he rested his tensed finger on the ignition button. All indicators still gave a *go* status as the count continued. At the ten-second mark, the count could be heard loud and clear over the loudspeakers. All eyes were affixed to the launch pad. "Ten-nine-eight...five-four-three-two-one."

At 10:37 hours, a fiery blast erupted from the base of the rocket as its engines came to life.

"We have ignition," said the launch controller. Massive clouds of gray and white smoke engulfed the entire pad area. He then announced, "We *have* lift-off."

The enormous rocket began its spectacular ascent on top of a violent, explosive pillar of fire. Its long white exhaust trail made a sharp contrast against the bright blue morning sky.

Observers heard a loud rumbling sound and felt strong vibrations under their feet while the ground shook. The rocket climbed higher and higher while they cheered and shouted—"Go—Go—Go."

The flight control room gave updates every few seconds while the rocket continued its ascent. Within three minutes, the rocket appeared as a tiny bright speck in the sky. Suddenly loud sonic boom was heard as it broke the sound barrier. Two minutes later, a fiery burst of exhaust could be seen as the second-stage engines roared into action. The spent first stage fell, helpless, back to Earth.

Corbin watched the launch monitors with intent. They indicated the rocket's speed, altitude, and angle of ascent. He glanced over to the launch controller. He was happy to give him a "thumbs-up."

When the rocket reached a speed of eighteen thousand miles-per-hour at an altitude of one hundred sixty miles, its engines shut down. Having achieved orbital insertion, flight controllers sent a remote command to the rocket releasing its payload of segments. After receiving confirmation of the payload release, Corbin's entire launch control team jumped up, shook hands and celebrated their first successful launch of the segments.

Afterward, Corbin held a Press briefing. A complete departure from his usual stoic personality, he expressed words of pleasure and delight while shaking hands with everyone in sight. He settled down in his wheelchair and began.

"WASA has taken the first step in the construction of our New International Space Station. Today's first launch and many others to follow will help ensure our success in building the orbiting station and laboratory.

"When completed, the station will set the stage for future missions to galactic destinations never before thought possible. I congratulate everyone in the program for a job well done. One week from today, we will launch a second Osiris rocket, which will carry the third and final segment of Mod One into orbit.

"After we place the last segment in orbit we will schedule a trip to the construction area with a crew of seven astronauts. They will be the first crew to go into orbit aboard our new X55 shuttlecraft.

"I can't tell you how excited I am with these plans. We hope that all our launches go as well as the one we completed today. I'll be happy to take a few questions."

Eden-459

He pointed to a woman wearing a bright yellow blouse and sunglasses. "Mr. Corbin, when do you expect to complete construction of the Mod One phase of your project?"

"Barring technical difficulties or weather setbacks, we expect to complete construction and have our team aboard by September 16. Assuming we are successful in meeting that time schedule and the Mod One performs as hoped, we can begin the launch of the eight spokes needed for the attachment of the outer modules."

"Thank you," said the woman.

Corbin signaled to a senior gentleman with his hand raised.

"Mr. Corbin," he said, "can you tell us a little about the team of astronauts that will man the X55?"

"Yes of course, Colonel Phillip Bennett will be skipper of the team. A veteran astronaut, he has my complete confidence in his ability to do a superb job. Second in command will be Colonel Oliver Barnes. He too is a veteran of several shuttle missions. Because of his strong space engineering background, he will head up the technical areas of the module's construction.

"The other five members of the team are Captain Lauren Brown, Captain William Anderson, First Lieutenant Charles Staeb, Lieutenant Salim Moussa and Lieutenant Richard Greaves.

"These astronauts, in my view, are the best and most dedicated ever gathered in one place at one time.

"I'll take one more question. Yes, sir?" he said, pointing to a gentleman in a flowered shirt.

"Mr. Corbin, how long will the team stay in orbit after the station has been built and how often will the X55 shuttle be making trips to and from the station?"

"Once the station has been built we expect our team to stay in orbit for at least one year. The X55 shuttle has a high degree of versatility, which gives us the option of making many intermediate trips. It also has the capability of carrying significant amounts of equipment and supply replenishment payloads and will visit the station on an almost weekly basis."

Martin J. Stab

Corbin looked at his watch. "I'm afraid that will have to conclude our briefing for today," he said. "I want to thank y'all for sharing a momentous achievement with us here at WASA. We congratulate the launch crew and look forward to our continued success."

Chapter 13

Following Corbin's Press briefing, U.S. Surgeon General Dr. Melvin Broderick, Corbin and a group of eight medical scientists and WASA officials met in private in a secured conference room. The meeting's prime agenda was to share top-secret confidential details concerning two of the astronauts included in the space program. Broderick carried the dossiers of Colonel Phillip Bennett and Captain William Anderson in his attaché case.

The attendees had no prior knowledge of the status of the individuals under scrutiny.

Corbin put all pretense of politeness aside. He rolled up his sleeves, loosened his tie and brought his wheelchair to the front of the conference table.

Having made ready to emphasize the seriousness and confidentiality of what he was about to say, he began.

"Thank you for coming. I must warn everyone that if any one member of the group leaks the slightest hint of the proceedings' content following this meeting, I will deal with him in the strongest way possible—short of execution."

Corbin's statement hit home—the group fixed their eyes on him with their full attention.

"We have asked you here," Corbin continued, "to apprise you of salient information concerning two of our top astronauts. I cannot over emphasize the importance of total secrecy as it pertains to information you are about to receive. Before we continue I must ask that each of you review and sign the Secret Information Access Agreement in front of you. Please complete it now."

While the group complied with Corbin's request, their faces grew taught with anticipation. They attended many meetings related to the mission plan, but this was the first time they had ever been asked to sign a document, which warned of severe Federal penalties for even the slightest breach of confidentiality.

After the forms were signed, Corbin collected them, put them into his briefcase and closed it.

"Good," Corbin said, "the Surgeon General and I have discussed the basis of our get-together in advance, and we will try to address all of your concerns." Corbin motioned to Broderick.

"Gentlemen," said Broderick, "the two astronauts in question are Colonel Phillip Bennett and Captain William Anderson."

He stood up and continued while pacing back and forth in front of the group.

"As you already know, both of these astronauts are scheduled to play key roles in our space program. They will be involved with the space station and later on, our first major deep space mission.

"There are no doubts as to their qualifications and ability to fulfill their responsibilities." When Broderick reached the center of the room he stopped, hesitated for a few seconds making eye contact with everyone in the room and said with emphasis, "Gentlemen, what you do not know is that they are both of *alien ancestry*."

Broderick paused, allowing his remarks to settle in.

The eight individuals in the group froze, staring back at Broderick. Several coffee cups dropped to the table, pencils fell from stunned fingers, and one gentleman who choked on his own saliva said, "Aliens! Alien astronauts? This must be someone's idea of a joke?"

For a moment, everyone sat stone still afraid to even take a breath, lest they miss hearing one word. Corbin sat back in his wheel chair enjoying their reactions.

"The full circumstances surrounding their origin are not important," Broderick continued. "The vital thing is that we have two exceptional astronauts capable of meeting the needs of our space mission.

"I can assure you there are no reasons, medical or otherwise that present me with any reservations whatsoever as to their suitability for the task at hand. We are fortunate to have them on our team and I am sure all of you will be pleased with their performance.

"I have one demand to make, however. What we share with you here must never leave this room."

Dr. Thurmann, a medical scientist had the floor. "What we have learned today has to be, without a doubt the shock of all time. Are you serious? Do you mean to tell me that aliens not only landed, but also have managed to gain entry into our space program? If you're not joking sir, and I have a feeling you're not, I have a lot of questions to ask." He was then interrupted.

"I find your disclosure difficult to believe," Dr. Patel an astro-biologist said. "Adding to Dr. Thurmann's comments, I want to know why we've had *encounters of the third kind* and weren't informed? How do we know these aliens do not pose hazards to humans? And if they are in actuality extraterrestrial, how and why did they become involved in our space program? How do we know they can be trusted? What do they look like?" He shook his head and started pacing. "I can't accept this without a full explanation."

"At first I was shocked too," Dr. Broderick said. "Let me explain a few things and then we can cover your questions."

"I want to be open-minded," Dr. Gregory Wang chimed in and said, "and listen to your explanations, but there must be some convincing reasons, not just for them being here on Earth, which is an obvious question in itself, but also as to why we allowed them into our space program. I do not understand what is going on here at all. I think you have made a big mistake and I agree with Dr. Patel...we should not trust them. They could be out to get us."

"May I continue?" Dr. Broderick said in a sharp tone. "I have made a complete review of the alien's dossiers with Director Corbin and have prepared some notes that should answer most of your questions. Please understand, however, we can't explain some of the reasons why the government did what it did in a number of areas."

Broderick started a slow walk around the room as he prepared to speak. The rustle of pages could be heard as he started speaking. He recapped most of the salient events and aftermath of the Roswell Incident of 1947 to the sheer amazement of the group.

When he finished he said, "I shall ask Director Corbin to take it from here." Broderick sat while the group continued writing their notes.

"Thank you, Melvin," Corbin said. "The government realized it had to prevent the aliens' arrival from becoming public knowledge. Can you imagine the fear and panic, not to mention the obvious spectacle, which would have ensued? As to what they look like—I can assure you they appear quite human. If they sat here with you right now you wouldn't be able to identify them."

Corbin almost laughed out loud, as he watched the assemblage nervously glancing around at one another—wondering.

"After the government realized the Roswell aliens were not hostile and posed no known danger, they decided to place them into surrogate families hand-picked by the Pentagon. Living with those families, they achieved full assimilation into our society.

"And yes, they even married and each fathered one son. That explains Phillip Bennett and William Anderson's family trees. Yes gentleman, they do have alien roots, but they're also half-human."

Dr. Patel interrupted Corbin's address. "I remember now," he said, "I met Colonel Bennett and had a lengthy conversation with him. Are you sure he's an alien?"

"Now *there*," Corbin asked, "do you see what I mean? I can assure you that Colonel Bennett is indeed half alien."

"Their abilities couldn't go unnoticed. We needed their innate capabilities and that is why they have been offered crucial positions in WASA's space program. Needless to say, they accepted the offer and that is where they are today. They have earned their place as vital entities for our space endeavors."

"How do we know they will be loyal to us?" Dr. Wang asked. "Having two of them on the same mission might give them persuasive influence over the rest of the crew."

"No, no, no doctor," Dr. Broderick said. "They don't even know yet that the other is an alien. And remember also, they are part human. They grew up on Earth and served with honor and distinction in our armed forces."

"Where are the original aliens now?" Dr. Patel asked.

"I'm sorry," Corbin said, "but that information must remain secret and it does not concern us here."

Dr. Hunt, an obstetrician assigned to WASA's Earth-based medical team voiced his concern. "You mentioned a pregnant female alien had perished in the crash. Do you know if an extensive autopsy of the unborn child had been performed?"

"Is that question necessary for our agenda?" Corbin asked. He wanted to keep the momentum going along *his* lines, not Hunt's.

"As you know, my specialty is obstetrics," Hunt said. "I am most interested in finding out about the alien physiology of both the mother and the fetus."

"Well put, doctor," Corbin said. "I'll try to get those records from archives as soon as I can. I don't think that information is pertinent to our work here today, however."

"Thank you," Hunt said with a smirk.

The panel had difficulty accepting all the explanations offered, but seemed satisfied their questions had been addressed and they had been brought into the loop.

"I think we're finished here for today," Dr. Broderick said. "I'm sure that we've raised as many questions as we've answered."

"Well I'll be. That has to be the greatest understatement of the century." Corbin thought to himself.

"In time," Broderick said, "you will learn more about our alien astronauts and I'm confident you will find their participation most valuable to our efforts in space. Once again, I must insist on strict confidentiality. We don't need *red meat* for the Press or public opinion problems at this juncture."

Corbin wanted to curtail the meeting before someone asked a question he did not want to answer. He had shared enough and did not want the group too well versed on his plan.

"Thank you for coming," he said, "and I would appreciate it if everyone would leave their notes behind on the table."

* * *

14 July 2012, 07:00 Hours
Kennedy Space Center

The weather again cooperated for the 10:16 hours scheduled lift-off of the second giant Osiris rocket. A flawless launch, it represented another major milestone when it accomplished the successful lifting of the final segment for the space station's Module One's construction.

Bennett's wife Eva and the other astronauts' families also visited Kennedy to observe the lift-off.

* * *

The X55 shuttlecraft, an advanced and larger successor to the X49 and X53 designs, had the unique capability of lifting off and landing using conventional aircraft runways. The long runways at Kennedy Space Center and Edwards Air Force Base were ideal.

The inclusion of four new SINERE rocket engines gave the craft the advantage of tremendous power and speed. The X55's advanced cockpit even enabled it to be flown by remote control if necessary.

A Hyper Laser Tracking System—designed and tested in Russia—made locating even the smallest orbiting objects easy. The X55 provided WASA with a superb vehicle to commute to and from the space station. The craft also had the capability to support a team of eight for up to sixty days in orbit without re-supplies of fuel, oxygen, or nutritional needs.

Chapter 14

19 July 2012, 06:00 Hours
Kennedy Space Center
First Operational X55 Shuttle Launch

The exuberant and brave shuttle crew shared their final meal with their families before launch. Led by Colonel Phillip Bennett, the excited crew awaited the start of their maiden trek aboard the new X55.

Just prior to Bennett's entering the van, which would take him to the shuttle, a news reporter approached. "How do you feel about the mission and the team?" he asked, making ready to take notes.

"We're ready and I'm confident the mission will be a success," Bennett said. "Three of us have space walked before. We've trained hard for the physical and mental challenges we face."

He shook hands with the reporter. "Now you'll have to excuse me—I have a flight to catch."

The reporter laughed and thanked Bennett for his time and wished him and his crew much success.

The X55 had been positioned on an apron area near runway number fifteen. The shuttle's ground crew made final equipment checks of the communications, propulsion, and computerized navigational and guidance systems.

At 07:00 hours, the crew boarded, strapped in, and began their routine pre-flight checklist. All systems received a *go* from Flight Control Center.

The Auxiliary Power Units (APUs) supplying electricity and high-pressure air needed prior to launch had been activated.

At 08:06 hours Colonel Bennett started the X55's engines and ordered the APUs removed. He kept the power controls at a minimum power setting and performed a slow taxi roll to the end of the eighteen thousand-foot runway. The crew braced for the awesome thrust soon to be experienced once the engines came to take-off power level.

The crew beamed with excitement over the anticipation of traveling aboard the first orbiting spacecraft to depart from the Earth using traditional runways. Their families watched and bid farewells from an observation post.

Colonel Bennett had been too busy to give any serious thought to his crewmember William Anderson, but for some reason felt he was a kindred spirit. He promised himself he would find the time to speak with him to investigate his impression.

08:15 hours

Bennett checked his instrumentation. He found everything normal and received a one-minute notice from Flight Control. At the start of a twenty-second countdown, he made a tight grip on the thrust controls and advanced the power level of the X55's engines to twenty-five percent. At 08:15:45 hours, Bennett received an okay to roll and released the brakes while throttling forward to ninety-five percent power. He advised Flight Control, "X55 is rolling."

They gave him a "ten-four" when an ear-splitting roar accompanied the craft while it raced down the runway. A long yellowish white exhaust plume emitted from its powerful SINERE engines. At the speed of two hundred seventy-five knots, Bennett pulled back on the control stick. The X55's nose lifted upward and in seconds the craft became airborne and sliced through puffy white clouds in its path.

The crew felt the effects of escalating G-forces. Climbing higher and higher, they reviewed the in-flight checklist and prepared for the rendezvous in orbit. Bennett gave Flight Control an "all-systems-go" status when his ship attained a speed of seven thousand miles-per-hour while climbing and continuing to accelerate.

After twenty-two minutes at full power, the X55 reached a speed of eighteen thousand miles-per-hour and an altitude of one hundred sixty miles. Engine power was cut and all became quiet.

Eden-459

In perfect position to scan for the Mod One segments, the crew listened for the ping of radio beacon signals transmitting in three-second intervals that came from the segments.

The flight navigator's calculations indicated the three segments' positions at an approximate distance of six thousand miles ahead or one quarter of the way around the Earth from the their position.

Bennett stayed on the safe side and made a slow increase of the X55's speed to gain on the target. While closing in, the crew reviewed their operational checklists and afterward took a one-hour rest period.

First Lieutenant Staeb checked the X55's communications equipment while Captain Brown ran the shuttle's on-board computers through a series of diagnostic routines. The excitement level of the crew rose as they looked forward to beginning their work.

In five hours, the X55's scanners and radio receivers made contact with both Mod One segments. They were spaced twenty-three nautical miles apart. In orbital terms, they were judged to be close indeed.

At twelve miles out Bennett made visual contact with the first segment and began a slow closure of the gap. He ordered a reduction of speed and an adjustment in altitude to match that of the target. When he came within a few thousand feet of the first segment he announced to Earth Base.

"We have a problem, repeat...we have a problem."

"Go ahead Commander," Base answered. "Explain the nature." Bennett's communication struck terror in the hearts of flight controllers. It represented their worst fears.

A problem on Earth could be addressed with a lot more ease and safety. Help could be summoned or workers might elect to abandon an area for safety. But problems in space, even small ones, could spell an alarming degree of danger.

The mood at the flight control center grew tense. No one moved, and they became more and more anxious awaiting Bennett's response.

"Bennett to Base."

"We read you *five-by* Commander," Base responded. "We're ready for your status."

"We're positioned an approximate distance of two thousand feet from the first segment," Bennett said, "but the segment is *rotating* at eight to ten revolutions per minute."

The control room buzzed with conversation. Every viable solution to correct the problem was examined. Director Corbin assumed control.

"Gentlemen," Corbin said. "It's obvious they are on top of the situation. Give *them* a little time to think it through to the best solution."

"Base to Bennett," Corbin said.

"Bennett here. Go ahead Henry." Corbin's authoritative voice had a soothing effect on Bennett.

"Y'all come up with a remedy for the spinning segment?" Corbin asked.

"I'm having Captain Anderson evaluate the situation," Bennett said. "He's tops with this kind of problem."

"Sounds good Phil," Corbin said. "Don't rush it. Keep your shuttle at a safe distance until you're ready to make a definitive move."

"Ten four," Bennett said.

Base and the X55 crew understood that because of the size and weight of the spinning three billion dollar segment, the task of stabilizing it presented a special challenge. Extreme caution had to be exercised to avoid a collision with the shuttle and possible loss of life.

Unless the segment could be stabilized for attachment to the other segments, it would become an expensive and useless piece of space junk. If that happened, a replacement segment would have to be built and orbited. It would delay the program for many months.

Captain Anderson reviewed every option to correct the situation. After careful study, he reported to Bennett.

"Bridge come in," Anderson said.

Eden-459

"Go ahead Bill," Bennett said. "Do you have a solution?"

"Yes, I advise using the *cocoon* method to stabilize," Anderson said.

"I believe you're right," Bennett said. "There's not much else to consider. It would be too dangerous to send a space walker with a portable thruster. Give me a minute to update Base."

The cocoon arresting procedure involved positioning the X55 at fifty yards away from the target. On command, an eighteen-inch wide Mylar tether tape, tipped with a sticky pod would then be aimed and propelled toward the target.

After successful attachment, the segment's spinning movement would cause the tape to enwrap it. After twenty to thirty wraps had been achieved, the segment would be considered cocooned.

At that time, the out-spooler operator would apply small amounts of drag, causing the spinning motion of the target to reduce until it stopped. The procedure would be complete when the target had stopped rotating and the wrapped tape had been cut away by a space walker. The crew could then safely continue their attachment tasks.

Bennett called base to announce their plan. "Bennett to Base, come in."

"Go ahead Phil," Corbin said. "What have you decided?"

"We're going to use the cocooning system. It's our best option," Bennett said.

"Sounds good, Phil. I'll sit in on this one in case you need me."

"Thanks," Bennett said. "Ten four out."

Bennett exercised caution while he shortened the distance between the shuttle and the dangerously spinning segment. At one hundred fifty feet away, he gave Anderson the okay to proceed with the cocooning operation. He also instructed Lieutenant Greaves to suit up and stand by for a space walk in case it became necessary to go outside the shuttle.

Captain Anderson powered up the out-spooling system for a five minute warm up. The tape spool held two thousand feet of tape. If he missed the target, he would be required to press a *cut switch* to preserve the rest of the spool. The cut function would also be used to sever the tape if an emergency release became necessary.

Bennett rotated the shuttle's position enabling the spooler system to face the segment. He called Anderson, "Bridge to Anderson, come in."

"Anderson here. I have our target lined up in my sight. I'm ready to release the tape."

"Do it," Bennett said. "Let's hope we get it on our first try."

Anderson gave a slow squeeze to the deployment trigger on the spooler. Following a snapping sound he observed the tape speed toward the segment. "Anderson to bridge."

"Go ahead Anderson," Bennett said.

"I'm counting wraps," Anderson replied.

"Great. Start applying drag when you reach twenty raps," Bennett said.

The segment became wrapped with at least twenty turns of tape. Anderson applied a gradual drag to the tape while Bennett compensated with short tiny bursts of the shuttle's attitude thrusters. Anderson recalculated the spin rate and reported to Bennett.

"Anderson to bridge. The spin rate is beginning to slow. Copy?"

"Good, I copy," Bennett said. "Keep the drag steady. I can feel the shuttle being tugged a little."

"Ten four Commander," Anderson said. "I feel it too, but now the tugging seems to be getting too strong."

"You're right," Bennett said. "If it gets any worse don't hesitate to use the cut switch."

"Wow Commander, what was that?" Anderson said. "Sir, I'm going to cut the tape right now."

The balance between the drag applied to the tape and the shuttle's offsetting ability to hold itself in stable position went out of sync. Bennett felt the heavy yanking action also.

Eden-459

"Bennett to Anderson, did you cut the tape?"

"I pressed the cut switch Commander," Anderson said. "But it failed to operate. We're still being drawn toward the segment."

"Keep trying," Bennett said.

He observed the segment had moved even closer to the shuttle.

"It's no use Commander," Anderson said. "I'm having Greaves go to the cargo bay. He will call you when he's ready to walk out and cut it manually."

"How much time do we have?" Bennett asked. "Never mind...it looks too close for comfort already. Call Greaves back inside. I am going to blast us away from the segment. Do you copy?"

"I copy Commander," Anderson said, "but Greaves used the manual override controls and opened the cargo bay. He's already out there walking toward the tape."

"Bennett to Greaves—come in," Bennett said into his radio. "I repeat—Greaves come in—come in. Get back inside—that is an order. I repeat—get back inside."

"He's not answering Commander," Anderson said. "I hope he gets himself clear of the spinning segment in time. If he's struck it'll be over for him."

"It's unfortunate, but you're right," Bennett said. "Bennett to Base, come in."

"Go ahead Commander," Corbin said. "What's your status?"

"We have the segment wrapped, but we weren't able to keep the shuttle in sync with it. The emergency cut switch failed. Greaves went out without clearance to perform a manual tape cut. I must tell you, he's placed himself in grave danger."

"How close is the segment now?" Corbin asked.

"Less than twenty—five feet," Bennett said. "If Greaves doesn't get out of its path when it rotates toward him, we're going to have a dead hero."

"Did you warn Greaves of the risk?" Corbin asked.

"Yes," Bennett said, "but he ignored it and continued on his own even after I called him back."

"Keep me updated," Corbin said. "We better hope that he's able to get out of this in one piece."

"Anderson to bridge, Greaves must have cut the tape, we're free."

"Good, but what about Greaves," Bennett asked, "did he get clear of the segment?"

"Stand by," Anderson said, "I'm checking now."

"Ten four captain," Bennett said, praying that Anderson would find Greaves unhurt.

But Greaves, unaware, became detached from his safety tether line after cutting the Mylar tape. When he attempted a return to the cargo bay by pulling himself back using the line, he realized his predicament—he was stuck where he was and the line had drifted out of reach. He had no way to move. He saw the segment coming toward him and made a frantic attempt to propel himself out of its way, but it was not to be—Greaves took a severe pounding and was thrown farther away from the ship.

"Anderson to Bennett, please come in."

"Go ahead."

"I'm sorry Commander," Anderson said, "you can close the cargo bay doors. I just watched Greaves trying to avoid the segment as it headed for him. But he must have lost his hold on the tether line and could not move out of its way fast enough. It struck him and catapulted him off into open space."

Bennett ordered Lieutenant Moussa to attempt to find Greaves's body for return to Earth for burial when the shuttle returned. But Moussa never found it.

The E—One suffered its first casualty.

Bennett filed the report of Greaves's death to Earth Base.

Later that day he made a somber entry into his journal:

"Today we had our first loss. The strong potential for accidents in orbit is always present since space is a dangerous and unforgiving place. It tolerates little in the way of mistakes.

Eden-459

Lieutenant Richard Greaves did not plan to be a hero when he joined the program. What happened to him today occurred when he made a brave and daring attempt to protect his fellow crewmembers, our shuttle and the loss of an errant segment. He accomplished his goal without regard for his own safety. He will always be remembered as one of the best, and a true hero after all."

In the weeks that followed, the shuttle returned with a new tape spooler system. The unit worked as it was designed and they finally were able to save the segment. After the first two segments had been connected, the crew began its search for the third, which came into view thirty minutes later. Bennett maneuvered the X55 and made a safe gain on the steady target.

The attachment of all three segments having been completed they connected the necessary cables and closed the Mod One's hatches. The crew of the Mod One began its environmental checks. Once they determined the Mod One safe, Barnes and Anderson oxygenated and pressurized the module and began checking all on-board equipment. After the Mod One came on-line, they removed their spacesuits and took up residence. Following the completion of their checklists, Barnes reported, "All systems go," to Bennett.

Bennett's vision of commanding a space station and later deep-space mission took another step closer to reality. He wasted no time in getting the station's programs begun on schedule. He would not accept even the slightest deviation by any of the crew.

* * *

Bennett radioed Barnes to tell him Captain Brown would accompany him on a space walk to the station. Once they arrived, Brown began the task of checking the Mod One's computers.

The following day Bennett went on their secure network to speak to Earth Base about the progress of the mission. He completed his routine report and asked to be connected with Director Corbin for a private conference.

Bennett heard brief static then Corbin came on the line.

"Sir," Bennett said, "can you assure me we have complete privacy?"

"Yes, why?" Corbin said. He decided to give Bennett time to speak before he jumped to any conclusions.

"Well sir, we had company last night," Bennett answered in a matter-of-fact voice.

Corbin remained silent. His immediate response: One of fear. He hoped whatever was out there did not prove to be hostile.

"Sir, we had company last night," he repeated.

"I'm here, Commander. I guess my mind drifted. What you just said reminded me of a similar incident on one of our other missions. All right, tell me about it."

"Sir, when the crew was resting, I spotted a circular craft about one mile out. I did not want anyone to be awakened so I turned off the object scanner alarms. Then I snapped a few digital pictures. It didn't seem to pose any threat, it just hovered in one spot as though it had been watching us."

"Hmm, I see...then what happened?" Corbin asked, with a slow and calm demeanor.

"After a few minutes it disappeared," Bennett said.

"All right, let's name this one 'Curious Lady' for our reference. I want you to send me those pictures for our people to analyze."

"Ten four, sir," Bennett said. He remembered his father speaking of the possibility that his planet might send scouts to look for him and Antar. Bennett wondered if it could have been one of *their* ships.

* * *

The following day Captain Brown went to the bridge with her computer in hand to review statistical programs with

Commander Bennett. She downloaded several files from Bennett's main computer via its infrared port.

A curious thing happened when Brown's computer started to receive additional data. "Commander," she said, "I thought you turned off your port."

"I did," Bennett said.

"Hmmm," said Brown, "my port was still active...I must have received data from someplace else."

"That's impossible, captain," Bennett said. "My computer was in normal operating mode."

"Does your wristband communicator have the ability to transmit via infrared?" Brown asked.

"No, and the only other thing even close to your computer was my hand."

"You mean the one with the onyx ring?" Brown asked.

"Yes," Bennett said, alarmed.

Bennett told Brown to open the file to review the unknown data she had received, but Brown asked if she could do it later on, as she was needed for a software problem at the communications section.

"That's fine, captain," Bennett said, "I'll see you when you're through."

That afternoon Brown went back to her quarters. She turned on her computer and opened the mysterious file to study its contents. It made no sense to her. It contained text data, but it was unintelligible. Believing it to be garbage data, she started to delete it, but stopped when she noticed several clear and defined characters among the general text. She saved and printed it.

She called Bennett on her communicator and advised him she had a hard copy of the file, but it made no sense.

"Why, captain?" Bennett asked. "What does it look like?"

"At first glance I thought it was garbage data full of alpha numeric print, but then I noticed a handful of special characters."

"Special characters?" Bennett asked. "What do they look like?"

"I can't explain, sir. I printed it though and I'll bring it to you."

"I want to see it now," Bennett ordered.

Commander Bennett did not tell Brown, but when she was gone, he experimented with his own computer. He placed the onyx ring next to his infrared port, turned on his computer and he too began to receive data.

He started to remember his father saying his onyx ring had special abilities, but Luxor never gave him any specifics as to what he meant.

Brown arrived at the bridge and gave Bennett the printout. He perused all six pages and found them unintelligible as had Brown, but he too circled a few unusual characters.

"Well, Commander, what do you think?"

"I don't know, captain, they are strange. I am going to scan these sheets and send them to Earth Base. Maybe they can make something out of them."

"Good idea, Commander," Brown said.

Bennett had a faint hunch that the 'Curious Lady' was responsible somehow, but all he could do was remain patient until he heard from Earth Base. He thanked Captain Brown for her help and dismissed her.

Early the next morning Bennett received a call from Earth Base.

"Commander good morning. This is Colonel Herbert McManus at the Pentagon. I had base patch me through to you."

"Good morning, colonel," Bennett said. "I suppose you called about the data I forwarded. Could you make anything of it?"

"Commander," McManus said, "Director Corbin and I spoke about your sighting and we think there's a possibility that the data received came from that craft. We're now trying to ascertain whether or not that ship may have been sent by your father's home planet."

"Why can't your people be certain?" Bennett asked.

"I wish we could," McManus said, "but the data are in a code we've never seen before. Our hope is that the transmission came from one of his planet's ships. Then we'll be able to break the code."

"Are you telling me you've had communication with alien ships before?" Bennett asked.

"Yes we have Commander, but the format and encoding of the new data are strange. When we figure it all out I'll get back to you."

"Colonel, anything else?" Bennett asked.

"Yes, we want this thing kept under tight wraps."

"Very well, colonel. I'll make sure there are no leaks."

"Good, and one more thing, Commander."

"Yes?" Bennett said.

"We want you to forward any new data you receive to us right away."

"I understand colonel," Bennett said.

After Bennett's conversation with Colonel McManus, he called Captain Brown and ordered her to delete the file she had received.

"As you wish, sir," Brown said, "but what did it mean?"

"Nothing, captain. We were just receiving stray signals from a passing communications satellite," Bennett said. He did not like to lie, but sometimes he had to.

Chapter 15

Once Mod One had reached full operational status, Bennett and Barnes returned to the X55. Captains Brown and Anderson stayed behind aboard the Mod One as the shuttle returned to Earth to pick up three additional astronauts. On its return to the station, the shuttle's cargo would include both spokes needed for the attachment of two of the eight outer modules.

The shuttle maneuvered away from the Mod One and began its descent to Earth.

After landing at Kennedy Space Center, Bennett, Barnes, and First Lieutenant Staeb attended a debriefing and then took three days leave with their families. The X55 was placed in a hanger for maintenance checks and outfitted for its next flight back to the station.

***

Meanwhile, Bennett met with Corbin to review the mission. They discussed Bennett's UFO sighting and studied the digital images he had sent.

"We'll keep our discussion to ourselves for the time being," Corbin said, with a stern edge to his voice.

"Fine," Bennett said, wondering why Corbin was being tight lipped.

"The pictures you took of the unknown craft are similar to others we have on file. Their origin is a mystery, but we computer-enhanced something which raised a few eyebrows at our Scientific Investigations Division."

"What, Henry?" Bennett asked, engrossed.

"The markings along the outer edge of the craft. It didn't take them long to find similarities with those found at the Roswell crash."

"That's curious," Bennett said. "I had a strange feeling there was a chance the craft could be from my father's planet. I wonder, what do you think?"

"That's a good guess," Corbin said, "but until they communicate we can't be sure of anything. Just keep your eyes open since they might be hostile. They may have put those markings on their ship as a disguise. Let's hope for now they're friendly, because we would be defenseless sitting ducks if they aren't."

That evening Corbin asked Bennett to join him at a vital planning session attended by the WASA medical staff. On their way to the conference room he said, "Phil, you and I have worked together for a number of years and I feel we've accomplished a lot of our objectives together."

"You're right Henry," Bennett said, "I'd say we've shared a pretty productive working relationship. Why are you bringing that up now? Is there something wrong?"

"Not exactly," Corbin answered, "but I just want you to understand that when we meet these doctors you're going to have to be open minded."

"Open minded?" Bennett replied, confused.

"That's right, open minded."

"Now you have my antennas up," Bennett snapped, "why don't you just get to the point?"

Corbin paused to gather his thoughts and started with hesitation. "Phil, WASA needs to know now, and I mean *now*, whether or not normal human birth is feasible in space. Phil, I cannot overemphasize the importance of the plan. If birth can be accomplished, they are going to go forward with something very big in two years. If not, their plans may be delayed for a decade or more.

"Everything hinges on that question. Our station provides the ideal test environment."

Bennett pondered the matter. "Henry," he said, "you are aware my wife Eva has volunteered to give birth on the space station, aren't you?"

"Yes Phil, I am," Corbin said. "Nevertheless, time is of the essence. So, before you meet the medical gurus you must know, they're already one step ahead of us."

"Do you mean they already have an astronaut couple who volunteered to have a child in space?" asked Bennett.

"It's not quite that simple Phil," Corbin said, "the couple they've targeted is already on the space station. Your astronauts Brown and Anderson."

"Brown and Anderson?" Bennett said. "I wasn't aware of a romance between those two." He was surprised at the unexpected scenario, but if the situation did not have an adverse effect on the mission, he thought it might be okay.

"Phil," Corbin said, "I didn't say anything about a romance."

"Right, you didn't," Bennett said, now a little on edge. "Henry, now why do I get the feeling I'm not going to like what I'm going to hear?"

"Phil," Corbin said, "here's the scoop."

Bennett's eyes narrowed and he could feel that dull ache on the side of his head.

"Listen Phil, what they did was necessary, for the good of all mankind. It isn't anything that..."

Bennett started to protest again, but Corbin was not having any.

"Phil, just listen and stop the histrionics! We are talking about a...our...we're talking about man's future in space. We have to experiment, we have to take chances and sometimes we have to go through the back door to accomplish our goals."

"Director Corbin," Bennett hissed between gritted teeth. "Back door? Just what does that mean?"

"Okay, okay, calm down," Corbin said, waving his hands at Bennett. We used an agent—a drug—in their food and water, something similar to Viagra, but stronger. Let us just say it does the job it is supposed to do. Love and romance have nothing to do with it. Nothing."

"Dammit Henry, what in God's name are you saying? I hope you are not telling me that you are *so* desperate to have a pregnancy in orbit that you have resorted to using drugs and deception. What about moral and ethical standards?" Bennett's eyes bulged as his jaw clenched.

Corbin looked straight at Bennett and shouted, "Phil! Tough if you have a problem with it. *I* gave the go-ahead. We need answers and we need them in a hurry. Candy and flowers have no place on a space mission. It is about life, death... and birth! I am not going to debate you. I don't give a damn what you think. I did my job and I expect you to do yours." He sat red faced wishing he could stand on his own two feet so he could punch Bennett in the face.

"Do you mean to tell me it's a done deal?" Bennett asked. "That's outrageous, Henry." Bennett started pacing.

"Look Phil," Corbin said, "we have no choice but to support the plan," Corbin said. "Face it, there's no way to stop it now. Even if I tried, by now Brown and Anderson have already completed the operation."

"You're not going anywhere until you tell me everything," Bennett said bolting to the front of Corbin's wheelchair. He leaned over him, grabbed the armrests and said, "I want the whole story *before* we go into the meeting."

Corbin again raised his arms in an effort to calm Phil down and took hold of his wrists. "Phil! Cool it!"

"I can't believe what's going down here." Bennett yelled. "Do you think Brown and Anderson are just a pair of laboratory animals? This is *my* command and I should have been in the loop on this. Why didn't you let me in on it sooner? They are two of my best people. How the hell am *I* supposed to explain everything to them?"

"Wait Phil," Corbin said, "before you go any farther off the deep end, hear me out. I know how you feel, but think about it. What they have done will address a lot of critical and important concerns. The results are vital in helping us to plan our entire future in space."

"I expect a scientific surprise once in awhile," Bennett said. "But what we're talking about here is horrendous. You should have realized how *they* would be affected. They are being treated like lab rats. Didn't you think they'd sooner or later discover that they were set up?"

Bennett was seething now and red faced as he continued his tirade. "How about this, they might even opt out of the mission. Henry—I need them. They are good people, the best. What then?"

"I guess you're right, that is a possibility," Corbin said, trying another approach to calm Bennett down. "And I do understand your resentment. But, the fact is I didn't even have to tell you anything."

"Tell me, Henry," Bennett was shaking. "Suppose after Brown conceives she decides she doesn't want anything to do with Anderson and resents him too? When she finds out what happened she could decide to leave the mission and I'll have no choice but to let her go."

"Phil," Corbin said, "I expect *you* to reckon this with them, and keep the spirit of our mission your first priority."

"Henry, I can't tell you how upset I am. Is there any way we can halt the plan?"

"No! By now, it has already begun. If they've taken food or water it's already too late."

Bennett blew his top. He picked up a vase filled with flowers that stood in a corner of the corridor and flung it down the hallway.

"Are you happy now?" Corbin said smirking. He turned to look both ways to see if anyone might have seen Bennett's outburst.

Bennett's fists balled. His face flushed with anger. He could not think of anything else to say. He started pacing again, shaking his head in disgust, and tried to regain his composure.

Corbin practiced cool patience as he waited for the volcano to finish erupting.

"Now I have a pounding headache, Henry," Bennett said after he calmed down somewhat.

"Here," Corbin reached into his jacket pocket, took out a medicine bottle and offered two pills to Bennett. "These will help."

"I don't like *pills*, Henry. What I need is some respect—from you, and WASA's medical people. You are our director, and you should never have let this happen. And another thing, I'm not holding anything back at the conference."

"Don't," Corbin said.

"I'm telling them what they did stinks and they used rotten judgment. Henry, I'm warning you, if anything like this ever happens again I'm leaving the mission."

Corbin nodded in agreement.

"Henry, tell me the names of the planners who helped you concoct this scheme," Bennett insisted.

"Not that it makes any difference now," said Corbin, "Doctors Hunt, Broderick, Richardson, and from the Pentagon, Colonel McManus."

"McManus? Who the hell *is* McManus?" Bennett yelled. "He was in on the Curious Lady incident, what's he doing with doctors?"

"Frankly Phil, the Pentagon selected him and I was not given any options," Corbin said.

He then collected his thoughts and used his uncanny power of persuasion to try to defuse Bennett's anger.

"Listen," Corbin assumed a patriarchal tone, "before we go in, why don't you just take it easy. Don't let them see you so upset. *You* want to have the upper hand. If you are too cavalier, *they* might just ask *you* to leave. How about it?"

Bennett shook his head and sighed.

They went into the conference room, and Bennett sat next to Corbin. He was adamant about making his feelings known to the panel. He whispered to Corbin, "I'm not going to take what they did to Brown and Anderson lying down."

The meeting began as the chairperson, Dr. Hunt spoke at length about the mission's plan concerning Brown and Anderson. To Bennett's shock, Hunt talked about Brown's pregnancy as though it was something that the two astronauts volunteered for.

Bennett's blood pressure ratcheted upwards the longer Hunt spoke. Corbin kept a sharp eye on him and at one point made eye contact. Corbin raised his hand toward Bennett and gave him a signal to hold back. The hand gesture Bennett returned spoke for itself.

Following Hunt's presentation, he opened the floor for any questions. Bennett raised his hand and was acknowledged.

"Dr. Hunt," Bennett began, "you just told everyone astronauts Brown and Anderson are cooperating with the childbirth experiment."

"Yes, I did say that," Hunt said. "Do you have something you wish to add?"

"You *know* I do doctor," Bennett said. "Maybe you can bamboozle these people with that lie, but you're not getting it past me..."

"What? Hunt said, "Why? What do you mean? His face flushed.

"You know darn well what I mean doctor," Bennett opened up with both barrels. "You and your genius medical staff hatched the whole thing. Why don't you tell these people the truth about how you and Colonel McManus set Brown and Anderson up?" Bennett went on as Hunt sank lower into his chair. "Go ahead doctor, explain how you arranged to have drugs put in their food..."

The attendees sat motionless listening to the discourse.

At that second Corbin tugged at Bennett's sleeve and whispered to him, "Okay Phil, that's enough. You made your point, now let's just leave so he can explain to his associates what it's all about."

With reluctance, Bennett followed Corbin out of the meeting, brushing against one of the doctors as he left.

Eden-459

In the hallway Corbin said, "Phil, please calm down. You got your point across. He's never going to admit anything in front of that group."

"I know that Henry," Bennett said, "but I had him on the hot seat and it was enjoyable. You know he deserved every bit of it, and more."

"Yes Phil, okay, yes," Corbin said, "but enough is enough. We have to work with these people for a long time."

"That's exactly why I had to get it off my chest Henry. I want them to know I'm no fool and I'm not going to let them play with my astronauts' lives like that again."

Chapter 16

Aboard Mod One, Lauren Brown and William Anderson worked on their scheduled tasks.

An introvert, Lauren Brown twenty-six and single, preferred reading a romance or mystery novel to socializing. She was not one to let her hair down. Although popular, she had more acquaintances than close friends.

A voluptuous woman of five foot seven with thick brunette hair, full lips and large dark brown eyes, she was considered a 'ten' in the eyes of most. Despite good looks and a winning personality, Lauren never saw herself as pretty. She had no attitude problems. Vanity was not a word in her vocabulary.

She could have had a life of comfort had that been her objective, but that was not what she wanted. She was impassioned to achieve her goal—becoming an astronaut—and to be part of the deep-space program. Her fellow trainees admired her strong work ethic and awarded her great respect. Her healthy attitude, along with strong intellectual abilities, made a more than favorable impression on the hierarchies of both NASA and WASA.

Raised in a rural Michigan town, Lauren was immersed in a strong climate of aspiration. Her father managed a small manufacturing plant while her mother owned a fabric and knitting store. She had what her mother liked to call "a good head on her shoulders." Her father, disappointed at first that she was not a boy, nevertheless adored her and respected Lauren more than anyone.

On her sixteenth birthday, she received a personal computer as a gift, which she used as a tool to hone her learning skills, and by the time she completed high school, Lauren and her PC became inseparable. Later she chose computer sciences as her college major.

Captain Brown received many offers from large computer software firms after earning her MA, but when Corbin's staff at NASA perused her resume, they called her within the week to discuss the possibility of a career in WASA's astronaut program. The idea thrilled her and she wasted no time arranging an interview. In just a few days, she received and accepted their offer.

Brown believed, as Corbin already knew, life-sustaining planets existed somewhere in our galaxy. She wanted to be part of WASA's challenge in finding them.

Brown's lone companion for the next three days was William Anderson, the thirty seven year old half-alien son of Antar. Like Phil Bennett, he had appealing physical qualities. He was of average height and build, and possessed an outstanding level of intelligence.

Bill had always been a loner. In grammar school, he socialized just enough to keep the gossipmongers at bay. He did not want his peers poking fun at him behind his back. But it strained him to be with the other kids. His high school years mirrored the primary ones. Dating, school dances, football games and after-hours student activities never held any interest for him.

After school, he either went home or to the library. His favorite books—anything pertaining to space. His passion for the heavens earned him the nickname "Astro." One he despised.

Bill spent a great deal of time with his father, Antar. He became the instrument through which Antar's devious plans would be implemented.

Antar knew that his son could travel in circles he himself could not. Being born on Earth gave Bill Anderson certain advantages. Antar despised humans and their weak minds and materialistic pursuits. With a definite purpose, he followed a course of brainwashing his son to instill the values and prejudices he held himself.

What appeared to the outside world as closeness and mutual respect between father and son was in actuality a series of lessons in manipulation, conniving and destructive hate. William Anderson learned his lessons well. He grew into a man with one purpose in life: To do what was necessary to ensure the success of his father's ultimate plans for his home planet, Sadarem. When the time came, he would unleash his father's will by making sure Earthlings would never colonize any other planet in the galaxy.

In college, Bill pursued the fields of mechanical engineering, astrophysics, and computer sciences.

He kept his social life on the back burner in deference to his goals and joined the Air Force's Officer Program following college graduation. He completed basic flight training and was later assigned to F-15 fighter jets.

When he applied to the astronaut program, his application was placed in a hold-file because NASA feared his quiet traits might not blend well with a crew on a space mission. But for some reason when the Pentagon's Colonel McManus learned of his status, he used his influence to override NASA's block and placed him on a short list for inclusion.

Anderson later became a member of the elite Top One Hundred Team.

* * *

Their work assignments completed, Brown and Anderson took a five-hour break for meals, exercise, and rest.

During their meal, they talked at length and shared their experiences from college to astronaut training. They enjoyed their amicable conversation, but for some reason they could not comprehend, their new platonic association began drifting away from simple casual chatter. Anderson began to see Lauren in a different light.

Lauren was comfortable with the way men gawked at her and at first did not give a second thought to Bill's eyes taking her in. But what she did notice was that she felt lightheaded.

"Bill," Lauren asked, "are you okay?" Thinking she could have been experiencing some adverse effects of microgravity.

"Yes?" Anderson asked, "why?"

"Because I'm feeling a little strange. Maybe it's the oxygen level?"

"That can't be," Anderson said. "I checked it thirty minutes ago. But now that you mention it, I feel a little dizzy too."

"For me it's as if I had one drink too many," Lauren said.

"Yeah," Anderson said. "That's about how I feel too. Look, why don't we try to get some rest? We did a lot today."

"You're right, we must be exhausted."

Bill's thoughts of Lauren became more and more erotic. He began to fantasize about seeing her naked and making love to her right there in Mod One.

Lauren returned a strange look—one he could not put his finger on. He moved to within inches of her as she began to remove all her clothes. She became more and more intoxicating to Bill. In just minutes, their irresistible and unstoppable passion led to the first known sexual encounter in space.

Little did the two astronauts know—it was not their own desires that drove them into it.

WASA declared their secret operation a complete success.

Several hours later, Anderson awoke with the worst headache he ever had. Earth Base radioed in for a routine status update.

"We have completed our task checklist and everything is up and running as planned," Anderson said. "Now we're resting."

"Ten-four out," Base answered.

Bill woke Lauren. She too complained of a pounding head. They hydrated themselves with juice and water and began work on another checklist of scheduled activities. Their assignments finished, they went to the galley for a snack.

"Bill, I can't believe what we did," Lauren said. "That wasn't like me. I cannot explain it. What happened to us?"

"I don't know either, Lauren. I have never felt like that with anyone. Believe me, that was the last thing I could have ever imagined happening."

***

Three days later at Kennedy Space Center, the X55 prepared to embark on its second trip to the space station carrying three additional astronauts, two spokes and other supplies, which had been loaded into the cargo hold.

Three new astronauts from the Top One Hundred Team arrived: Dr. Maria French, MD, OB-GYN Specialist, who headed the station's medical program, Major Thomas Corell, of the Astrophysics and Scientific Group, and Captain John O'Riley, a member of the Astrological Navigation team. The astronauts represented a welcomed addition necessary for the schedule to come.

All well-seasoned astronauts, Captain O'Riley's background included six years with the Air Force as a pilot. Major Corell's specialty, Astrophysics, enhanced the team's scientific acumen for the many sophisticated experiments planned for the space station. Dr. French's superb medical credentials spoke for themselves with regard to the upcoming needs of the Medical Unit.

***

Bennett had a brief meeting with Director Corbin before the shuttle's departure.

"Henry," Bennett asked, "did the Pentagon decipher those transmissions from that alien ship?"

"I thought they told you," Corbin said.

"Told me what?" Bennett asked.

"They ended up taking the printouts to your father for interpretation."

"So? Was he able to help?"

"Yes," Corbin said, "but I want you to get in touch with Colonel McManus at the Pentagon for further orders before the E-One mission gets underway."

"Here we go," Bennett said. "I feel like a mushroom again. It sounds like they've got a plan I'm not in on." He glared at Corbin, but gave in without a fight. "Okay, I'll be sure to do that. But you know Henry—it bothers me when I am by-passed. McManus seems to be getting his two cents into everything."

"What can I say," Corbin said. "The Pentagon calls the shots when it comes to aliens."

"*I* can see that Henry," Bennett said. "Maybe I'm a little leery of McManus because he seems to have just popped up out of nowhere. Now he has his hands in almost everything we do."

"I know," Corbin replied. "But I'm sure they've checked him out. Remember, he's in the Pentagon and if we can't trust them, who can we trust?"

"I hope you're right," Bennett said, unconvinced.

Chapter 17

The X55 readied for another shuttle trip to the space station. The astronauts boarded and strapped in, and receiving clearance from flight control, made their scheduled departure at 09:20 hours. The successful launch took them back into orbit. By that afternoon, they pinpointed the station's position and Bennett began his approach. He prepared to make the first direct docking to the Mod One, without a space walk.

On arrival, Bennett positioned the X55 against the Mod One's docking port like a veteran. Not even the slightest thump. Once in position and secured, they opened the hatches of both the X55 and the space station.

The X55 crew boarded the Mod One. Bennett noticed that the module had been set-up and completed according to plan. He met with Captains Brown and Anderson to review their accomplishments, and gave them an update regarding the installation of the spokes they brought.

Bennett picked up on the vibes between Anderson and Brown, but did not say anything.

Following a tour of the station, Dr. French performed a routine physical on Brown and Anderson. She found them in perfect health, but French made a note on Brown's chart about red marks on her neck.

She too picked up on the vibes between she and Anderson.

When French later reported her observations to Commander Bennett, he just nodded.

"Thank you, that's all for now, doctor."

* * *

Commander Bennett assigned the task of installing the spokes to Barnes and Staeb. Barnes operated a remote robotic arm while Staeb fastened them to the exterior mounts on the Center

Module. Meanwhile, Anderson completed all connections for the internal systems.

Barnes, second in command, piloted several additional missions to and from Earth. During those shuttles, two more astronauts traveled to the station: Major Dawn Perkins, Astronomer, and Captain Paul Batty, a Computer Engineering and Design expert.

Major Perkins would operate the Telescopic Equipment Unit in outer module six, using the new H-5 Infrared Gas Laser Telescope for experimentation and investigation of distant stars and planets beyond the solar system. Her previous work experience at nationally recognized planetariums made her an invaluable asset.

Captain Batty an MIT graduate, worked along with Major Perkins in collecting data received, and storing it in the ship's main computer files. Their work was performed in module two, the Computer and Communications module.

Upon completion of the center module and the installation of all eight spokes, the station was ready for the attachment of the eight outer modules. They finished the task prior to the scheduled deadline of August 2012.

* * *

25 August 2012

Dr. French called Bennett and requested permission to speak with him at the bridge. She arrived at 09:00 hours with a concerned look on her face. "Commander," French said, "we have a situation involving two crewmembers which needs your immediate attention."

"Tell me about it doctor," Bennett said. "Are they ill?"

"If you define *pregnancy* as an illness," French said, "yes."

"So you're telling me we have an expectant mother on the station?" Bennett asked, attempting to appear a little surprised and judgmental.

"Yes Commander," French said. "The three-day period that Brown and Anderson spent alone last month will bear more fruit than WASA expected."

Bennett turned and looked at his monitors to break his eye contact with Dr. French. He had to decide whether or not to tell her the truth now or later. After a few moments, he heard French speak.

"Commander," French said, "how do you suggest we handle this?"

"I'll schedule an official meeting with them later today. For now, doctor, let's keep our conversation confined to the bridge, and I'll update Base."

"Commander," French said, "there's one more thing I think you should know about Lauren Brown."

"What, doctor?"

"The blood work I did as part of her physical showed the presence of a very unusual drug."

"Doctor," Bennett said, "you mentioned Brown's blood work, but not Anderson's correct?"

"Yes," French responded, "why?"

Bennett recalled Corbin saying the food and water aboard the Mod One had been spiked. He stared out an observation window tapping his finger against his lips and wondered how it could be that Anderson's blood work did not show the presence of any drugs.

"Commander," French said, "did you hear me?"

"Oh...yes, doctor. I do not know anything about drugs. Send it to Dr. Hunt at Earth Base and let him follow up on it," trying to make light of her question.

"I'll do that right away Commander."

Bennett called Barnes to the bridge.

"Yes, sir?" Barnes said approaching Bennett.

"Barnes, I want you to tell Brown and Anderson to report to me at 15:00 hours today," Bennett ordered.

"Yes sir," Barnes said turning to leave.

"One more thing, Barnes. Please stop at my quarters and get my bottle of aspirin," the Commander said pinching the bridge of his nose.

"Yes, sir," Barnes said.

"Commander," French asked puzzled, "you've been using a lot of aspirin. Is there something *I* should know?"

"Just stress headaches, doctor."

"Really, Commander. How often do they occur?"

"Once a week." Bennett lied.

"I suggest you come to the medical unit for a complete check-up and an MRI. And I mean as soon as possible."

"I'm fine, doctor. It's been hectic here and the stress has taken its toll." He decided to let French in on WASA's scheme. "Doctor, what I'm about to tell you stays between you and me."

"Consider it safe, Commander."

"Doctor," Bennett said, "WASA factored Brown's pregnancy into the mission plan." He paused peering at French.

"Factored? Do you mean it was planned?" she asked, not believing what she heard.

"Let me tell you—that's all you need to know at this time," Bennett said.

"But Commander," French said disturbed, "we're not sure if a fetus can develop normally in a weightless environment. There may be serious complications from a medical standpoint. And who will bear the responsibility if something goes wrong?"

"Doctor," Bennett said, "in the end, it is WASA's. They conjured everything up without a thought to ethics or decency."

"*WASA*, Sir? Weren't Brown and Anderson consenting adults?" French asked.

"Look doctor, I'll level with you," Bennett said. "Without my knowledge the WASA medical team, including your colleague Dr. Hunt, planned for Brown and Anderson to be left alone for three days aboard the station."

"So what? Didn't they have a work schedule to follow?"

"Of course, but WASA also knew they had to eat and drink during that time. In short, Brown's pregnancy was not the result of their falling in love or a passionate liaison."

"I think I get the picture, Commander," French said. "May I ask, are Brown and Anderson aware of what's been done?"

"No they're not, doctor," Bennett said. "But I feel in all fairness I'll have to tell them soon."

"Better you than me, Commander," French said.

"I'm telling you right now, doctor, unless there's a good reason, I'm not going to allow you to abort the pregnancy, nor am I recommending Brown or Anderson be taken off the mission. I am prepared for whatever might happen when they learn the truth. Now please excuse me, I have a lot to do."

Bennett at least was relieved that WASA's scheme was not his doing. "Damn those scientists," he said under his breath, as French left the bridge.

On the way back to the medical unit, French thought about WASA's reckless approach to childbirth testing in space. She thought it might just work, but she never would have done it that way.

Dr. French also had concerns about Bennett's health. Her younger brother had suffered similar pains and died from a brain tumor within a year.

Ten minutes later Barnes activated his communicator, "Commander, your request has been forwarded. Brown and Anderson will be there at 15:00 hours."

"Ten-four, out," Bennett replied. He felt he needed to sit down with these two astronauts to let them speak their minds and to ease any anxieties they might have. He reached the conclusion, however, that when the time came, Dr. Hunt must be the person responsible for unveiling the complete circumstances of the scheme.

15:00 hours

Brown and Anderson, both a little nervous, entered the Command Bridge. Bennett greeted them and asked them to sit at the navigation table. Dr. French was already there.

"Barnes," Bennett said, "please man the bridge."

"Yes sir," Barnes said, as Bennett joined the others at the table.

Bennett stared at Anderson. "I think you know why I've asked you and Captain Brown here," he said, thinking again that he knew this man.

"Yes, sir," Anderson said. "Dr. French told me Lauren is pregnant."

Bennett decided to let them have the floor before he commented.

Brown sat mute as the two of them discussed her condition. She bowed her head and studied her folded hands. She did not like being talked about while she just listened. She had no idea what to expect, but the thought of being reprimanded for something she had no control over was not acceptable. Lauren raised her head and looked straight at Bennett with defiance in her eyes. "Commander," she said, "we never intended for this to happen. We're not at all sure how it did."

She looked at her unwitting partner. "Bill, tell me, what do you think?"

Anderson cast a sideways glance at Bennett and saw him looking at Dr. French. He looked at Lauren. She seemed pale and afraid. He decided to support whatever she wanted to do. But, he mused, he wanted the child—it might fit well into his objectives if she gave birth to a male.

"Lauren, I know how you must feel," Bill said, "but it's the same for me. I can't tell you what steps to take. The decision has to be yours, but you have my complete backing for as long as you need me."

Lauren started to say something when Bennett interjected. "My role is not to pass judgment. You are not here to be chastised, I just wanted to open the lines of communication and to allay your fears and let you know I am always here when you need me. Dr. French," he continued, "your job is to care for Captain Brown and make sure she and the baby are well. Also, what was said here at the bridge stays here. I do not want to hear our conversation parroted among the rest of the crew. Is that clear, Dr. French?" he said, turning a steely eye on her.

French nodded. "Yes, I understand, sir."

"Captain Brown?" Bennett asked, listening for her acquiescence on the secrecy of the matter.

"Yes, sir."

Bennett turned to Bill Anderson. "And you, Captain Anderson?"

"Yes, I understand, sir."

Bennett felt relieved that the couple did not dwell on the details of the matter. "Let's plan on meeting in two weeks and we'll talk again," he said.

Before Anderson left, Bennett asked him to visit with him in his quarters at 19:00 hours. He had something he wanted to clear up, unrelated to the present situation.

They all left the bridge.

"Barnes!" Bennett called out. "My headache came back. Get me three or four aspirin tablets and I'll have my seat back now."

"As you wish, Sir," Barnes replied.

Bennett placed a call to Corbin. "Henry, thanks to you and your unscrupulous doctors, Captain Brown *is* pregnant. It looks like I'm going to have to tell Brown and Anderson the truth if Dr. Hunt doesn't do so soon."

"I figured that," Corbin said. "I'll talk to Hunt. Let's hope Brown makes the right decision when she learns everything."

"The right decision, Henry? How would *you* feel if you were in her shoes? As I told you, if she wants to return to Earth I am prepared to let her go. Thanks to you and your scientists."

"There you go again," Corbin said. "You must *always* have the last word."

"That's right," Bennett snapped back. "I'm not WASA's puppet. If they want to jerk my strings on this mission, let them get another marionette. I know my duty and I will do it *my* way. Now I need to know one more thing before I end this communication."

"What's that, Phil?" Corbin asked, bristling.

"I want to know why Anderson's blood work didn't show the presence of drugs."

"Well...I don't know, Phil. A...let me find out from them and I'll get back to you on it."

Bennett switched off the communications line. He knew he rode the edge with Corbin again, but felt he was in the right and that Corbin knew it.

When Brown and Anderson maneuvered their way back to their duty sections, they both shook their heads in wonder.

"What happened back there?" Lauren said. "I don't understand the Commander's logic at all. I thought we would be facing a reprimand, not be given the keys to the executive wash room."

Anderson laughed and put his arm on her shoulder. "You acted like a perfect Trojan back there. I am impressed. I don't think I would have reacted as well if it had been me."

Lauren moved away from his grasp and said, "Uh, let's not get too close here. I don't know how I feel about you right now, not that I don't like you, but it's just a little..."

Bill pulled his arm away. "I understand. I'm not sure that I like it, but I think I understand. Who knows what will be? For now, I will play by your rules. Is that okay with you, Lauren?"

"Yeah," she said with a wry smile, "that's the way it has to be, at least for now, *captain*."

"Fine with me," Anderson said.

"Bill, the more I think about how Bennett treated us at the bridge, the more I wonder if he was holding something back."

"I've been thinking the same thing. Maybe we should have told him how strange we felt, you remember, right after we ate. Are you thinking what I'm thinking?"

"Do you mean drugs?" Lauren asked.

"Yes, maybe," Bill said, "and for some reason I get the feeling he knows more about this than he's willing to admit."

"Bill, let's leave it for now. We'll be talking to him soon enough, and when we do we'll try to get to the bottom of this."

"Okay, Lauren. Later."

Chapter 18

At 19:00 hours, Anderson arrived at Bennett's quarters as planned.

"Come in, captain," Bennett said. "Bill, I want to talk to you about something I discovered in your personnel dossier." He picked up Anderson's file and handed it to him.

Anderson looked at Bennett and flipped through the pages until he found the section he assumed Bennett referred to.

"Commander, I think I know what interests you."

"Let me first tell you something about me I don't think you're aware of," Bennett said.

"What's that, Commander?"

"Bill, my dossier reads like yours."

Anderson inched closer to Bennett, who held his hands out to Bill. "My father is Luxor," Bennett said.

"Yes I know," Anderson said. "I overheard conversations at the Pentagon when your name came up."

"Is that so Captain?" Bennett said. "I didn't know that I was so popular there. I thought I was going to surprise you."

"It doesn't matter Commander," Anderson said, "we're here now. I notice the scars from the extra fingers are almost gone from your hands too."

Both men stared into each other's eyes, emotions churning. Bennett felt a sense of kinship. Anderson—hostility.

"I think I recall where I've seen you before our mission got underway," Bennett said.

Bill lowered his head in an effort to remember something buried deep in his memory. "Where's that, Commander?"

"Weren't you at a briefing at the Pentagon a few years ago?" Bennett asked.

"Yes, yes, I was," Anderson said, "I remember now."

"My wife Eva and I went there for the same reason," Bennett said. "In fact, we passed you in the hallway."

"Right, you turned back to look at me just as you got on the elevator."

"We met with General Williams. He had the personality of a stone," Bennett smirked.

"I met with Colonel McManus. He seemed genuine," Bill said suppressing a sneer.

"Oh yes, McManus—I know of him," Bennett said, as he thought to himself what a strange and unsavory character McManus was.

Bennett approached Anderson and shook his hand, his mind racing to the future. What indeed would the two of them be able to accomplish? Bennett knew Bill's request for inclusion on the E-One's coming mission had been accepted by WASA and he was looking forward to serving with him.

He was hopeful they would travel the universe together with their offspring, and if they had any luck, return to their fathers' home planet. It was a momentous time, a new beginning.

"Captain—Bill—we'll talk again."

"Fine, Commander, I'd like that," Anderson said with an expression Bennett could quite not make out.

Anderson left Bennett's quarters looking content, but what Bennett did not realize at that time would later prove to be a shock. Both of their fathers shared a mutual distrust of each other.

Antar and Luxor in fact, came from different home planets. The Pentagon's real decision that they be placed apart from each other during their assimilation reflected their true feelings. Though warned by Luxor's surrogate father Dr. Bennett, the Pentagon never suspected the animosity would carry on to one of the alien's offspring: William Anderson.

During the ill-fated alien ship's mission to Earth, which ended at Roswell, Luxor's superiors assured him Antar's allegiance was strong and not predicted to falter, but Luxor still had reservations.

Antar and Luxor never communicated with each other during or after their assimilation. The Pentagon insiders had faith

Eden-459

in Antar's son William Anderson, but had Phil Bennett known the truth about Anderson's father, he never would have approved of Anderson's participation in the up-coming space mission.

Anderson had another secret, which held the potential to threaten the entire space program. Colonel McManus's true allegiance did not belong to the Pentagon. He was an alien from Sadarem and was transported in secret to Earth several years earlier. It was he who spearheaded the covert plan to have Anderson father a child with Lauren Brown. The hope was that the child be male.

* * *

A week later Lauren Brown called Bennett after speaking with Dr. Hunt from Earth Base.

"Commander," Brown said, "I need to talk to you. May I come to the bridge?"

"Yes, make it in thirty minutes."

"Fine, Commander, I'll be there."

Bennett received a call from Corbin at Earth Base as he waited for Brown's arrival.

"Hello, Phil," Corbin said. I got an answer from the Pentagon as to why Anderson's blood work didn't show any drugs."

"Great Henry, what is it?" asked Bennett.

"I spoke to Colonel McManus," Corbin replied, "who told me that the drug might not have shown up in Anderson because of his alien physiology."

"I see Henry," said Bennett. "But we're talking about a foreign substance being introduced into the blood stream. Something would have had to show up."

"Phil, I don't see a problem here, so why should you look for one?" Corbin asked.

"Okay, Henry, okay. I guess the explanation will have to fly for now, but I have to tell you this entire situation is sticking in my craw and I intend to see it through one way or another."

Making her way to the bridge to speak with the Commander, Brown rehearsed her agenda. She understood Bennett was not part of the scheme she and Anderson fell into, but she wanted to explain her feelings to him anyway.

"Commander," Brown said as soon as she saw him, "I had a serious talk with Dr. Hunt who told me everything and I'm not happy about it. He took full responsibility and explained you didn't take part in it, but believe me, that doesn't help."

"I'm sorry," Bennett said, "but you should know I never would've approved their plan had I known. It should never have happened."

"I believe you Commander," Brown said. "I understand it wasn't your doing, but I've decided not to have the child here on the station. I'm so upset over what they've done." She lowered her head and tried without success to hide her tears. "I'm requesting that you remove me from the mission. I'm going to have my baby on Earth."

"I understand," Bennett said, "and if that's what you want to do, I won't stop you. I had hoped you would stay, but I cannot say I blame you. Does Anderson feel the same way?"

"After what Dr. Hunt told us," Brown said, "he feels it's not our child at all, but WASA's, and he could never accept it as his own."

She hesitated before adding in quiet tones, "He said if I opted for an abortion, he wouldn't object."

"But Lauren, isn't that your decision alone to make?" Bennett asked.

"Yes Commander it is, but my emotions have been in turmoil since I found out what happened.
Sir...I also know about Anderson," she continued, after a brief pause.

"What do you mean?" asked Bennett, freezing in place.

"Commander, I know he's part alien. He told me everything."

"Oh, I see," Bennett said. "I must tell you that I feel despite everything, you have nothing to fear from him. But again, the decision is yours. Tell me, do you think there is any chance you could ever feel something for him?"

"No," Brown said, "I don't think so."

"I understand, and I thank you for being candid. I'm sure it's been difficult for you."

"Yes, it has. But I'll get through it." She smiled at Bennett—a smile which lit up her face, one which also put him at ease and seemed to melt away some of his anxiety. "And you know what, Commander? I'm going to have my baby."

"That's great, *major*, great."

"Excuse me Commander...*Major*? You called me major."

"Oh yes," Bennett said with a grin, "I'm sorry about that. I should not have been so nonchalant about it, but both you and Anderson have been promoted. You both deserve it. Congratulations."

Chapter 19

November 2012
Kennedy Space Center

The team reached another milestone with the orbiting of Module Two. After its installation, the X55 returned to Earth to pick up Module Six. Commander Bennett and Colonel Barnes shared the piloting during the sequential lifting of the eight outer modules into orbit. One by one, they attached them to their respective spokes, completing the station's entire construction phase.

By the end of November, three scientists had been carried to the station, bringing the number of personnel to eleven. The long and tedious task of final testing and checking of all on-board systems followed. The X55 stood by as a precaution.

Earth Base, pleased with the team's accomplishments, completed the mission agenda. The initial crew settled in and made their final preparations for their one-year stay in orbit.

* * *

24 December 2012

The space station's construction having been completed and operational, gave Bennett the green light to begin its rotation.

He ordered the crew to secure everything and strap down into their seats. Then he powered up the thrusters in modules four and eight for six seconds. Rotation began. He repeated the thrusting until the station reached one revolution per minute, which provided enough pseudo-gravity in the outer modules to equal that of Earth's. After achieving stable rotation, the crew was ordered to the outer modules to acclimate themselves to the simulated gravity.

Bennett reported with pride to Earth Base that the New International Space Station was complete and then exchanged Holiday Greetings. The crew took a twenty four hour rest period, giving them ample time to celebrate the Holidays and rest in advance of the arduous scientific schedule to follow.

* * *

During the break, Bennett again asked Anderson to join him at his quarters. Following a meal they talked at length about their grandfathers' origins and all that had occurred since the Roswell crash of 1947.

"Bill," Bennett said, "we all have a lot to be thankful for. Are you aware that the Pentagon and the government plan to help our ancestors defend themselves with a nuclear deterrent in the future?"

"Yes," said Anderson. "McManus filled me in on that plan, but from what I can see, by the time we're able to reach them, it may be too late."

Bennett hesitated from making a disclosure to Anderson about the Pentagon's future secret plan to expedite a weapons transfer to an alien ship. He trusted Anderson so far, but realized telling him everything held no benefit.

"Bill, what was your father's reaction when you told him you wanted to volunteer for a mission to his home planet?"

"He said he would have done what I did. He was upset because he would never see me again, but saw the importance in linking the two planets for future growth and development."

"My father felt the same way," Bennett said.

Anderson went along with Bennett's expectations. He could not tell him his father would never have tolerated the linking of the two worlds. Both Andersons believed the people of Earth to be aggressive, evil, and domineering. Anderson's feelings toward earthlings mirrored those of his father. He would rather see the Earth destroyed than have it associated with his father's world. Though he did not hate Bennett, Anderson's secret charter to stop any Earth mission from approaching his father's planet had to be carried out at all costs.

That was the real reason he applied for a position as an astronaut. Aided by his secret alien operative inside the Pentagon, Colonel McManus, he got the job. By the time Bennett discovered his horrendous plan it would be too late.

Chapter 20

The space station's modules had been designed for the most effective and efficient use of every square inch of space. Its total square footage came to more than six thousand.

The initial crew of twelve astronauts and five scientists had an endless schedule of experimental research to perform in the fields of astronomy, medicine, physics, biology, botany, human cell and gene studies, human physiology, pharmacology, and metallurgy.

Awaiting orders from Earth Base, the crew kept busy acclimating to life in space. They adjusted to weightlessness, special diets, and a rigid exercise routine.

Lieutenant Colonel Oliver Barnes, second in command received a promotion to full colonel. His outstanding performance would have a great influence on the success of the mission.

He served in the military as a pilot, and after his commitment, he returned to school where he earned a graduate degree in physics. He never married, and at the age of thirty-five entered the space program through NASA.

A lone child, he had no next of kin, having lost his parents in a tragic car accident during a vacation in North Carolina. An aunt on his mother's side had died young, and two uncles on his father's side were killed in action during the Viet Nam War.

Known for his quiet and calm demeanor, he seldom became riled and approached problems with cool cleverness and efficiency. As Bennett's right-hand man, he often counterbalanced Bennett's often seen short fuse.

His unwavering ability to get things done and do what he was told made him even more of a valued asset. During his screening for the mission, he was asked by WASA interviewers why he wanted to be part of the deep-space program.

Barnes sat quiet for a few moments surveying the room and ceiling with his eyes. He started to remember.

"My entire family gone, no loved ones left and no ties." He bowed his head into his hands for a second, fighting the emotions that bubbled to the surface.

What indeed was his reason for going on such a dangerous mission? Would he ever return to Earth?

"I have nobody left here on Earth," he said. "The program needs people with few if any family commitments, and it's a great personal challenge. I love space and space exploration. What better occupation than to offer my life to something bigger and more wondrous than anything I could ever hope to achieve? I have no real life here...I want my life among the stars."

The screening panel thanked him for his candor.

Barnes went home after the interview, made himself a Caesar salad and poured a glass of wine. Had he said the right things, he wondered. Should he have been that truthful? Perhaps he should have given them a pat answer. But he could not. He could not be anything but truthful and honest. He wanted the job, he wanted the challenge, and he wanted the chance to have a surrogate family, even if it was in space. He ruminated as he munched on his salad. The phone rang.

He got the job.

* * *

Bennett held a briefing with the entire crew in attendance and reviewed the station's status, discussed the operational plan, and laid out his expectations for the coming months.

During a question and answer period, he addressed all the concerns the crew had and reviewed assignments for each astronaut group.

Majors Perkins and Corell worked together in the Telescopic Equipment Unit, which mapped the galaxy and used the new and powerful H-5 Infrared Gas Telescope for the charting of planets, stars, and asteroids.

Dr. Edmonds a neurosurgeon and scientist assisted by Dr. Karley had a schedule of experiments designed to study the long-term physiological effects of microgravity on human cells.

Doctors French, Edmonds, and Karley built a comprehensive cryogenically stored inventory of human, plant, and insect DNA.

The frozen inventory included hundreds of human sperm and ova for studying test-tube conception in space.

The use of in vitro fertilization and artificial insemination would be used as viable alternative options for maintaining a satisfactory birth rate during deep-space voyages lasting longer than the life span of the initial crew. Using live human sperm and fertile ova, their research studies expected to uncover many secrets regarding fertilization in orbit.

The crucial nature of human reproduction on deep-space missions placed the research at the top of the mission's priority list.

A sophisticated new Micron-Scan-Eye microscope used in the research gave them the ability to view and image human cells in a way not possible on Earth. The specimens would be placed in a neutral saline solution and injected into what looked like a crystal ball. The cells, after being polarized by tiny electrical pulses, aligned themselves into the path of a laser beam. They could then be observed from all angles, even from the inside out, without damage.

Another area of research was the study of viral organisms. A number of experiments involving live infectious bacteria and viruses sought to ascertain whether current antibiotics could be used to treat crewmembers with maximum results in space.

Viral mutation and spread in an enclosed environment could be catastrophic.

*　*　*

Until her reassignment back to Earth to have her baby, Major Lauren Brown, along with Captain Batty, designed and tested software programs that archived and managed the mission's immense banks of data. They transmitted their findings to Earth Base each day for analysis, and review.

Doctors Maria French and Kaitlyn Mallard maintained the crew's physical and mental well- being. Any signs of illness would be addressed on the spot. They had the responsibility for the operation of the Medical Surgical Unit, which had the capability of handling everything from a simple muscle sprain to complex heart and neuro-surgical procedures.

Dr. Mallard, also a hypnotist, used her techniques for an array of treatments. Sleep induction and pain control headed the list.

The responsibility for all on-board navigation rested in the capable hands of Captain John O'Riley. He made constant checks of the station's position and recommended any course or speed corrections. He also monitored the station's scanners for possible collisions with other orbiting objects and studied galactic maps for future missions.

Every section gave status reports at four-hour intervals.

Each crewmember wore a wristband voice communicator, which provided instant communications with the bridge and all other crewmembers. Special codes had been programmed into the system to be used in the event of an emergency.

A Code One required the recipient to call the bridge immediately. Code Two warned of critical system failures—a subsequent digit indicated specific locations. Code Three informed the medical staff and officers of a medical emergency. A special Code Ten would indicate an internal security threat.

First Lieutenant Staeb's responsibility fell in the area of computers, communications and electronic maintenance. His background in these fields made him key in the critical area of equipment maintenance. He kept a large inventory of testing equipment and replacement parts and coordinated his activities with Earth Base and the Commander at all times.

The bulk of the crew's assignments had been geared to research and preparation for future deep-space voyages.

The station's galley hosted a wide variety of foods. Sixty percent of their meals came from tubular, push-up, and squeeze containers. Nuggets and pellets of grains and dried fruits were always available. Water and juices were ingested using flexible squeeze bottles equipped with check valves to avoid spillage. Should a spill occur, a sixteen-inch long disposable device resembling a hypodermic needle was used to vacuum the debris.

Dry foods, though less problematic, needed constant vigilance to avoid stray particles floating about the modules. Bacteria growth from the particles could cause both health and equipment problems.

The difficulties in handling food in zero gravity became apparent from day one when a crewmember lost control of her gelatin dessert and sticky little red blocks started floating about the galley. But, the routine became manageable after a few weeks.

The crew kept the galley spotless at all times. All food wastes would be placed in airtight sealed destruction bags for incineration in a microwave waste unit. The powdery tan-colored remains found a new use as fertilizer in gardening experiments and food production. Non-organic waste materials were compacted and placed in special export containers for transport back to Earth via the shuttle.

On a deep-space mission, non-recyclable and non-organic materials would be jettisoned.

* * *

Every crewmember exercised daily, which aided in maintaining the proper condition of their bodies' muscular and vascular systems.

Proper physical conditioning would be aided with the use of tension exercises, a walking drum, and push-pull devices. The astronauts received a four to six hour personal rest period each day for hygiene and sleep.

Dr. French maintained meticulous current detailed medical records for every crewmember. She recorded their daily food intake and general physical condition. She would also provide recommendations for adjustments as necessary. All nutrition and conditioning protocol had been well rehearsed during the astronaut-training phase. The crewmembers' space diet was begun weeks before their trip into orbit.

Medical problems were natural. Dr. French had the authority to order any crewmember back to Earth for treatment if necessary. The next shuttle would exchange the ailing crewmember with a replacement astronaut.

Chapter 21

Experiments aboard the station bore fruit.

Live sperm cell studies revealed a surprising discovery. Doctors Edmonds and Karley spent two months working with samples using a special camera synchronized with a powerful electron-eye microscope.

Viewing the tapes, the doctors observed the individual sperm had a rounded shape compared to the usual pear shape found on Earth. Also, their mobility level appeared to be much higher. In Earth-based studies, sperm were much less active.

Sperm having a greater activity level would provide a dramatic increase for the chances of successful fertilization. The WASA scientists believed microgravity was responsible for the differences in the sperm's shape and vitality level. In addition, the life span of the sperm had more than doubled.

The experiments were repeated thirty-five times with the same result, which intrigued Earth Base scientists. The big question, which had to be answered, was whether normal fetal development could take place in the weightless environment.

Fortunately for the scientists, Major Brown's pregnancy answered many early questions. She agreed to participate in the study for as long as she stayed on the mission, provided no harm came to her unborn child.

During an MRI of Brown's fetus Doctors Edmonds and Karley observed something never seen before: The existence of neural pathways from the fetus to the mother's brain via a second umbilical cord. It was a far departure from ordinary fetal development.

Earth Base doctors had concerns as to the possibility of fetal abnormalities with regard to Brown's baby, but for the time being concurred, it would be imperative the baby reach full term. They also requested amniotic fluid, blood, and DNA samples be sent to Earth Base for analysis.

The X55 made another round trip to Earth and brought back Eva Bennett, Commander Bennett's wife, and a scientist Dr. Sandra Lauder.

Dr. Lauder had an extensive background in viral research and her work was crucial to understanding the behavior of different viruses in the space environment. She also had strong credentials in the fields of antibiotics and astrobiology.

* * *

Eva Bennett thirty-seven years of age, completed her astronaut training and came as a volunteer to join her husband for the purpose of conception and birth aboard the station. She was also slated for inclusion in the future E-One's deep space program.

If similarities between the Brown and Bennett pregnancies could be found, questions would be both answered and raised.

As Eva boarded the station, Bennett saw something new in his wife. She seemed slow in her motions and her face looked a little paler than normal. He chalked it up to the exhausting flight.

When she spotted him, she moved toward him with an enormous smile and outstretched arms.

Bennett's arms encircled her and they shared a lingering kiss. "How did you like the ride?" he asked.

"I have twenty-five hundred hours of flight time back on Earth," Eva said. But none of it could have prepared me for that."

Up close, Bennett could see the fatigue around her eyes and suggested she rest for a while. She slept for two hours. Refreshed, she was given a tour of the station.

Later they enjoyed a private meal, talked to their earthbound relatives via videophone, and retired for the day. Bennett told her about Brown's pregnancy in full detail.

Eva never realized anyone else aboard the station had been involved in a childbirth experiment. She thought she was the only one, but that was okay with her, she looked forward to the camaraderie of another mother and child.

"I never said I had to be the first," Eva said. "Just to know I did my part is enough for me. Phil, I am curious though about some of the things you said about Lauren's pregnancy. If it's so unusual, is there anything we should worry about?"

"I'm not a doctor, but from what Dr. French said, her pregnancy is proceeding at a normal pace. Also, Dr. Edmonds theorized since neural pathways from the unborn fetus to the mother's brain exist, there is a good possibility she could download her knowledge to the fetus. If that becomes a fact than there's a good chance that the child could be born with an astounding level of intelligence."

"My goodness," Eva said, "do you realize what that could mean?"

"Remember our meeting at the Pentagon when we read about the findings during the autopsy of the pregnant alien?" Phil asked.

"Yes, but how is that connected to Lauren Brown's child?" Eva asked.

"The child's father is William Anderson," Bennett said. "Bill's father was the other alien who landed with my father at Roswell. His name is Antar."

Eva's eyes opened wide and she wondered, "*What might they look like...these strange and different little beings?*"

"Oh, now I remember," Eva said. "By the way, did Brown know he was half-alien from the beginning?"

"No, but there's a lot more to the story than two people just having sex. Someday I'll fill you in, but for now you need your rest."

Since Barnes manned the bridge, Bennett relaxed for a few hours. It had been a productive day and now the crew rested.

Chapter 22

January 2013

Lauren Brown went to the medical unit for her five-month check-up when Dr. French noticed how advanced her pregnancy seemed. To French she looked closer to her ninth month.

"How are you feeling?" French asked.

"I feel pregnant, doctor," Lauren said, a little fatigued.

The inertia force scale revealed she had gained twenty-two pounds.

"Lauren, have you changed your eating habits?"

"No, why doctor?"

"You've gained more weight than normal. I want to do another sonogram just to be sure everything is okay. Your baby is by all accounts fine, but in view of your weight gain I'd like to make certain."

"Doctor, you're making me worry. Do you think there is a problem? If there is, tell me." Lauren's heart began to beat fast and the fetus's movements grew more active.

"Believe me, Lauren, I have no reason to think there's a problem. The additional scan is just precautionary."

Despite Dr. French's assurances, Brown still felt nervous.

"Okay doctor, as long as you're sure. When do you want to do it? I won't rest a minute until you do."

"We can set you up right now, if that's okay with you."

Lauren took a deep breath and slowly exhaled, calming down a little. "Fine Dr. French," she said, "let's get it over with!"

French had Lauren put on a gown and positioned her on the examination table. She palpated Brown's lower abdominal area and found nothing unusual except for the fact the pregnancy had advanced. French applied a gel lubricant and turned on the sound scanner.

"Watch the monitor with me so you can see your baby," French suggested.

Eden-459

Manipulating the scanner with skill, doctor French made an 'Hmmm' sound as she went over the area several times.

"Doctor, is everything okay?" Lauren asked on guard.

"Everything looks fine except for one thing."

"Why, what's wrong?" Brown said, almost bolting from the table.

"You're closer to full term than you should be," French said.

"Oh, is that all?" Lauren said, "You scared me half to death." She wondered out loud, "But how can that be, I conceived just five months ago?"

"I know that, Lauren, but don't worry. It seems the fetal development has accelerated. Just keep following your normal routine. I'll update Earth Base, they'll need to know the latest findings before you get there."

"Oh, doctor, I forgot to tell you, I've changed my mind about going back to Earth and I asked the Commander if I could continue with the mission."

"I'm happy to see you've changed your mind," French said. "That's very good news. You'll be a fine asset."

"Being an astronaut is what I've always dreamed of," Lauren said. "I just couldn't give it up."

"I have no objections to your staying on and I'll bet the Commander is delighted too," French said.

"Yes, he is."

Dr. French held back some serious doubts out of concern for Brown. The most unusual finding she had ever seen started to unfold. Accelerated pregnancies just do not happen. She made a prompt call to Dr. Hunt at Earth Base.

Following French's update, Hunt conferred with WASA's medical colleagues in Europe and the United States regarding Brown's pregnancy.

The acceleration may have resulted from one of two things: An unknown genetic anomaly or the fact that fertilization and fetal development had occurred in a weightless environment. As far as the maternal-fetal neural pathways, medical experts around the world were dumbfounded.

They knew the father was half-alien, but they needed to take a cautious approach. Unless evidence surfaced of serious defects or malformation, abortion would not be considered an option.

The following day Commander Bennett received a call from Dr. French. "Commander, I have Eva with me at the medical unit. She wants to speak with you."

"Put her on," Bennett said.

"Phil, I'm pregnant!" Eva blurted out.

"That's fantastic news, darling and everything's fine, right?"

"Dr. French says it is, and she thinks I'll have our baby in October."

A silence prevailed. Eva thought the connection had broken.

"Hello...Phil, are you there?"

"Yes, I'm here. Sorry, I just got one of those piercing headaches again."

"Please come and see Dr. French, I'm worried about you. You never did go for that MRI. Can I tell her you'll stop in later?"

"Okay, tell her I'll be there late this afternoon."

"Good," Eva said. "Those headaches scare me."

"I know. Don't worry, I promise I'll see her later today."

Bennett's migraines became more and more debilitating. Barnes sometimes found him at the bridge's main console holding his head in pain. He did not go for the MRI. He knew he should get checked, but feared being taken off the mission if any abnormality existed. His burning desire to go on a future space mission became an obsession. As long as he could control the pain, he would stay in the program. He hoped it would soon go away for good.

* * *

Added to the excitement over the on-board pregnancies, several scientific accomplishments had been achieved.

Dr. Mallard discovered her use of hypnosis in the space environment proved effective in dealing with stress and even physical pain. Crewmembers needing therapy seemed to go under her complete control much easier than they did in Earth's gravitational environment.

In one incident, a crewmember sustained a crushed finger. Mallard helped the patient shut down his pain receptors as French sutured the wound.

Because of that successful treatment, she felt confident she could apply her hypnotic techniques to lessen the pain of labor and delivery.

French saw advantages to the use of hypnosis in childbirth. She decided that she would allow Mallard's assistance in the delivery of Lauren Brown and Eva Bennett's babies using hypnosis instead of anesthesia, even if a Caesarian section had to be performed.

Hypnosis also worked well for sleep induction. Since the routines aboard the station set specific rest periods for every crewmember, the ability to fall asleep proved difficult at times. Hypnosis reduced the need for sleep inducing drugs and became the preferred treatment.

* * *

Captain O'Riley and Major Perkins made great strides in mapping vast expanses of the galaxy. They found that by echoing high intensity radio wave frequencies off planets, they could measure distances with incredible accuracy.

That finding had given WASA engineers the green light to develop and build two Scout-probe vehicles that could travel far ahead of a space ship during a deep-space voyage. The potential navigational and collision avoidance benefits would be enormous.

The Scout could also detect the presence of dangerous black holes that could ensnare a ship like a fly in a spider's web. Also, an unmanned Scout could be orbited on a temporary basis or even landed on a planet by remote control, which would enable it to send back images and surface samplings to the main ship for scientific analysis.

Major Corell's work with the H-5 Infrared Gas Telescope had yielded the discovery of many new celestial bodies that could be reached within one hundred years traveling at a fraction of the speed of light.

He had documented twenty-five planets deemed worthy of exploration by WASA for the purpose of finding an acceptable habitat for humans.

One planet mapped was located on the near side of the galaxy appearing to have all the main ingredients needed for life, but the finding could not be confirmed until future missions traveled closer. Two-thirds the size of the Earth, the planet contained twenty percent less water with an oxygen rich atmosphere and a three hundred day annual cycle.

It had one moon and orbited one hundred million miles from its sun. Most other planets in the galaxy were positioned too close or too far to their suns to ever support human life.

What Major Corell deemed as a chance discovery, was in fact the planet, Xeron—the birthplace of the two Roswell survivors—Luxor and Antar.

WASA's choice of vector placed the E—One on a definite path for the solar system in which Xeron resided.

No chance discovery at all—Corell would later learn that he followed a previously planned course.

Chapter 23

WASA scheduled a conference to review the space station's progress. Corbin put out a request for all senior staff and officers to attend, as well as the Press. His agenda covered everything that had taken place aboard the station to date. Bennett and his crew participated via video conferencing.

Corbin looked back at Bennett on the video screen. "Hello Commander, nice of you to be with us. How are things up there?"

"Everything has been going well here Henry, and I want you to know the entire crew has been patched in."

"Why that's great!" Corbin said. "We want all of you folks up there to know how much we appreciate the fine job y'all are doing."

"The space station has been a great success," Bennett said, "and I want to thank each of the individual crewmembers as well as all those who have supported, and continue to support it there on Earth. I'm also happy to announce that we have two pregnancies in progress aboard the station."

He omitted the questionable circumstances surrounding Brown's conception.

Corbin then announced a new mission plan to travel to planets on the near side of the galaxy.

"We will use the new E-One space ship for the mission," Corbin said, as he unveiled a twelve-foot model of the proposed craft. The audience voiced its strong approval.

Corbin tapped the microphone and asked for quiet.

"Our model E-One contains removable sections for your inspection. The phenomenal new craft will be over eight hundred feet in length and two hundred fifty feet wide at its widest point. If stood on end, it would be more than half as tall as the Empire State Building, in New York City.

"As you can see, the craft has a delta shape. When the mission reaches the outer limits of our solar system, its two rear aerodynamic wing sections will be removed to function as two Scout vehicles.

"The ship's total square footage counting its four decks will be over seven hundred thousand square feet even after equipment installation. The delta shape will help deflect and protect the ship as it travels at ultra high speeds from any collisions with objects it might encounter.

"Three command centers are planned: One in the nose, one in the center, and one aft, which are all redundant for reliability and flexibility during emergencies.

"Two docking and cargo ports are included in addition to four air-locked hatches, which are to be used for exterior maintenance and other operations which will require external vehicular activities.

"Movement aboard the ship would be difficult and time consuming given its size," Corbin continued. "To alleviate this problem, a simple and efficient personnel carrier has been designed which will be routed to all major areas of the ship. We have nicknamed it the *E-train*.

"Three carrier cars holding up to six passengers will make their rounds about the ship at a top speed of twelve miles-per-hour. One additional flatbed carrier car is included in the plan to be used to move large pieces of equipment and supplies. Monitored by computer, the train will travel inside climate-controlled tunnels. But, when external loading or off-loading is required, the system can be vented by bridge control to match the outside space environment. It would then be necessary for workers to wear spacesuits while performing their tasks.

"When in carrier car mode, a Call Car Button is pressed at an entry point. Within seconds, a train entry hatch will open to allow passengers to enter their car. Once inside, a destination code can be selected on a keypad that will command the car to take them to any one of fifty-six locations aboard the ship.

Eden-459

"During operational testing at maximum speed, engineers said the tight turns and twisting action reminded them of amusement park attractions."

The group chuckled at the analogy.

"The E-One will have incredible amounts of thrust using a larger version of the SINERE engine employed on the X55 shuttlecraft. There will be two banks of eight engines mounted in the rear of the ship. Having over two hundred forty million pounds of thrust, the ship will be capable of operating with an enormous payload and attain a maximum safe velocity of five hundred thousand miles-per-hour.

"The ship's upper deck includes a farming module capable of producing enough output to feed the crew for an indefinite period. Given the E-One's vast and complex systems inventory, it's not possible for me to cover everything at this time, however, we've invited Doctors Bogort and Werner to our meeting and they will be staying with us afterward to answer your queries."

Corbin opened the floor for questions.

"How much do you anticipate the cost of the project to be?" a gentleman asked the panel.

"We estimate the cost to be near six hundred seventy-five billion dollars," Corbin said. "WASA's Financial Director Mr. Kohler reported we have already received funding commitments of three hundred billion dollars from the international membership. Also, our Chinese and Japanese partners have voiced their intention to increase their level of funding."

A woman near the podium stood. "Since the mission will involve people who will never see Earth again, how do you plan to have an adequate staff for the ship as crew members die? Also, why do you think the global members are willing to put their money into the program?"

"Ma'am, your questions are well taken," Corbin said, "and you are right, it is a concern. At present, we have about one third of the ninety-five astronauts needed to begin the mission. We are, however, aggressively recruiting candidates from the entire globe until we meet our needs.

"Those who volunteered have gone through a thorough screening and have accepted the challenges, uncertainties, and the obvious fact of no possible return to Earth.

"Most of the personnel who will reach their final destination will have been born during the voyage. They will be at an advantage since their entire families will be with them. Also, those born on the ship will have little sentimentality or allegiance for Earth.

"Other important facets of deep-space voyages lasting many years are the psychological and emotional effects from living in close quarters for a long duration. Our experience aboard the International Space Station went a long way toward helping us understand the phenomenon."

Director Corbin took a drink of water and glanced at the wall clock.

He continued, "There have been some reports of behavioral and psychological changes during atomic submarine tours lasting over four months. It is not possible to know how successful we will be with humans living in a closed-rigid shipboard environment for many years on end.

"Regarding your second question," Corbin said, "the funds are coming in simply because it is the hope of many to find a new planet to inhabit."

A gentleman to Corbin's left raised his hand. "Sir, what type of defensive weapons would your crew have at their disposal if threats should arise during a mission?"

Corbin leaned over to Dr. Werner and asked him to respond.

Werner stood up and walked to the podium. "We believe threats from an alien source are only a very remote possibility, but should it happen, the E-One's defensive laser weapons inventory would be preferred. Also, the ship's arsenal includes a quantity of nuclear weapons."

"Can you be more specific," the gentleman then asked, "about the types of nuclear weapons to be used and why they might be needed?"

Eden-459

Werner glanced at Corbin for a second before divulging more information about the E-One's nuclear arsenal. Corbin nodded his assent.

"Some things must remain secret regarding our E-One's weapons arsenal," Werner said, "but I can tell you it will include an anti-missile defense system with capabilities for offensive use. The nuclear weapons inventory will be included only as a defense in case a major threat should arise."

Despite the eager show of hands, Corbin closed the meeting and reminded the attendees they were invited to visit with the panel along with Bogort and Werner at the E-One model display.

Chapter 24

Commander Bennett met with his wife Eva, Dr. French, Colonel Barnes, Majors Anderson and Brown, and First Lieutenant Staeb. He recapped the station plan and informed the group he had received orders to add two more modules. "They will be pan caked onto the Center Module," Bennett said. "One will provide housing and a nursery for the newborns while the other will accommodate the influx of new astronauts for our future deep-space mission."

The following day Bennett spoke to Dr. French.

"When is Brown due doctor?"

"It should happen soon," French said. "I've asked her to report to medical in the morning for a check-up."

"Very well doctor," Bennett said, "please keep me informed."

When Major Brown arrived, Dr. Mallard assisted as French performed a follow—up exam.

"Doctor," Brown said, "I must tell you something strange has been happening with my baby."

"Strange, Lauren?" French said. "What do you mean?"

"When I relax and I ask my baby to move, it seems to respond."

Dr. Mallard asked, "What do you mean by move?"

"Let me try to explain," Lauren said. "In my mind I tell my baby to move its foot, and I know I feel something. Or, I'll just think about it keeping still so I can sleep and it seems as though the baby settles down."

"Are you sure, Major?" French asked.

"Yes I am, doctor," Lauren replied.

"How many times has it happened?" French asked.

"Maybe twenty or thirty."

"Major," Mallard asked, "would you mind giving us a demonstration while we perform a scan?"

"Of course not, doctor."

"Major," Dr. French said, "if what you are saying is true, we'll have another *first* to announce to Dr. Hunt." She set up the sonogram unit as Mallard helped Brown onto the exam table. She attached tie-downs to help keep her steady. French then began scanning and asked Brown to attempt a mental instruction to the fetus.

The first command Lauren gave her baby was to clench its fists. Two tiny fists closed as the doctors watched the scanner in amazement.

French nodded to Mallard, who acknowledged she also saw it. French asked Brown to have the baby open its fists. The fists opened. Mallard nodded to French.

The next request was to have the baby move both arms up. The baby did that too.

"See?" Brown said, feeling smug.

The doctors recorded the entire sequence of events for study by Earth Base. French thanked Brown for her cooperation and told her the videotape would be sent to Dr. Hunt for his review.

"Are you feeling any labor pains yet?" French asked.

"Sometimes I think so, but if they are labor pains, they're mild," Brown said.

"Major," French said, "your baby is low and it may enter the birth canal within twenty-four hours. I want you back here early tomorrow as a precaution. Until then you must rest."

"Fine, I will," Lauren said with excitement. "Please, doctor, can you tell me if it's a boy or a girl?"

"Do you want to spoil the surprise?" French coaxed.

"Yes, please tell me."

"Okay Lauren. It's a girl."

"Oh thank you, doctor, thank you so much for telling me."

After she left, French called Dr. Hunt regarding Brown's unusual revelation.

"Nothing similar has ever been seen," Dr. Hunt said.

"It has now," French said. "I'll send the tapes on the next shuttle."

"Fine, doctor," Hunt said. "And one more thing. Later this year, assuming all goes well, can we have both the Brown and Bennett babies brought to Edwards for an evaluation and work-up?"

"I don't see any reason why not. I'll speak with the Commander about it."

"Thank you, Dr. Hunt said, "get in touch with me in a few days."

Later that day the shuttle arrived carrying the first of two add-on modules for Center Mod One, then returned to Earth to pick up the second. After both add-on modules had been positioned, four space walking installers connected them to opposite sides of Mod One with the help of a robot mini-tender nicknamed the *Tug*.

Given the designation of Mod One A and B, the family-living and personnel modules, they each provided an additional one thousand square feet of living space housing three to four couples at the station. Their modular design enabled expansion by adding identical units as the on-board population increased.

Commander and Eva Bennett wasted no time in setting up their living quadrant adjacent to Mod One's entry making it convenient for him to get to the bridge.

* * *

At 09:00 hours the next day, Major Brown reported to the medical unit. "Good morning Lauren, how are you feeling today?" French asked with tenderness as she gave her a big smile.

"I feel wonderful doctor," Brown said, "but let me tell you what my baby did last night," Lauren said, animatedly.

"My, my Lauren, it must have been something!" French said, laughing at Brown's exuberance.

Eden-459

"Oh yes it was," Lauren giggled. "My baby must have been dreaming she was playing soccer or something. She wiggled and kicked her feet...I thought she was going to jump right out!"

French and Mallard chuckled. "That sounds like a typical healthy girl to me," French said in an effort to reassure her.

Let's get you onto the table and have a look." The familiar crisp snap of her surgical gloves could be heard.

"Lauren, the baby has moved quite low into position and you've begun to dilate," French said. "How often have you been having contractions?"

"Once in awhile, but they didn't seem strong...oh...my goodness...except for that one." Lauren pulled herself up on her elbows, inhaled deeply and let out a loud sigh. "Now I know what real labor pains are."

Dr. Mallard wiped Brown's face with a cool cloth and said, "It looks like we'll be having our crew's new addition soon."

"Is everything all right?" Lauren asked.

"Yes Lauren," French said, "now I want you to just stay right where you are and try to relax. We're here for you."

Brown laid back on the table while the doctors prepped her for delivery and started an IV with Oxytocin—a labor-inducing drug. She relaxed and fixed her eyes on the overhead lamps, and began to reflect on all that was happening to her. She thought, "Here I am in labor, one hundred sixty miles above the Earth. I knew the program held a lot of excitement, but I never expected anything like this."

Almost asleep, she pondered, "My baby will be born soon. Her father is half alien. Suppose it turns out, she is not normal. No, she will be fine. All those movies I watched only reflected someone's imagination...crinkled foreheads, pointed heads, funny shaped ears. How could they know what alien newborns really look like? Besides, Bill Anderson is pretty good looking and so is Commander Bennett..."

"How did I become the test platform for WASA? It's funny, I probably would have volunteered if they had only asked, but that is all history now. I must be strong, take it minute by minute and live my life with my daughter, no matter what. Deep in my heart, I always did want a daughter. From here on it's up to me to make the best of it."

Another powerful contraction broke Brown's musings. She let out a cry, "Doctor!"

"We're here Lauren," French said, "another one?"

"Yes doctor, and it was strong," Brown gasped. Fifteen seconds later, "Here comes another one," Brown yelled.

French checked on the progress. "Let's have a look at you Lauren. My, my," French said, "that two-hour nap and a little help from Oxytocin sure changed things."

"Now doctor? The baby's coming?" Brown asked excitedly.

"Yes Lauren," French said, "and don't worry about those silly things you talked about in your sleep."

"I talked in my sleep?" Brown asked, embarrassed, "you mean you and Dr. Mallard heard everything I was dreaming about?"

"That's not unusual Lauren," French said, "we've heard a lot worse."

"Dr. Mallard," French said, I'm ready." She turned on the overhead surgical lamps. "Here we go Lauren," French said. "On your next contraction I want you to follow it up with a great big push."

"Okay doctor," Lauren breathed.

"Everything will be fine, Lauren. Show me that beautiful smile."

Brown smiled back, but at that, second a contraction developed. "I feel one doctor," Brown said, "it's a strong one."

"Good Lauren," French said, "as soon as it begins to subside, push hard."

The contraction tapered down and Brown pushed as hard as she could. French looked at Mallard and said, "One more like that and we will have the baby."

Eden-459

On the next contraction, Brown took four deep breaths and pushed.

"That's it Lauren," French said. "One more good push should do it...yes, here she comes. Oh! What a beautiful child you have," French crooned. "Just a second," French said urgently, blinking in astonishment. "Dr. Mallard, I think you should take a look at this."

"What's wrong doctor?" Brown cried out. "Is she okay?"

"Stay calm Lauren," French insisted. "The baby looks fine, but there's..."

"There's what doctor?" Brown panicked, trying to sit up.

"No Lauren, don't get up and please stop wriggling," French said. "Just lay back and let us handle everything. Give her a shot of Demerol doctor, stat!"

After the injection, Brown quieted as French and Mallard studied another first. The umbilical cord appeared normal, but an additional cord existed they could not explain. Its diameter was less than two centimeters. Dr. French performed thousands of deliveries, but never came across a *second umbilical*.

"Maybe the extra cord contains the neural paths to the mother?" Mallard said.

"I'm sure of that." French said. "Look here, the cord is attached to the back of the baby's head, but I don't know what I'm supposed to do with the other end."

"Did Dr. Hunt send us any information?" Mallard asked.

"No, definitely not," French said sternly. "Get on the voice line to Base right now. I don't want to do anything until we hear from Hunt."

French cradled the baby in her arms with a gentle touch as she checked her vital signs. Everything seemed fine so far. She let nature take its course and allowed the placenta to expel itself from Brown's own contractions.

Dr. Mallard's attempts to reach Dr. Hunt failed. All she could ascertain was that he was on a flight to Houston.

"Keep on trying," Mallard told WASA's message center. "Tell them it's very urgent."

Then another problem arose. The newborn's lips and skin began to turn blue. A sure sign of oxygen deprivation, French placed an oxygen mask on the baby's face. She noticed the baby stopped breathing altogether. Panic set in as she made a desperate attempt to resuscitate the baby, but it did not seem to be working. The baby's color worsened.

"Mallard!" French yelled, "I need your help, stat. Give her a few good hard slaps on the buttocks."

A whack sounded, but no cry. "Again doctor," French ordered. "Harder!"

Mallard slapped the baby's buttocks harder than she wanted, but then the baby gave out a gasp and a loud screeching cry...and another, and another. At last, the child began to breathe on her own again and her color began to improve.

French sighed with relief and said, "Thank God...a little longer and we might have lost her."

Brown remained half-asleep through the entire ordeal.

In just minutes after the close call, French received a call from Dr. Patel on her communicator. "I'm sorry I couldn't get back to you sooner doctor," Patel said, "we've been unable to reach Dr. Hunt."

"I understand doctor," French said. "Dr. Mallard and I delivered Lauren Brown's baby. There was a tense moment, but now she's stable. However, we still have a problem."

"Go ahead," Patel said.

"There's an additional umbilical cord attached to the back of the baby's skull," French said, "can you advise us as to what to we should do with it?"

"Yes," Dr. Patel said, "but didn't you get the special procedure information we sent regarding births of partial alien ancestry?"

"No, I never received it," French answered, confused.

"I don't understand why you didn't get it. We instructed Colonel McManus to forward it to you over a month ago," said Patel.

Eden-459

"Doctor, to *hell* with McManus!" French exploded, "the extra umbilical, what do we do with it?"

"Just cut it one-half inch from its attachment pod on the skull," Patel instructed, "then cold pack everything and send it to us."

"Very well, stand by," French said. She cut the mysterious umbilical cord with a surgical scissors. "It's done doctor. What should we do about the remaining pod?"

"Nothing," Patel explained, "in a few weeks it will dry up and flake off. New hair growth will take place at the site and you'll never know it was there."

"That's it doctor?" French asked surprised.

"Yes," Patel said, "that's all there is to it doctor. It will take care of itself from there."

After the procedure, Brown awoke. "My baby, where's my baby?" Brown asked.

"Here you are Lauren," French said placing the child in Brown's arms.

"What happened doctor?" Brown asked. "Do we have a problem?"

"No, well nothing we couldn't handle, she'll be fine," French said. "By the way, what are we going to call this little one?"

"Elaine," Lauren said smiling. "It's my mother's middle name.

Following the ordeal, French called Commander Bennett while Mallard contacted Anderson.

"Commander," French said, "we have our *first* baby girl. Mother and daughter are doing just fine."

"That's wonderful news doctor. Everything's normal?" Bennett asked, with a slight edge of concern in his voice.

"She's five pounds eight ounces, in perfect health and a beauty," French answered.

"That's great, doctor. Does Anderson know yet?"

"Yes, Dr. Mallard has him on the line now," French said.

"Good," Bennett replied.

When French noted Mallard's conversation with Anderson had ended, she inquired, "What was Anderson's reaction to hearing he's the father of a beautiful and healthy baby girl?"

"He said he's glad for Lauren," Mallard said, "but he had hoped it was a boy."

"What else did he say?" French asked wondering about Anderson's insensitive attitude.

"Nothing, nothing at all," Mallard replied.

"Strange," French pondered. "Did he at least say he'd come to see his daughter?"

"No," Mallard said. "He just gave a polite thanks for the call and signed off."

Anderson could not tell Dr. Mallard what was going through his mind. Having a daughter was the last thing he wanted. If it had been a boy, it would have been a perfect fit for his scheme to take over the E-One before it ever reached planet Xeron. As far as he was concerned, it would have been better to abort the pregnancy.

June 2013

Major Brown's baby Elaine progressed well while Eva Bennett's pregnancy reached its fifth month. Eva's was accelerating at the same rate.

On June 15, Eva went to Medical for a pre-natal check up, and to her surprise, French told her to expect the baby within the next day or so. Eva shared the same special ability Brown had of communicating with her unborn child through the neural paths to the fetus's brain.

"Doctor, will everything be all right?" Eva asked.

"Eva, Lauren and her baby have been doing well, and your baby's development rate matches that of Elaine's. I see no reason whatsoever to worry and we will do everything possible to ensure you have a healthy baby. By the way, you said you wanted a boy didn't you?"

Eva's eyes widened with excitement. "Oh doctor, it's a boy?"

"Yes, it is!"

"Phil will be delighted," Eva said. "We both wanted a son."

Dr. Mallard asked Eva if she was willing to allow her to use hypnosis during delivery and Eva gave her consent, on condition of course that Dr. French would approve.

The next day Eva called Dr. French and informed her she was having regular contractions. French told her to report to the Medical Unit at once. On her arrival, French explained that a second umbilical existed, but not to worry about it.

"From what you're saying doctor," Eva said, "can I assume Lauren's baby had an extra cord?"

"Um hmm, and I just want you to be aware of it so you are not frightened when you see it," French explained.

"Thank you for telling me doctor. I would've been pretty shocked if you hadn't told me what to expect."

"Eva, believe me when I say it was quite a surprise for us too," French said. "But as you've noticed, little Elaine looks fine and she's in perfect health."

After Dr. French explained the extra cord to Eva, Dr. Mallard relaxed her for a few minutes and began hypnosis. Once placed in a mild hypnotic state, Mallard had Eva position herself onto the delivery table.

French observed dilation had begun and she prepped her. Eva labored for two hours while the doctors stood ready for the imminent birth of the baby.

"How do you feel?" Dr. Mallard asked.

"The contractions aren't hurting anymore."

"Let's begin pushing," French instructed Eva. Three pushes later, the baby was born and introduced himself with a loud cry.

"Just look at this child," French said. "He's perfect," and placed the baby onto Eva's breast.

Eva's joy when seeing her baby brought her to tears. "Call Phil...I mean Commander Bennett...no, I mean my husband," Eva said confused but laughing.

"He's already on his way," Mallard said. "Eva, are you feeling any pain?"

"None whatsoever, doctor."

"Wonderful. We can thank Dr. Mallard for that," said French. Congratulations. Did you decide on a name for him yet?"

"Oh yes, doctor. Phil and I decided on Paul Phillip."

"Now...there's a name with class," Mallard said. "*Paul Phillip Bennett.*"

French called Earth Base to report the details of the birth to Dr. Patel. She also asked if they found anything unusual with the tissue samples she had sent from Brown's delivery.

"As a matter of fact, they did," said Patel. "Brown's samples were quite uncommon."

"Uncommon, doctor? How?"

"Let me just say the DNA Helix is, well...different," Patel said.

"Um, I see, but how?" French repeated.

"I'm convinced it has something to do with the father being part alien," Patel said, "but we're not sure yet."

"Thanks doctor," French said, "please let me know when you find out more."

"I can assure you we will."

As the weeks passed, the newborns developed at a rapid rate, but their other special qualities would not be understood until much later.

Childbirth in space had been accomplished. A crucial milestone in the space effort had been reached.

Chapter 25

The following month Dr. French received a call from Dr. Hunt. "I'm sorry you couldn't reach me when Brown gave birth," Hunt said, "I was on the water with my new boat and for some reason my cell phone stopped working."

"I understand," French said, "things like that happen. Dr. Patel helped us with the removal of the extra umbilical."

"Good," Hunt said. "I understand the Bennett baby arrived too."

"Yes doctor, he's a beauty," French said. "So far he's doing well."

"Did Dr. Patel tell you about the Brown baby's DNA problem?" Hunt asked.

"He said he made some unusual findings, but he didn't mention any special problem. Can *you* add anything that we should know?" French asked.

"I'm afraid I must," Hunt said.

"Afraid? What do you mean doctor? What's wrong?" French asked alarmed.

"I'm sorry doctor," Hunt said, "but the child will have to be *terminated* and sent to us."

"Terminated? No…Why? She's doing fine doctor," French said, with an emotional tone. "I can't believe you're telling me this. My God...there better be one hell of a good explanation as to why."

"I'm sorry, but the child is not normal," Hunt said. "If we allow it to survive, serious physiological problems will develop."

Dr. French became choked up and unable to speak. All her observations pointed to the fact that Brown's baby was healthy and normal. She could not fathom taking the child's life on Hunt's directions. She thought, "It would be nothing less than murder to take the baby's life."

She decided to speak with Bennett before saying another word about the child to Dr. Hunt. "Let me get back to you doctor," French said. "You can't expect me to carry out this type of order with blind obedience."

"The sooner you do what I say, the easier it will be for you and Brown," Hunt answered. "Remember too, I gave you a *directive* from a higher authority and it must be carried out."

Stunned, French said, "I'll get back to you by tonight. Over and out." French covered her face and sobbed.

Dr. Mallard overheard French's conversation with Hunt. She never saw French that upset. "What's wrong?" Mallard asked. "What did Dr. Hunt say?"

French closed her eyes and shook her head.

Mallard asked again, "What happened? Please tell me."

"I don't think I can handle this," French said.

"Handle what," Mallard insisted.

"They want us to terminate the Brown baby...they maintain there is a problem with her DNA," French said embracing Mallard for comfort.

"I don't believe it," Mallard said. "Elaine looks fine. Did he say it was an order or just a recommendation?"

"An order," French said. "Then they want the remains sent to them."

"No! This can't be real doctor," Mallard said, "it must be a bad dream. A nightmare."

"I wish it was," French said. "But it's not. They want us to kill Brown's child because *they* think the DNA has some defects they do not understand. I cannot tell Lauren—Commander Bennett must get involved in this right away. Please call and tell him we have an emergency and need to speak with him."

"I'll call him right now," Mallard said as she pressed the call button on her communicator.

"Before you do," French said, "don't tell him what it's about, even if he asks. Just say it's urgent—we must see him."

"As you wish."

Chapter 26

Commander Bennett had just arrived at the bridge after a long night's sleep. His eyes still puffy, he peered out of an observation window and looked down at Earth. He thought to himself, "What a beautiful and peaceful looking planet. No wonder my grandfather's ship found it inviting."

But his moment of serene thought came to an abrupt end when his communicator started pinging a medical emergency- *Code Three*.

His mind had not yet cranked up for the day's work and he said out loud, "Why do these things have to present themselves so early in the day? I hope it's just a routine request for equipment at the Medical Unit. Sometimes Dr. French thinks the mission will fail of she runs out of something."

Bennett hesitated, but after pressing the *return call feature* on his communicator, Mallard's voice came on.

"Good morning Commander, we have a serious situation and need to speak with you as soon as possible," Mallard said.

"What does French need now?" Bennett asked.

"This isn't a request for supplies, Sir. The matter is serious, and we must speak with you right away," Mallard said.

"Very well," Bennett responded. "Oh, can you please bring me something for a headache. I think I'm going to need it."

"We're on our way."

On arrival to the bridge, they handed Bennett a packet of tablets. Bennett noticed French and Mallard had been upset.

"Thank you doctor," Bennett said taking the medication. "What's going on? You two look as though we've had a death."

"It's not your fault Commander, but *that* was a poor choice of words," French said. "The fact is that if we follow a directive we just received from Earth Base, there *is* going to be a death."

"What are you talking about? I know they think they are gods at times, but this sounds ridiculous. Get to the point doctors, what's going on?"

Bennett took three tablets.

French looked at Mallard and began to sob again. Mallard became too choked with emotion to speak. With difficulty French began, "Commander, Dr. Hunt just told us we must *terminate* the Brown child."

He bowed his head in thought for a moment then bolted straight up. "Did I hear you right?" Bennett asked. "They want us to terminate Brown's child?"

"Yes Commander, I'm afraid you did," French said beginning to sniffle. "They stated that her child's anomalous DNA will predisposition her to develop serious future physiological and psychological problems."

"I pray Lauren Brown hasn't been told," Bennett said.

"Of course not Commander. And if we do have to follow their order, I could never be the one to tell her," French said.

"Dr. Mallard," Bennett said, "please push the red button there in the center of my command panel. I think we need to have a chat with Director Corbin. Both of you stay right here with me."

"This one Commander?" Mallard asked, pointing.

"Yes, just press once. I'll take it from there."

When Mallard pressed the button, the communications system performed an automatic voice connection from Bennett's console to Corbin's office and home phones. It was 06:00 hours when Corbin's phone rang and Mrs. Corbin answered. She shook him and said, "The phone!" she shook him a second time, "The phone Henry, pick it up!"

Corbin answered sounding dazed, "Hello, Corbin here."

"I know how happy you must be to hear from me, Henry," Bennett said.

Corbin noticed the lack of frivolity in Bennett's voice. "Happy Phil? What's happy about six in the morning?"

Eden-459

"Nothing Henry. I'll get to the point," Bennett said, firmly. "Are you aware WASA and the Pentagon medical team have decided we should terminate Brown's child?"

Corbin hesitated contemplating his answer to Bennett's question. He knew a firestorm of protest was on tap. He read the memo regarding the decision to terminate Brown's child the day before and thought, "I should have notified Bennett myself. Now, *I'm* on the defensive."

"Phil, I received the memo yesterday," Corbin said. "I needed some time to digest it."

"You blazing fool!" Bennett yelled. "Why in God's name didn't you bring it to my attention right away?"

"I told you Phil…I needed time," Corbin said.

"Where's your head Henry…up your backside?" Bennett said, as he gave Corbin a verbal pounding. "Didn't you even *suppose* French and Mallard would get the directive too?"

"They did?" Corbin asked surprised. "Who's responsible for that? I never signed off on it."

"Your charming Dr. Hunt told them this morning," Bennett said in a raised voice. "Are you going to tell me it was a mistake?"

French and Mallard sat stunned listening to the discourse between Corbin and Bennett. In their hearts, they prayed that it *was all* just that—a mistake. But then Corbin said something that struck them deep in their hearts.

"It's not a mistake Phil," Corbin said. "The recommendation specified the child be terminated." I'm sorry, it's out of my hands at this point and I have no authority over WASA's medical panel."

Bennett's eyes bulged with anger and frustration. He knew he had to put *his* career and maybe the entire mission on the line to save Brown's child. But if that is what it took, he was ready.

"Henry, I warned you the last time they foisted something like this on me," Bennett said. "Remember? When they drugged Brown and Anderson?"

"Yes…I remember."

"What did I tell you I planned to do if they tried it again?"

"I know. I know Phil. You said you would leave the mission."

"That's right and I meant it. Get this straight, Henry," Bennett said in a clear loud tone of voice. "Go to the White House if you have to. The child will not be harmed. If I don't get a call from you by tomorrow telling us the child is off the hook, then you better be prepared to see Brown, her child and *me* getting off the shuttle for the last time at Kennedy tomorrow night."

French and Mallard chimed in, "Tell him we'll be there too."

"Phil, I heard you...and your doctors. Let me see what I can do."

"Tomorrow night Henry," Bennett reminded him. "I'm dead serious about this."

"Over and out," Corbin said.

"Dr. French," Bennett said, "I want you and Dr. Mallard to go back to your routines for today. Tonight I am packing my things. I suggest the both of you might want to do the same."

"We couldn't stay either," French said. "We're with you Commander. If they force us to comply with the order, neither of us has the heart to do it anyway."

"We're agreed," Bennett said. "Be at my quarters by 20:00 hours tomorrow."

Bennett planted the onus on Corbin for straightening out the whole mess. He decided if they insisted on terminating Brown's child as planned, he would indeed resign.

At 20:00, hours the next day French and Mallard arrived at Bennett's quarters. But, he was not there. After waiting fifteen minutes, they made a somber decision to go back to their own quarters to finish packing for their trip home.

At 21:00 hours, while they packed there was a knock on French's door. French opened the door to find that it was Bennett carrying a large box under his arm. French said, "I guess it didn't work out Commander. It looks like you've packed your personal belongings too."

Eden-459

"Oh no," Bennett said. "This box just arrived on the shuttle. I thought you and Dr. Mallard would like to see what's in it before I present it to Lauren Brown."

Bennett opened the box to show them what it contained. French and Mallard's eyes widened while they both broke out in huge smiles and sighs of relief. It contained twelve sets of toddler space garb. The name embossed on the front read: *Elaine Brown-Astronaut*.

Chapter 27

The space station reached its sixth month of full operation without major technical setbacks.

A remarkable and important metallurgical discovery was made when an experiment produced a new hybrid metal alloy. Named *Tilumium*, it had even greater qualities than those of Titanium— the ability to withstand twice the temperature, less than half the weight and three times stronger. The discovery represented a major breakthrough for aircraft and spacecraft design and durability, but the new alloy's most valuable property was its ability to deflect and stop high levels of space radiation.

Until now, a serious concern for space travel was the ability to include effective shielding of the ship to protect crewmembers and sensitive equipment from radiation in space.

Prior to the new alloy's discovery, metals capable of shielding the crew had to be so thick that the weight of the craft reached unacceptable levels.

Tilumium made it possible to design and build much larger, stronger, lighter and safer space vehicles. It would be used as the primary metal throughout the construction of the new E-One spaceship.

As the station's mission progressed, construction of the E-One had begun at a new hanger built at Edwards Air Force Base, California. Hanger Nine became a self-contained city of activity designed to accommodate the enormous physical and logistical scope of the E-One project.

Edwards proved ideal since it had some of the longest runways in the world. The frequent dry and clear weather and its remote location in the Mojave Desert provided a high level of safety and security.

Most of the nearby population consisted of military and civilian contractor personnel. The more than three thousand men and women needed to build the ship came from all over the world.

In spring of 2014, the E-One's sixteen SINERE engines underwent static testing at Edwards. During the scheduled weekend tests most non-essential personnel were asked to leave the vicinity in avoidance of the dangerous noise levels generated by the engines. During testing, the ground shook. Civilian authorities within a hundred mile radius received calls asking if an earthquake had occurred.

By fall, the E-One's construction neared ninety percent completion, as hundreds of on-board systems were being installed and tested. Its electrical power requirements equaled that of a small city. The ship's computer and guidance elements surpassed state-of-the-art levels and had multiple redundancies.

Piloting the E-One's launch into orbit required at least seven astronauts. The balance of the mission's personnel and gear would be lifted in sequence by shuttle prior to the E—One's arrival at the station. The full mission payload could only be loaded in orbit, because the craft's superstructure could not withstand the stress of the full weight during launch.

Though enormous, the E-One spacecraft was light in weight, since the new versatile metal alloy, Tilumium had been used wherever possible.

Weather conditions for the launch required close monitoring since crosswinds above twenty-five knots would be dangerous.

While the E-One received its finishing touches at Edwards, the space station's crew carried on, as equipment and supplies were lifted to the station.

Additional living modules had been stacked onto the existing ones for housing, training and supplies in preparation for the mission.

Over one hundred twenty shuttle flights carried cargo to the station. Large items had to be tethered nearby until the E-One's arrival.

At Edwards, propulsion engineers completed tests of all sixteen SINERE engines and installed them onto the E-One.

A low-speed test roll down the runway had been performed while the ship had been positioned onto its one-time launch undercarriage system. It supported E-One on rails similar to train tracks. Following the test roll, all support and environmental equipment received their final certifications. The E-One was deemed ready for its 7 December 2014 mission launch date.

A steady flow of volunteer astronauts made the shuttle trip to the space station in preparation for the E-One mission. Astronaut candidates received a thorough screening for their suitability to participate in a *mission of no return.*

All prospective candidates received extensive background checks. WASA, the Pentagon and Commander Bennett had to feel confident that the astronauts selected had volunteered for the right reasons.

A list of warning flags assisted the screening personnel in identifying potential undesirable participants. In addition to personal interviews, and psychological testing, the screening panel communicated with the candidate's immediate family, neighbors, church leaders, and the Medical Information Bureau.

Candidates who had any prior psychiatric treatments, recent divorces or child support responsibilities, or had been taking medication for any mental or emotional illness, were summarily excused from the program.

By mid-October, seventy-three astronauts had been recruited. There were twenty-four married couples among the crew. Six couples were engaged and planned marriage during the voyage. Husband and wife astronaut teams received preference.

The number of mission volunteers to date raised WASA's expectation that a full crew of ninety-five would be present and ready by November.

The astronauts came from all over the world, from every race, religious and ethnic group. Most ranged in age from twenty-five to thirty-five.

Living the rest of their lives in a long-term closed environment would place a heavy strain on every crewmember.

Eden-459

The medical staff anticipated the need for medical or psychological assistance, and was prepared to administer treatment.

Chapter 28

The Bennett and Brown babies had been progressing well, but the same could not be said for Eva Bennett since she had been ill for several weeks. Dr. French decided she should be returned to Earth for medical care, and had her shuttled back for special attention at Edwards.

Following a series of tests, the diagnosis indicated she suffered from an acute form of multiple scleroses. The disease had progressed at an alarming rate. She had been experiencing blackouts and periodic falls.

Bedridden, Eva asked that her husband and son travel from the space station to Edwards to be at her side. Lauren Brown and her daughter also made the trip for Elaine's evaluation.

A special team of medical experts had been dispatched to Edwards to study both space children for the first time. Dr. Hunt was expected to accompany them and head the group, but for some unknown reason he never arrived.

When his medical colleagues at Edwards called his Pentagon office regarding his whereabouts his secretary told them that as far as she knew he had left for Edwards two days ago.

Commander Bennett arrived at the medical facility when the doctors who treated Eva informed him of the grim prognosis. Eva would be lost to the disease within days.

Eva clung to her husband and son when they arrived, but after only a few precious moments with baby Paul in her arms, she lost consciousness. An unexpected and serious complication later developed, making matters worse, when both babies turned blue and went into acute distress, all vital signs failing.

Bennett in a panic summoned the doctors to help Eva and had his son rushed to intensive care for evaluation. Elaine Brown was already there.

The doctors determined that the infants were having difficulty due to the Earth's oxygen mix. Once the babies were stabilized, they decided to return the infants as fast as possible to the space station to avoid putting their lives in jeopardy.

The infants were placed on a shuttle for an immediate return to the station. When Dr. French saw them, she reported a rapid improvement in their vital signs.

The next day Dr. French called Bennett to give him the good news. His son Paul and Elaine Brown made a full recovery. But Bennett had bad news to share with French—his beloved wife Eva had passed away.

Bennett requested immediate cremation for his wife. He then took a somber three-day leave to Santa Barbara, California to visit Eva's parents and attend a special military funeral service in her memory. He never realized how many people's lives she had touched until then.

Few if any in the congregation could hold back their emotions during Father Antonio Carlo's eulogy. A military honor guard completed the service and presented both the United States flag and a WASA banner to Bennett. After 'Taps' was played, he presented the flags to her parents.

When Mass ended, he turned to leave the church with her parents at his side to find there had been standing room only. As he walked to the front doors of the church, a touching message was expressed in the faces of everyone there. Eva was dearly loved and would be deeply missed by many. Henry Corbin, who made a special trip in her honor, comforted Bennett and Eva's parents at a reception line outside the church.

The following day Bennett boarded the next shuttle back to the space station, taking Eva's ashes with him.

During the return trip to the station, Bennett's mind was filled with dark and painful thoughts. Carrying Eva's ashes brought home the reality of his tragic loss. She was part of him, the loving part. He would go forth without the only woman he had ever, or would ever love.

Chapter 29

November 2014

 The astronaut crew reached full strength for the E-One's intrepid voyage into the galaxy.

 The final details of the mission plan had been reviewed repeatedly by WASA. Mistakes were not an option. The mission promised to be the largest, most complex, expensive, and challenging ever conceived for the exploration of the galaxy.

 On November 21 the rollout ceremony for the E-One took place at Edwards. Despite the searing desert heat, several thousands attended the ceremony, along with dignitaries and WASA representatives from around the globe.

 At 11:00 hours, the Air Force Band marched onto the tarmac outside Hanger Nine. A special grandstand had been built for the occasion, draped with flags from every country that participated in the E—One's funding and construction.

 The President, a number of Senators and Congressmen, and a host of military officials sat under the United States "Old Glory." Next to them, key WASA officials, including Director Henry Corbin, Commander Phillip Bennett, and Co-Commander Barnes. Dignitaries from other nations sat adjacent to their countries' flags. A large WASA banner proudly hung across the front of Hanger Nine.

 While the slow moving mammoth hanger doors opened the band struck up a medley of patriotic songs from each participating country.

 Everyone in attendance stood up when the nose of the E-One became visible as it rolled out of the hanger. The entire construction crew, wearing their blue WASA hard hats, also wore a look of pride as they walked alongside the craft.

 A crescendo of applause arose for the E-One's first public debut. Cameras clicked incessantly.

Eden-459

Suddenly it seemed from out of nowhere, a fly-over by the latest Air Force F28-stealth fighter jets roared overhead adding to the excitement.

But all eyes soon shifted back to the E-One. Its sheer size overwhelmed the crowd.

"It's a wonder anything that large could be launched into space," said many onlookers.

After the band finished playing, the Base Commander, Air Force Lieutenant General Frederick Stapleton took the microphone. He welcomed everyone to Edwards Air Force Base and told the audience how honored he and his staff felt to be part of the upcoming mission.

"We feel privileged having our base here at Edwards selected as the construction site for the E-One space ship," Stapleton said. "I wish to take this special opportunity to express my thanks to all the military and civilian leaders from around the world for their unparalleled cooperation and assistance.

"I will try to be brief because of the heat. Let me say what we've accomplished here is not just a technological marvel, but proof positive that together we can build a better world for all mankind by sharing our resources, talents, and technology for peaceful means."

Applause broke out.

"I'll be retiring soon, but will always feel honored to know I was a part of the greatest human space mission ever endeavored. Thank you."

Next, Director of WASA, Henry Corbin spoke. "Ladies and gentlemen I would like all of us to reflect for a moment on one of our fallen astronauts: Commander Bennett's wife, Eva."

The group grew silent.

"She made great contributions to the program and became a dear friend to all of us at WASA. Everyone who knew her will miss her. Her husband, Commander Bennett sends his sincere thanks for all the comforting prayers, cards, and gestures in her memory. Please take a moment of silence and prayer to honor Eva Bennett."

The audience stilled and bowed their heads in respect while Air Force Chaplain Charles Banney read a biblical passage.

Corbin rolled his wheelchair to Bennett's side and offered him a few personal words of comfort. They embraced, not just as co-workers, but also as friends. Bennett no longer had any doubt that deep down, Corbin indeed had a heart.

"Ladies and gentlemen," Corbin continued, "just look at what we've been able to accomplish, together," he said, pointing to the E-One. "What's most important, however, is not its enormous size, but rather what went into it. Vital here is the passion of every worker involved in its construction.

"In my years with NASA and now WASA, I have never witnessed such dedication, hard work, camaraderie, cooperation, and professionalism as I've seen here. Those qualities have been evident from the drafting of the first blueprints until today. What a remarkable achievement for the international community.

"Their positive attitude will help ensure a successful mission.

"We must continue this cooperation and superior work ethic and support every need of our devoted Commander and crew as they journey far into space. We are confident we will do what it takes for their sake and for the future of mankind. We are happy to tell you that Commander Bennett, along with his young son Paul, will continue with the E-One program. Please allow me to introduce the E-One's Captain, Commander Phillip Bennett."

Wearing his silver and blue spacesuit with a noticeable WASA logo patch visible on the front, Commander Bennett shook Corbin's hand and turned to the audience.

"This is the day I've been waiting for," Bennett beamed.

The audience gave a loud cheer.

"As you know, this will be my final opportunity to meet with you in person. We have a team of special astronauts who will be traveling billions of miles with me to distant places in our galaxy.

"We face the challenges ahead knowing we have your support and your prayers. The space frontier holds many known and unknown dangers. Along the way, we will face death, isolation, and uncertainty. Our hope is that we can meet and overcome all of these. With the help of God, we will find another world for all of us. Your endeavors here will help make that dream a reality. Please keep us in your prayers. Thank you and farewell."

After shaking hands with the President and other dignitaries, Bennett made a brisk exit from the stand.

The President of the United States walked to the podium and spoke extemporaneously.

"The United States would like to thank every nation from the four corners of the globe for their cooperation and for getting the job done, and done well.

"The mission we are about to undertake is one of challenges, foresight, hope, and bravery. We in Washington are excited and proud of what *you* have accomplished."

He paused to beam in appreciation at the WASA personnel. "WASA represents the joining of the best of the best when it comes to space technology. We have a lot to learn about space and there are many surprises and dangers out there.

"Again, I thank everyone from home and afar for making this day possible. We wish the crew of the E-One a safe and fruitful voyage and want them to know our prayers will be with them always. God bless our astronauts. Thank you."

The audience offered long and enthusiastic applause and afterward attended a reception at 12:00 hours as the ground crew inched the E-One back into the hanger.

At the reception, visitors viewed the E-One up close. Following the gala, each of the visitors received a poster of the E-One and a group picture of the astronauts.

For the next week, Commander Bennett and Co-Commander Colonel Barnes stayed at Edwards to familiarize themselves with the ship.

Back on the space station, advanced training and procedure drills took place in anticipation of E-One's arrival. Every crewmember had their task assignment prior to departure. All medical needs had to be met before the mission began. Astronauts received a final bailout opportunity during special screening and counseling.

Bennett and his officers returned to the space station two weeks prior to the E-One's launch to make a thorough check of the mission inventory. Enough food had been stocked to nourish the crew for at least two and one half years, which gave the E-One's farm system ample time to grow replenishments.

The upper deck of the E-One had enough farming area to grow food for the entire crew for an indefinite period. The primary growing technique used, *hydroponics,* employed a capillary action water trickle containing needed nutrients, which would cascade over the plants' suspended roots. Special lamps would be used during times when exposure to natural sunlight was not available.

To augment the crew's food source and provide needed protein, the E—One's top deck included an on-board fish farm. A second benefit from the large fish tank would be gained when its rotating water acted as a gyro, helping to keep the ship's course stable.

The ship's wastewater recycling and reclaiming systems received sound testing.

The hospital, pharmacy, and dental modules had all been made ready and operational, and stocked to handle everything from a root canal to open heart surgery.

One week from the scheduled launch, the E-One received last minute preparations. Spectators began camping out around the base to get a ringside seat. Crowd control and security concerns prohibited entry to the base proper by any unauthorized visitors. Observers did not need to be in close proximity to the runway since anyone within ten miles would have a bird's-eye view.

Three days prior to the launch, WASA staff personnel arrived at Edwards to view the start of the mission. The President announced his intention to attend.

Eden-459

* * *

The three-day countdown began.

Excitement rose. News teams set up shop at designated locations around Edwards.

Day two of the countdown.

Enthusiastic crowds of onlookers had been growing by the hour. Dozens of military officers and civilian WASA personnel from all parts of the world made the trip to Edwards to witness the unprecedented and historical event.

On the space station, the crew awaited the E-One's arrival. Once there, the transfer of fuel, equipment, supplies and personnel would begin in earnest.

Chapter 30

The E-One's ground crew positioned the ship on the tarmac and performed final pre-launch inspections. It took on one hundred thousand gallons of water—more than enough to get the E-One to the space station. Almost one million additional gallons, which were earlier lifted to the station and tethered in tanks, would be added when it docked.

Ninety nine percent of the water used by the crew would be recycled. That ability gave the E-One the needed insurance of an adequate water supply for its crew for an indefinite period of time. During the voyage, if additional water was needed, the ship's hydrogen and oxygen supplies could be recombined to form usable water.

7 December 2014
E-One launch at 21:00 hours

At a command bunker built for the E-One's launch, WASA officials headed by Corbin and his staff watched the minute-by-minute countdown.

Two hours before departure the crew took their last meal on Earth. For them it had been both a happy and an emotional time. The base chaplain, Reverend Captain John Sully joined them at the table. He led them in prayer, blessed the food, and offered thanks.

They did not talk about the obvious. Their mood had been shaped into one of eerie silence. They all shared the common knowledge that their fates brought them together on a one-way voyage for the rest of their lives.

After their meal, the chaplain gave the crew a final blessing and presented each of them a gold crucifix on a chain. Even First Lieutenant Staeb an atheist, placed one around his neck.

A short while thereafter, they left the dining hall and boarded a van, which took them to the E-One spaceship. Each crewmember stepped off the vehicle and paused to take in one last breath of Earth's air.

One by one, they made their brave walk up the entry ramp and boarded the ship.

Some of them turned back for a last glimpse, as others just proceeded.

Major Butler lagged behind for a few moments to say goodbye to his mother who made the trip despite her pain from terminal cancer. Following a long embrace she said, "Tony, promise me you'll look for Papa when you get to the heavens."

"I will Mother, I promise, I will."

As he turned away, his eyes welled. His mother swayed from both illness and the awareness it was the last time she and her only son would be together. She grabbed on to his arm. He stopped to look at her one more time and said, "I love you, mom. I must go now," he said, taking a heavy swallow.

She let go, crossing her hands on her chest, "God bless you my son," she said.

Butler walked up the ramp and into the ship unable to look back.

Entering the E-One, the astronauts were greeted by hundreds of red, green, blue, and amber indicator lights that brought the ship's instrumentation and displays to life. They stationed themselves at the bridges, four in the Forward Command, two at the Aft and one in the Center.

At sixty minutes and counting the entry hatch was secured and the crew busied themselves with pre-flight checks. The launch-flight pilot, Major Anton Butler, a thirty-five year old seasoned Marine test pilot and astronaut, initiated voice contact with the command bunker, Earth Base at Houston, and the space station.

While the countdown progressed, the station passed over the West Coast.

"We're ready for you," Commander Bennett radioed Butler. "See you in a few hours."

"Ten-four, Commander," Butler responded, "we won't waste any time getting up there."

At 20:50:00 hours, Major Butler got the go-ahead to start the ship's engines. He brought the power level to five percent, which caused a bright orange glow to radiate from the rear of the craft. Following a five-minute warm-up, the engines were ready for some real action.

Spectators and officials monitored the E-One with an intense expectation of the momentous roar and fiery blast that would soon come from the ship's sixteen powerful SINERE engines.

20:59:00 hours Major Butler received the command from the Flight Control Bunker to increase power to thirty percent. The glow from the engines erupted into a blinding plume of bright white-hot flame. The evening sky lit up and a low frequency rumbling sound spread through the air and shook the ground.

Observers watched the scene with great anticipation, and at exactly 21:00:00 hours, Major Butler applied a vice-like grip to the power level controls. The flight control officer gave him an "Okay to roll." Butler responded with a "Ten-four, we are rolling," as he pushed the power controls to their maximum thrust position.

The E-One's engines spewed forth a spectacular and blinding quarter-mile plume of orange-white exhaust. The engines' roar sounded like a continuous deafening thunder roll as the E-One raced down the launch rails. By the time it reached the halfway point down the runway, the E-One's ground speed reached three hundred knots, lifting its nose upwards at a seven-degree angle. Within a matter of seconds, it became airborne and assumed a near vertical ascent as its one-time launching carriage sped off the end of the railway tumbling helplessly into the desert night in a cloud of dust.

During the E-One's awesome launch into the night sky, the crew endured incredible G-forces contorting their faces. But, even heavier were their hearts, since they knew they had just left the planet Earth *forever*.

Eden-459

With the Earth fading into the distance, and their inexorable climb toward the heavens, the stark reality of their mission began to settle in.

Butler took his last glimpse of home. His eyes glazed as he pondered the future. His mind became filled with nostalgic thoughts. Only tomorrow existed. From now on, there was no turning back.

"Men," Major Butler said, over the ship's intercom, "we must be strong and not let our feelings interfere with our tasks. We are the space faring 'Vikings' of our time. We can do this and we will succeed."

While the ship rose, the fiery exhaust plume wagged far behind the craft lighting up the sky. The thunderous blast from its powerful engines grew even more deafening. Windows began to rattle hundreds of miles away. Suddenly, a loud bang sounded, like the finale to a fireworks display when the ship broke the sound barrier.

In a matter of twenty to thirty seconds, the E-One appeared as a bright speck in the sky as it sped with increasing velocity toward its rendezvous with the space station. Everything quieted. The E-One's voyage into the heavens had begun.

The voice box at the Command Bunker elicited a welcome sound. It was Major Butler reporting. "This is E-One," said Butler, "we have no reds, no vibrations, and we're on course."

Corbin clapped his hands while his staff at the bunker jumped with joy. Everyone cheered, shook hands, and hugged one another. An exuberant Bennett then radioed from the space station and offered his congratulations to Butler and his crew on their successful liftoff.

Butler cut back on power once the E-One reached a velocity of almost eighteen thousand miles-per-hour attaining orbital insertion. Next, he plotted the exact location of the space station for the rendezvous.

He used a special navigational program to control the E-One's approach. In just five hours, Butler had the station in range.

The station's entire crew watched in awe as the huge craft made its approach.

"Major," Bennett said, in voice contact with Butler, "I'm happy to see everything went well and we're looking forward to seeing you and your crew at Dock One. We have quite a reception planned for you."

"Ten four, Commander, and we have a little something for you too," said Butler.

"Oh, what's that, colonel?"

"Mr. Corbin said you wanted a DVD of *The Ten Commandments* so I have it with me. I also have *Casablanca*, some *Flash Gordon* selections, and another one of your favorites, *Gone With The Wind*."

"Well now, he does keep his promises, doesn't he? I'll give him a call to thank him later. I have a surprise for you too, major."

"Great, Commander, what is it?"

"You'll see when you get here."

"Ten-four Commander," Butler said laughing. "We should be docking in about thirty minutes."

"Ten four major," Bennett said.

The E-One's crew maneuvered the ship to the station's Port Dock One. It moved in sync with the rotating space station and once in alignment, latched on. The crew opened the external airlocks of both the E-One and the station. An audible loud rush of air was heard as the pressure equalized between the crafts. A green indicator lit indicating it was safe. Major Butler and his crew then entered the space station.

Butler approached Bennett, gave a sharp salute, and introduced his crew. Bennett congratulated him for a fine job in getting the E-One in orbit. He invited the launch personnel to enjoy a meal with the station's crew and meet the senior officer staff for the E-One mission.

The crews exchanged greetings. Bennett introduced Butler as *Colonel*.

Eden-459

"Good job Colonel, congratulations," said Bennett while smiling and shaking Butler's hand.

Butler, a little amazed but nevertheless proud, thanked Bennett for the promotion.

"Commander," Butler asked, "was the promotion the surprise you spoke about?"

"The promotion is one of them, Colonel," Bennett said smiling. "And here's the E-One's crew manifest. Look under the D's for the other."

Butler's eyes scanned the list until they came to the name of Captain Diana Domenico, Space Navigator—and Butler's former college sweetheart. Though they had kept in touch on occasion, she never informed Butler about her involvement in the space program.

"Commander, where is she?" asked Butler.

"Right behind you, colonel."

Butler turned around and there she was.

"Colonel," Bennett said, "why don't the two of you go get reacquainted and when you're through, come to the bridge."

* * *

The loading process for the E-One's supplies and equipment began in earnest. First, the larger tethered modules that dangled about the space station like a child's mobile were moved into position. One by one, the crew un-tethered, and migrated them to the E-One using remote tugs and mechanical arms.

The supplies included: Nuclear fuel, water tanks, purification units, oxygen, food supply modules, electronic packages, defensive laser weapons systems, Moon and Mars scanning and communications payloads, and medical supplies.

After three weeks of exasperating effort the last of the equipment and supply transfers from the space station to the E-One had been completed. The next task required a team of astronauts to board the E-One to inspect its environmental readiness and critical systems.

Once the E—One had been deemed up to standards, the mission crew began to board. Commander Bennett and his senior officers went first. They exercised the E-Train carrier car system as it took them to their assigned bridge positions. From the bridge, all other personnel received instructions as to the location of their duty stations and living quarters on deck three.

It took a dizzying full day for the entire crew to bring their personal belongings onto the ship, familiarize themselves to the ship's layout and survey their duty sections.

Four general-purpose modules were available for social activities. Multi-denominational religious services would be held every seven days. Crewmembers who prayed daily had access to the ship's chapel.

Recreational modules offered a wide array of activities. Hobbies, crafts, video games and movies were plentiful. The ship was equipped with a superb library and a computer and communications center.

Physical fitness machines and a rotating jogging drum helped to provide the needed exercise regimen for the entire crew. A daily routine exercise program would be essential for the maintenance of muscular and vascular health. No exceptions could be made without the ship doctor's approval.

Educational programs would be provided both aboard the ship and via communications channels. An almost unlimited selection of courses could be found for almost any topic from medicine to astrophysics and engineering. Certain job classifications required constant study and re-certification—the medical field in particular.

A daily security detail of three persons wearing special security badges loosely monitored the ship. Any serious problems would be brought to the attention of the Commander for resolution.

Given the high degree of professionalism among the mission's astronauts and scientists, serious interpersonal problems were not expected. In the end, the Commander would have the final say regarding any disputes between his crewmembers.

Eden-459

* * *

Each section reported a ready status on December 17. Commander Bennett gave final departure instructions to the officers and crew. He offered everyone one last chance to bail out of the mission and return to Earth. Not one crewmember requested permission to go home. Routinely in touch with Earth Base, Bennett announced the E-One would be ready to shove off on December 21.

Chapter 31

21 December 2014
The E-One began its journey

At 06:00 hours, the crew of the E-One made final preparations for their voyage to the stars. The Forward Bridge officers, Commander Bennett, Colonel Barnes, Colonel Butler, Major Anderson, and First Lieutenant Staeb coordinated status with the Mid and Aft Bridges and monitored all systems.

At 07:00 hours, Bennett announced that in fifteen minutes there would be a video and voice address for the crew.

He intended his address to be a motivational talk for the rigors to come. He expected there would be serious mental and emotional trauma for the crewmembers once the ship left the station and ventured into deep space.

At 07:15 hours, Bennett started speaking. Every video monitor and voice speaker carried his message. Following, Earth Base would also send their farewell message.

"Good morning this is your Commander," Bennett began.

A dense silence spread throughout the ship. Bennett continued in a slow and somber tone. "We have received permission to embark at 08:00 hours today. Our ship is ready, I am ready, and I want all of you to be ready as we begin this historic, exciting, and challenging journey.

"We have undocked from the station and are distancing ourselves several nautical miles away prior to main engine start. This afternoon after traveling for seven hours and ten minutes at thirty-five thousand miles-per-hour, we will make a near-pass of the Moon. Our plan calls for releasing a remote-controlled payload, which Earth Base will take command of, and land on the surface. After the Moon operation, we will set our course for Mars.

"I want you all to know I am experiencing the same profound emotions you are. During training and briefings we informed you that the mission we are embarking upon is a one-way voyage.

"We must look reality head on and prepare for the inevitable. Failure is not an option. Our job is finding a New World, land there and begin the proliferation of humanity. This is a special task for special people. I know and believe everyone on this mission fits that description to perfection.

"Always keep in mind you are not alone in your fears and doubts, and in order to aid our adjustment and build strong bonds with our fellow astronauts aboard the ship, I encourage everyone to keep our goal in sight every single day.

"It is time for all of us to buckle-up and prepare for departure. Once we have stabilized our speed and set our course, do not hesitate to seek advice and assistance from the medical staff in dealing with your anxieties or problems. As we begin a fifteen-minute countdown to thrusting, please lock down your duty section and strap in. Thank you, good luck, and Godspeed."

Following Bennett's message, Earth Base was patched in for their final farewell to the E-One's crew.

"We are proud of all of you aboard the E-One," Director Corbin said, "and we will be praying for you as you begin your journey. You have chosen a noble but difficult task. We will fully support your every need.

"Years of preparation and hard work have given you the edge to fulfill your mission. On behalf of the WASA team, I wish you the best of luck and success as you go forth for the benefit of humankind. God Bless all of you."

The ninety-five astronauts aboard the E-One spaceship were ready to depart for their journey into a life in space. The time for stretching their physical, mental, and emotional muscles to the limit had finally arrived.

During the journey, the E-One's entire crew's mettle would be tested. Danger, uncertainty, birth, joy, sadness, and death would be their constant companions. Only two of the *original* crew, the space-born Paul Bennett and Elaine Brown, could ever realize the fruits of their labor, if they survived long enough to get there. The others would be born on the way.

Everyone shared the same dreams, the same hopes, and a common goal: To bring man to a new planet, a new home.

* * *

In compliance with WASA's order, Commander Bennett called Colonel McManus for further instructions regarding the alien ship's message received by the space station. He expected by now his father had been able to interpret the data for the Pentagon.

He patched a secure voice line to the Pentagon and asked to be connected with Colonel McManus. Instead, General Williams took his call.

"General, Director Corbin instructed me to contact Colonel McManus prior to our departure from the space station."

"Commander," Williams said, "I've been briefed. You will be working with *me* instead of McManus from now on."

"Sir, may I ask what happened to Colonel McManus?" Bennett asked, wondering if perhaps McManus took ill.

"Never mind him, Commander. Let's just say he's out of the picture," Williams replied, the tone of his voice signaling to Bennett the matter was closed. But Bennett knew he could push him.

"What's going on?" Bennett asked. "What do you mean he's out of the picture?" Refusing to acknowledge Williams's cue.

"Now is not the time, Commander. We do not want anything interfering with the task at hand. You must focus on what *you* have to do, not on our problems here on Earth."

"If that's a direct order Sir," Bennett said with a slight edge to his voice, "I have no alternative."

"First," General Williams said, "allow me to tell you that the following information *must* be held in strict secrecy."

"Understood, general."

"Fine Commander," Williams said and proceeded with his orders. "Once your ship enters Stellar Space you will rendezvous

Eden-459

with an alien ship. It will be prepared to receive a marked payload of nuclear weapons, which you will be releasing from your inventory. They will retrieve it and continue on to their home planet."

"General, this sounds a little risky to me," Bennett said. "How will we be sure we are communicating with a friendly ship?"

"It's simple commander, your main computer has been programmed with a time-dated message containing a special code word which will be given to you on the day of rendezvous with the alien ship. After you transmit the code they will offer a response which only your computer will recognize and prompt you to begin the transfer."

"Very well," Bennett said, "but sir, I have a question."

"Yes, Commander?"

"General, did the decision to transfer the weapons come after my father interpreted the message?"

Williams hesitated then answered. "Yes, and that's all I am at liberty to say at this time."

"General, I'm not satisfied with your answer," Bennett said, "I get the feeling something is being withheld? I am in charge up here. It is *my* crew, *my* ship that is on the line. When should I expect full disclosure?"

"I'll fill you in with every particular after the weapons transfer."

"I have one more question, general," Bennett said.

"Go ahead."

"McManus? What's up with him? Is he okay?"

"Commander, you don't stop until you get what you want, do you?" Williams asked, giving in to Bennett's persuasiveness. "What I'm going to tell you must not be shared with anyone. Is that clear Commander?"

"Yes, I understand sir."

"That information is as strange as it is confidential," Williams said.

"Strange—strange, General," Bennett said. "How so?" Bennett had always thought something about McManus did not sit well with him.

"Commander, since your voyage is about to begin I think I can at least share what happened to McManus without compromising security. Last week he never reported for work and when we checked his office we found every one of his computer hard drives had been formatted and his desk emptied of everything. It appeared as though he had never been there. I also sent a secret service team to his home in Leesburg."

"What did they find?" Bennett asked.

"Absolutely nothing. No papers, no computer, no clothing, no trace of anything showing he was ever there."

"Unbelievable," Bennett said a little frightened.

"We even sent a forensic team to go over his entire house," Williams explained.

"Well?" Bennett prodded.

"They were about to give up until one of the team decided to check the pipes in his bathroom for residue," Williams explained, "and he found hair samples. They compared the hair DNA to the DNA from a nail clipping they found on his desk."

"Did they match?" Bennett asked.

"Yes, but that is when things took on a very strange twist," Williams eluded.

"Twist," Bennett said. "What do you mean?"

"The samples showed McManus to be alien."

"An alien? He was an *unknown* alien in the Pentagon? How the hell did he pull that off?" Bennett asked.

"We checked out the real Colonel McManus and found out the last time anyone remembered seeing him was when he went camping at Mt. Rainier Park in Washington State."

"Are you telling me there's been an abduction and identity theft?" Bennett asked. "What about *his* family, didn't anyone miss him?"

"The plan must have been well researched," Williams said. "The real McManus had no close personal friends and no next of kin."

"Do you have any idea where the bogus McManus went?" Bennett asked.

"We know he took a military hop to McCord Air Force Base," Williams said. "There, he rented a car and drove to Mt. Rainier. They found the car ditched in a ravine, but no trace of him from that point on."

"This *is* quite mystifying General," Bennett said. "What's your guess?"

"I don't have a clue," said Williams, "but it might not be a coincidence that around the time he disappeared, McCord Air Force Base started receiving credible reports of UFO sightings over Mt. Rainier."

"General, I have to tell you, you sure have a hell of a way of making a guy feel secure," Bennett said. His head started pounding again.

"I understand how you must feel. I would find it unsettling also. But our hands are tied. I'll patch in to you if we learn any new facts." Williams said. His voice took on a quiet tone, "There's one more thing Commander, and I apologize for not telling you sooner. Dr. Bennett passed away a few days ago."

Williams heard Bennett catch his breath and waited out of respect for Phil to speak. Bennett regained his composure and cleared his throat, "General, my surrogate grandfather was special to me. Now I've lost two people I loved very much. How is Lucy?"

"Don't worry Phil, she will be looked after," Williams assured him.

"Do you have anything else?" Bennett asked the General.

"Yes, there is something else Commander," Williams said. "Remember Dr. Hunt?"

"Yes of course, what about him?" Bennett asked.

"If you recall he never showed up at Edwards when your son arrived for his checkup."

"I did think that was curious at the time. Did you ever find out what happened?" Bennett asked.

"Not exactly Commander," Williams said, "the Coast Guard found his thirty-six foot boat adrift in the Atlantic. The keys were in the ignition in the off position."

"No one was aboard?" Bennett asked, dismayed.

"That's affirmative Commander. Nobody and nothing could be found," Williams said. "I guess the best way to describe what happened would be to say he just vanished."

"That's incredible, first McManus and now Hunt," Bennett said.

Chapter 32

The E-One had been positioned three nautical miles from the space station when Bennett called Anderson, "Bill, come to the bridge. I want you to be here when we begin main engine start."

"Thank you, Commander," Anderson said, "I'm on my way."

When Anderson entered the bridge and strapped in, Bennett switched on the ship's intercom.

"We will begin engine thrusting in five minutes," Bennett said. "If you are not already secured at your positions, do so immediately." Five minutes later, he gave the order to start eight of the E—One's sixteen engines, bringing them to a forty percent power level.

For the first time, the entire crew felt the awesome thrust of the E-One's SINERE engines. Their faces contorted, and some of them blacked out as they felt their eyes being forced back into their sockets despite the fact they were wearing gravity suits.

The suits maintained an adequate blood supply to their brains during the effects of high G-forces. The enormous rate of acceleration even had the ship's veteran astronauts wondering whether the superstructure could withstand the stress. Because of the intensity of the acceleration, they could not even move their fingers. When Bennett radioed each section for a status update he sounded as though he was speaking with a mouthful of stones.

A huge stream of exhaust gases followed the E-One as it streaked away from the space station and out of sight.

Those able to see aft watched their home planet fade away until it appeared as a small blue-white marble with swirling white clouds.

Others just could not bear to watch. Many of the crew became choked with emotion, knowing they would never return to Earth.

All the training, preparation and counseling could not dispel the cold hard reality of that simple fact.

After twenty-five minutes of acceleration, the ship approached a speed of thirty-five thousand miles-per-hour. Bennett ordered all engines shut down. The crew felt a welcome relief regaining their ability to move about. Bennett, however, developed a severe headache.

"Barnes," Bennett said, "maintain the ship's course—I have to see Dr. French right away."

"Are you all right, Commander?" Barnes asked.

"Yes, just a pounding headache."

Bennett understated how much pain he felt. He even avoided using a carrier car because he feared the slightest jolt would aggravate his suffering. He thought his head would explode, but despite his excruciating pain, he slowly made his way arm over arm toward the Medical Unit. Every heartbeat became punishing.

Barnes called Dr. French to tell her the Commander was on his way. He also followed Bennett's progress on the ship's internal camera monitors, which enabled him to give Lieutenant Staeb Bennett's exact location.

Staeb rushed to the scene and found Bennett immobile with his eyes closed. "Commander, are you all right?" Staeb asked.

"I had to stop for a minute," Bennett whispered. "The pain in my head is terrible." He labored with each movement he made.

"Commander, let me help you."

"That's okay Lieutenant, I can do it."

Staeb could not bear to see his Commander struggle.

"Commander," Staeb said, "we have to get you to medical, please let me help. Put your arms over my shoulders."

Bennett did not argue. They traversed the ship inch by inch, Staeb making a great effort to handle Bennett with care.

"I can't thank you enough, Lieutenant," Bennett said when they reached Medical. "I appreciate the assist."

"No need for thanks, Commander," Staeb said.

After leaving Bennett in good hands, Lieutenant Staeb went to the bridge and reported to Barnes.

"Colonel, I didn't say anything to the Commander since he had enough to deal with..."

"I'm listening...report," Barnes ordered.

"Well, maybe it's nothing, but at the time I was helping Commander Bennett to the Medical Unit we passed Major Anderson."

"Go on," Barnes said. His instincts told him something was not right.

"Anderson had to have seen the Commander holding onto my shoulders," Staeb said. "What's strange is that he didn't even ask what was wrong or if he could help. He just looked at us and left the area," Staeb said.

"Did Bennett see him?"

"No I don't think so," Staeb said, "his eyes were closed."

"Hmmm, that *is* strange, Lieutenant," Barnes pondered.

"That's what I thought too," Staeb replied, reliving the incident in his mind's eye.

"Thanks for coming to me with this information," Barnes said. He planned to inform Bennett about Anderson's strange behavior at the appropriate time.

"Commander, you look horrible," Dr. French said seeing the look on his face. "What's the matter?"

"I can't tell you how bad my head hurts. It started right after acceleration began."

"Get to the exam table," French said, motioning to Mallard to help him. "I'll give you something to relieve the pain."

Bennett complied. Within two minutes, the pain abated.

"Commander, while you're here I insist we do that MRI you've put off."

"Ah...all right doctor, go ahead," Bennett said. "I can't imagine ever wanting to have another episode like that one."

"We have to get to the bottom of this once and for all. Relax Commander as Dr. Mallard and I set up the machine."

French had Bennett lie still as she moved him under the MRI unit and scanned his brain with precision.

Afterward French reviewed the images with Mallard. The news was not good. French went to Bennett's side and gave him the test results.

"We spotted what's causing the pain, Commander," French said.

"Let's have it," Bennett said.

"Commander, do you ever have visual difficulties, with these headaches?"

"Yes I do, sometimes. The vision in my right eye blurs every once in awhile. Why?"

"Commander, you have a marble-sized mass located between your pituitary gland and the back of your right eye. It appears to be quite soft, so I doubt if it's cancerous, but we'll have to rule that out with a biopsy and tissue pathology."

"You must be kidding doctor. I don't have time for this! You have to do something about it now," Bennett said.

"We have to wait to allow the swelling to subside before we can perform any procedures," French said. "The heavy acceleration must have exacerbated your condition. I want you to plan on coming back before you order any further accelerations."

"Why don't I stop back a few days after the Moon payload drop?" Bennett asked.

"Perfect, Commander," said French. "The swelling should be reduced by then. I want you to take two of these tablets with food twice each day. They'll help."

"Doctor, do not talk about this with anyone," Bennett said standing to leave. "I can't have the crew chewing fingernails."

"Right Commander, don't worry," French said. "You're going to pull through just fine."

Bennett left the medical unit and returned to the bridge. On the way he discarded the medication he had been given, tossing it into a waste bin.

Eden-459

When he arrived, he thanked Colonel Barnes for taking the helm.

"Commander, what happened? Are you okay?"

"I feel better now, thanks."

"Do the doctors know what's wrong? Staeb reported you got there okay, but that you were in a lot of pain."

"I was, but I'm all right now. Don't worry, Barnes, we have a terrific team of doctors. Incidentally, what I say is just between us. You're the only one I'm confiding in." Bennett paused. "They found a small tumor behind my right eye."

"A tumor...are they sure?" Barnes could not meet Bennett's eyes. He was fond of him and did not want to see him suffer. He put his hand on the Commander's shoulder. "I guess that explains all the headaches," Barnes said. "How are they going to treat it, Commander?"

"That depends."

"On what?" Barnes asked.

"If it's cancer, that's one thing, but if it's benign they'll have more options."

"Commander, my prayers will be with you."

"Thanks Barnes, now let's get back to work."

They maintained their speed, and continued toward the Moon.

Bennett's pain abated for the time being, but he could not stop worrying about the tumor. The thought he might not be able to continue as Commander put him in emotional turmoil. He prayed his health would return to normal.

* * *

In seven hours, the E-One reached the vicinity of the Moon and then released a remote-controlled communications and scanning module payload. Earth Base took control of the module's descent. Once settled on the surface, it would serve as an important communications link for the E-One and as a tracking device for objects traveling through the solar system.

The Moon project having been completed, Bennett gave an order to power up the E-One's engines to twenty-five percent. He for one wanted to avoid the severe G-forces of rapid acceleration, and knew that particular percentage of power would lessen the chances of causing another painful episode. After a forty-minute burn, the engines had accelerated the ship to over one hundred thousand miles-per-hour, and the eager crew went about its daily routines with vigor.

Bennett reported to the Medical Unit for his biopsy, as scheduled.

"Commander," French said, "did the medication I gave you help?"

"No doctor, I threw it out."

"Why did you do that, Commander?" French said.

"I have a thing about drugs."

"The purpose of the drug was to reduce swelling. I don't prescribe medication for the hell of it Commander, and I expect my patients to do what I tell them."

"Can we just do the biopsy procedure please?" Bennett ordered.

"By all means, Commander," French said. She knew when to pull back and she did not want to cause him any unnecessary stress.

"Go to the exam table and Dr. Mallard will prep you. We'll have to put you to sleep for the procedure."

Following the biopsy, Bennett recuperated for several hours in sickbay. Afterward, moving in slow motion, he made his way back to his quarters to rest. Barnes manned the bridge. By 20:00 hours that night, the results of the biopsy would be ready.

He received the call upon waking from a nap.

"Commander," Dr. French said, "I have some good news and some news that we must talk about."

"Do I have cancer?"

Eden-459

"No Commander, the tumor is benign, but there are some things that need addressing regarding treatment options."

"Options?"

"Rest, and come to the Medical Unit in the morning and we can go over it then."

"Right, doctor, I'll be there first thing."

In the morning, Bennett reported to Dr. French as promised.

He, along with French, Edmonds, and Mallard, reviewed the MRI images.

"Commander," French said, "we have three avenues to choose from in treating the tumor. Dr. Edmonds, will explain."

"Commander, here's where the tumor lies," Edmonds said drawing a circle around the image with a marker. "First, we could do nothing—which would greatly increase the risk of the tumor growing and putting pressure on your brain. Another approach would be to shrink the tumor using radiation therapy, but that method would require several follow-up treatments and we could damage your pituitary gland or the healthy optic nerves of your left eye. We cannot take the chance of damaging the pituitary at any cost.

"The last option is safest and will offer a permanent cure. But it does have a major drawback."

"You mean surgical removal of the tumor don't you?" Bennett asked.

"Yes Commander, but since the tumor has attached itself to the optic nerve, I'm afraid you will lose sight in your right eye."

Bennett looked at French and Mallard. The thought of losing sight in one eye nearly brought him to tears.

"We understand this isn't an easy decision for you to make," French said, "but in our opinion it's the best one."

"Thank you for explaining everything. Let me think it over for a day or two and I'll get back to you."

"I am sorry, Commander," French said. "I wish I had better news."

Bennett left the Medical Unit and headed to the bridge. For two days, he contemplated his options. On the third day, he called Dr. French.

"Doctor, tell Dr. Edmonds to schedule the surgery. If wearing a patch is the worst thing I'll have to endure, I consider myself blessed."

After listening to Bennett's comment Dr. French remembered the many times she had to advise patients of their treatment options. Sometimes they became depressed and felt sorry for themselves.

French thought, "what a strong man Bennett is. His courage must have played a major part in WASA's decision to make him Commander of the E-One's mission."

Chapter 33

On the day of Commander Bennett's surgery, Dr. Edmonds explained the procedure to him in detail. Access to the tumor would be gained through the hard palate in the roof of his mouth. The surgery, though intricate, was expected to be a complete success.

"Commander," said Edmonds, "you shouldn't experience too much pain from the surgery. I'm sorry you will lose vision in your right eye, but it's a fair price to pay for a complete cure."

"I agree. You and Dr. French have my total trust. But...the loss of vision, I guess there are worse things. I'll be satisfied as long as I'm able to continue commanding the ship."

"Commander," Dr. Edmonds said, "you are a courageous man. I have seen people go to pieces over a lot less."

"Thank you, doctor."

"Commander are you ready?" Edmonds said as he started the IV drip.

Bennett gave Edmonds a double "thumbs up."

"Here we go...now count down from one hundred," Edmonds said.

During three hours of delicate surgery, the team successfully removed the tumor. Bennett recuperated in the Medical Unit.

"How are you feeling, Commander?" Dr. Edmonds asked when Bennett awoke.

"I feel drowsy, but almost no pain at all," Bennett answered.

"Good. You will feel some discomfort for a few days, but don't worry about it. It's normal."

"How did it go?" Bennett asked.

"It went well, Commander," Dr. Edmonds said. "We did additional testing on the tumor and I'm happy to report it was definitely benign."

"Thank God. I have been praying for that answer all along. When can I get back to work?"

"You are a trooper, aren't you, Commander? You may return to the bridge whenever you feel up to it," Edmonds said. "But give yourself at least two days of complete bed rest."

"Thank you Dr. Edmonds, and you too Dr. French," Bennett said.

One week later Bennett went to Dr. French for removal of the surgical sutures.

"Commander," French said, "this will pinch a little. Do you want me to give you a local anesthetic?"

"No thank you. Save it for someone sensitive to pain."

* * *

After several months the medical staff at last found time to get some rest and concentrate more on the routine needs of the crew. Several more pregnancies occurred and became top priority.

The Brown and Bennett babies seemed happy and content in their surroundings, which gave the newer mothers a sense of security. A number of female crewmembers helped care for Commander Bennett's son, Paul.

Drug therapy and hypnosis proved useful tools in reducing the crew's anxiety. Dr. Mallard also found excellent results with group therapy. In her sessions, Mallard consistently raised the crew's hopes by discussing the possibility of finding another planet every bit as beautiful and hospitable as Earth.

* * *

The ship neared Mars, as per the mission plan. The second communications and scanning module payload would be released and remotely landed on the Martian surface. The E-One had to

Eden-459

reverse its position and start six of its main engines to slow the ship down to fourteen thousand miles-per-hour.

When the module descended to an altitude of forty-five thousand feet over its targeted landing site, its large parachutes would deploy allowing it to make a soft landing on the Martian surface.

The E-One approached its operational window to begin the Mars procedure. The ship reversed position and slowed down over the drop zone. During the release, a major problem arose when the payload snagged on part of the cargo bay door.

Bennett had the situation evaluated by Barnes, who reported that resolution would require three space walking technicians to exit the ship to free the payload.

He needed two crewmembers to accomplish a cut-and-release procedure and a third to maintain the tricky tethering lines to ensure no tangling occurred.

Barnes went over the duty roster and selected the first two names. They were telemetry specialists, Lieutenants Adams and Kessler. He called their quarters, but no one answered. Then he put out a "call bridge" message to them via the wrist communications system. But, still no response.

Adams and Kessler were in the galley having lunch. Nearby, Lieutenant Priscilla Collings was also eating. She heard the sound of their communicators and expected them to respond. To her dismay, they ignored the message.

She noticed that something did not seem right about the way they were carrying on. They laughed at almost everything they said to one another. Judging their behavior highly unusual for officers, she did her best to eavesdrop on their conversation. She was determined to learn what they were talking about. To hide her interest she pretended to be reading a manual.

What she overheard was anything but funny. They talked with ease about drugs they *borrowed* from the pharmacy. Then they spoke about commandeering a Scout vehicle and taking it back to Earth.

Kessler's communicator sounded again. "I better answer this one," Kessler said laughing. "Maybe I won a free trip to Mars."

Collings took advantage of the diversion and left the galley. She hoped that Kessler and Adams had not taken notice of her proximity. She turned one last time at the galley's exit to see if they had paid any attention to her—both of them gave her a piercing, cold, hard stare.

Fearing they realized their blunder, Collings went straight to her quarters. She wrote everything down she could remember hearing. When she finished, she placed the note into an envelope, marked it '*Confidential*' and addressed it to Commander Bennett. She radioed Lieutenant Charles Staeb, her fiancé and got his voice mail.

Just then, she heard a heavy knock on her entry hatch. She observed a tiny shadow along the bottom edge and held her breath, not making a sound.

The lone message she left for Staeb was that she had written a confidential note about Adams and Kessler and would handle it later with Commander Bennett.

"The sliding door is secured," she thought, "if it's Adams and Kessler they'll go away if I don't answer." Another knock sounded, only a little louder.

It might not have been them, but she could not take the chance. She stood alert and quiet and waited it out.

She remained perfectly still for five minutes and noticed the shadow had disappeared.

"Phew!" she thought. Whoever it was left the area. It could've just been Charles."

Using restraint, Collings gingerly slid the door open a fraction and peered out to see if all was clear. The passageway leading to the carrier car entrance was empty.

She grabbed the passage rails and pulled herself to the carrier car as fast as she could. After boarding, she pressed the stop selection button for number thirty-four, where her fiancé Lieutenant Staeb worked. To be extra safe she kept her finger on the override button, which caused the car to travel directly to her stop. Speeding toward her destination, she realized that she never locked her living quarter's hatch.

"I can't believe I did that," Collings thought. "It was probably Charles anyway—I hope."

But—it was not Charles. It was Adams. When she left her room, he came out of hiding, entered her room and after rummaging around for a moment, found the envelope addressed to Bennett.

"Where's Charles?" she said entering the electronics module.

"He's not here," said Captain Everett, an electronics technician. "He mentioned he would try to help out with that space walk."

"How long ago did he leave?"

"No more than ten minutes," said Everett. "If you go to cargo bay two you might catch him. Better yet, call Tanaka, he needed someone to manage the tether lines."

Collings thanked him for the information and called Tanaka on her communicator.

"Captain Tanaka?"

"Tanaka here."

"Lieutenant Collings—do you still need someone to help with the tethers at bay two?"

"Yes, are you volunteering?" Tanaka asked.

"Yes," Collings answered.

"Thanks, but you better hurry, they're nearly finished suiting up."

"On my way Captain. Please tell them I'll be there shortly."

"Ten four." Tanaka called Adams and Kessler to tell them Collings was en route.

Collings caught up with them just before the space walk began. She suited up and clipped her safety line to a hook close to the cargo bay hatch.

Martin J. Stab

She was still under the impression one of the space walkers was Lieutenant Staeb. But, it was Adams and Kessler instead. They had their helmets on and visors down, which prevented her from recognizing them.

In minutes, Adams and Kessler completed the task of freeing the payload. Collings noticed they just stayed outside and talked over their one-to-one communications radio. She repeatedly motioned to them to come in.

After ten minutes, they did. Once inside the bay Adams cut Collings's safety line while Kessler grabbed her and shoved her out of the bay into open space.

They waited fifteen minutes before calling the bridge to report an accident.

"Lieutenant Adams to the bridge, come in."

"Go ahead Adams," Bennett said.

"Commander, we've completed the payload release—but lost Collings," Adams said.

Chapter 34

"What do you mean you've lost her?" Bennett barked. "Where is she?"

Bennett removed the patch from his right eye and flung it against the wall in anger. He put on his narrow dark sunglasses. "Now talk to me, you fools," Bennett said. "What happened?"

"We don't know, sir," Adams said, "we don't know what happened. One minute she was right there with us and the next minute she was gone."

"My God! Are you telling me she's marooned out there in space?" Bennett asked, furious at this point.

"Sir," said Kessler, "we didn't see anything unusual—all of a sudden she was just gone—out of sight."

Bennett was outraged and wondered how a crewmember could just disappear. He ordered Barnes to take a rescue team straight to the cargo bay to investigate. "Stay where you are," Bennett ordered Kessler and Adams. "We're scanning the area for her, and Colonel Barnes is on his way."

Barnes and a team of four rescue personnel rushed to the cargo bay. "What happened to Collings," Barnes asked Adams and Kessler on his arrival.

"When we reentered the hatch we didn't see her," Adams said, "she just vanished."

Barnes went to the cargo bay area and checked Collings's safety line. It had been cut clean. He called Bennett.

"Commander, it doesn't look good, I believe we've just had our second casualty of the mission."

"What happened?" Bennett asked, seething now.

"I found her tether line cut clean," Barnes said.

"Cut?" Bennett yelled, "what do you mean cut?"

"It couldn't have been a line failure," Barnes stammered, "it was severed clean with a cutting tool."

"There'd better be a good explanation," said Bennett. "I want answers...I want answers now! Bring Adams and Kessler to the bridge on the double!" Bennett demanded.

Within minutes, Barnes, Adams, and Kessler reported as ordered.

Bennett aimed both index fingers directly at Adams and Kessler's faces, "Talk men. One of you must have seen something. You are the only ones who can shed any light on what happened. What did you men see?"

"Commander," Adams said, "all I remember is that when we were ready to leave the airlock Collings seemed upset and we heard her babbling something about we would all be better off if we just died."

"Kessler," Bennett said, "did you hear Collings say that?"

"Yes sir," Kessler answered, sweat pouring down his face. "But, we never thought she was serious about it."

"Colonel Barnes told me that Collings's tether line was cut clean. Am I supposed to believe she cut her own line?" Bennett asked. He doubted the veracity of these men and wondered if there was more to this than was apparent.

"Commander," Adams said, "we don't have any other explanation. We are just as shocked as you are Sir. I hope you do not think we are involved. We liked Collings and had no reason to hurt her."

But, Bennett noticed something in Adams's face that bothered him. Adams kept averting his eyes when he spoke, never looking straight at him. He could not put his finger on it, but he sensed there was something amiss. He did not want to accept their explanation, but with no other information or proof of any wrongdoing, his hands had been tied. He dismissed Adams and Kessler to their quarters with the order to stay there until advised otherwise.

After they left the bridge, Bennett looked at Barnes with a cold hard stare. "Colonel," Bennett said, "I don't know what happened out there, but I'm not buying their story. What do you think?"

"I can't say Commander," Barnes said, "I just don't know anything about Collings. Can I suggest that we contact Dr. French? Maybe she can help with this."

"Good idea," said Bennett, "but first call Captain Millette and tell him I want Adams and Kessler kept under surveillance until further notice. Also, have him search Collings's quarters for a possible suicide note. Is that clear?"

"Yes sir," Barnes said, "I'll also program Adams and Kessler's wrist-band communicators to ping their locations every five minutes."

"Good," Bennett said. "I'm going to find out what happened if it's the last thing I do.

Bennett stormed back to the command panel. "Barnes, let's get French and Mallard in here with Collings's file."

Barnes called Medical and ordered doctors French and Mallard to report to the bridge on the double with Lieutenant Collings's medical file.

They complied and proceeded to the bridge with the file. They had no idea of what had happened to Collings.

On arrival they found Bennett positioned with his hands behind his back, feet splayed, a look of rage on his face.

The doctors did not know what to expect. "Yes?" Dr. French said. "Commander, what is it? What's happened?"

"Lieutenant Collings is dead."

French and Mallard looked at each other bewildered.

"Dead?" Mallard said, "How? What happened?"

"There's an allegation that she cut herself free from her tether line during an external operation," Bennett said, rolling his eyes upward.

"Why in God's name would she do something like that?" Dr. French asked.

"That's what we're going to find out," Bennett answered. "I'm going to start with the two of you. What I want to know is whether or not she was being treated for depression? And if she was taking any medication?"

"Yes to both," said French. "You're not thinking drug-induced suicide? If you are, I cannot agree. The medication we prescribed has no history of causing suicidal episodes. By the way, we examined her only last week and she checked out fine. In fact, she was all upbeat and excited about her upcoming marriage."

"Maria," said Mallard, "isn't it possible she was repressing her anxiety? It's possible that could happen, and if it did she could have succumbed to a deep-seated psychosis."

"Doctors," he said losing patience, "enough of the armchair theories, she's not fine today, she's dead and her remains are out there!" He pointed outside the ship. "We can't even find her to give her a proper funeral."

"But...but..." Dr. French stammered.

Bennett cut her short. "Never mind the buts. Doctors, I need you to put your heads together and give me something I can sink my teeth into. Dr. French, do you concur with Dr. Mallard?"

"Well," French started, "if she left a suicide note or told someone she wanted to end her life, then I'd buy it. Right now I'm at a loss."

"During their questioning," Bennett said, "Kessler said that just before she disappeared, she talked about wishing she could die. Now you are telling me she was happy and had a bright future. It just does not add up. For now, I have no choice but to report to base the death was a suicide. What do the two of you think about that?"

"Commander," Mallard said. "We just don't have enough to go on to certify her death as a *definite* suicide."

"I feel the same way," French said. "Unless we get more information it should be classified as *apparent suicide*."

Bennett did not feel comfortable with what he had to report to Base, but felt apparent suicide would have to suffice for now. Nothing else made any sense. He could not imagine that Adams and Kessler made up the entire story.

"That's it then," Bennett said. "Put that on her death certificate. But I'm launching an investigation to delve into every facet of her behavior on this ship since we left Earth—Adams and Kessler's too."

"Very well, Commander," French said. "What can we do to help?"

"I want a full audit of the pharmaceutical inventory. Pay particular attention to mind-altering and anti-depressant drugs, the ones that are addictive."

"Yes sir, but why?" French asked.

"I'm not one hundred percent sure, but I noticed something strange about the way both Adams and Kessler acted while they were being questioned," Bennett said.

"In what way strange?" French asked.

"Never mind that now," Bennett said. "Doctors—get back to me in twenty four hours."

Dr. French felt both insulted and ignored. She did not like being dismissed as if she were a junior officer. But she knew she had to obey orders before anything else, and left the Bridge to implement them.

Following the briefing with French and Mallard, Bennett called the ship's chaplain and requested a special funeral service in Lieutenant Collings's memory. When the announcement was made, the crew was shocked and saddened. But there was someone who felt the loss even more than the rest. It was Lieutenant Charles Staeb. When he heard the news of Priscilla's death, he wasted no time calling the Commander and asked to speak with him.

Bennett consented. When he arrived, Bennett noticed Staeb's eyes were red and his face looked drawn.

"Lieutenant, I've never seen you look like this," Bennett said. "What's wrong, are you ill? Has something happened to you?"

"Sir, I guess you weren't aware of it, but Priscilla Collings and I had been seeing each other for some time."

"No lieutenant, I wasn't." Bennett now understood Staeb's condition. "I'm sorry for you. It's a tragedy for all of us."

"She was a wonderful person and I loved her very much," Staeb said. "We had planned marriage." Staeb's eyes welled and he shook his head from side to side, as he reflected on his last moments with her.

"If I knew how to comfort you better I would," Bennett said. "It's horrible when we lose someone we love. I suddenly lost my wife Eva just before the mission began, and I'm able to empathize with you."

"I am sorry, sir," Staeb said. "I know how you must have felt."

"And I still do," Bennett said. He looked away for just a second remembering Eva.

"Commander," Staeb said, "Priscilla was a beautiful, sincere, and happy woman. I cannot believe she would commit suicide. There must be some other explanation. It just cannot be. I will never accept that. Never!"

"I understand lieutenant, try to stay calm. Right now, it is the only thing that fits. Adams and Kessler insisted they heard her say she wanted to end her life because she was depressed over the mission."

"Sir!" Staeb said, "Did I hear you say Adams and Kessler?"

"Yes, why?"

"Commander," Staeb said. "You didn't see the note Priscilla sent you?"

"What note?" Bennett said, alarmed. "I never received a note."

"Then it must still be in her quarters," Staeb said. "She left me a voice mail mentioning it—and Adams and Kessler."

"I never received it," Bennett said. "Do you know what it was about Lieutenant?"

"No sir, I wish I did. She only said she didn't want me involved and would take care of it on her own."

"It is obvious there's something here we need to delve into," Bennett said. "But there's not much we can do right now. I have begun an investigation already. One way or the other I will get to the bottom of this. When we learn something definitive, and I'm confident we will, I promise I'll let you know."

"I appreciate that, Sir," Staeb said.

Eden-459

"Don't mention it, Lieutenant. Be strong, no matter what."
"I'll do my best, Commander."

Bennett called Dr. French as soon as Staeb left the bridge. "How is the inventory going, doctor?"
"We're on it, Commander. We should be able to wrap it up in time."

Chapter 35

The following day Bennett's wristband communicator flashed a Code Ten, which signaled that an internal security issue existed. The call came from Dr. French. She and Dr. Mallard wanted to see him as soon as possible. Bennett pressed the return-call button and told them to report to the Bridge.

He received a ten-four in return and awaited their arrival. Barnes, always at his side, asked if he should stay once they arrived.

"Yes, you'd better stay," said Bennett. "This could be serious."

Within minutes, French and Mallard arrived.

Bennett noticed the concerned look on their faces.

"Doctors, I want Colonel Barnes to sit in on this" Bennett said.

"Fine Commander," French said, "he should hear this too."

"Well, let's have it."

French handed him several pharmacy inventory sheets with notes on them.

"Commander," French said, "we are missing a large quantity of the drug, Alprazolam. To be specific, it is a psychoactive medication prescribed for anxiety disorders."

"What specific kinds of anxiety disorders?" Bennett asked.

"Panic attacks," said French, "phobias, insomnia, muscle spasms and ringing ears."

"That sounds like a drug we all need," Bennett said. "Have you prescribed the drug?"

"Yes Commander," French said. "It's a fine drug and has significant value when used properly. But it's not something anyone would want to play with."

"What could happen if the drug is misused," Bennett asked.

"Number one," French said, "the drug can be habit forming. And two—there are side effects to deal with, like sleepiness, memory and coordination problems. Three, overdosing could lead to confusion, loss of consciousness and could be fatal."

"I see," said Bennett. "Are you sure that the drug is missing—not just misplaced?"

"Yes we are Commander," French said. "We dispensed a dose yesterday and noticed the shortage."

"There's no mistake, doctors?"

"Correct Commander," Mallard said, "we are certain, and besides, the quantity missing is quite large and would never have been prescribed in that dosage."

"I see," said Bennett, "how much of it is missing?"

"About one-eighth of the total drug supplied from the start of the mission—or twenty-five hundred, twenty-five milligram tablets."

"Did I hear you right?" asked Bennett, "did you say twenty-five hundred tablets?"

"Yes, you did," French answered.

"Well then, what's your opinion?"

"Commander I hate to say it, but they must have been stolen," French said.

Bennett came alive. If it had not been two respected doctors informing him of the missing drugs, he would never have believed what he heard.

Turning to Barnes he asked, "What do *you* think?"

"Doctor," Barnes asked, "is there any possible way we can trace who's taking them?"

"Yes Colonel there is," French said. "We could install a hidden security camera aimed at the pharmacy cabinet. Then, with the Commander's approval, take a routine blood sample from every crewmember."

Barnes turned toward Bennett nodding his head in the affirmative.

"Excellent suggestion doctor," Bennett said. "Start today. It's obvious that whoever is using the drug has a serious problem and we must get to the bottom of it as soon as possible."

"Very well, Commander," French said. "Dr. Mallard and I should be able to complete the tests within three days. I'll report back to you as we progress."

"Right. And one more thing," Bennett added, "if anyone refuses the blood test let me know without delay."

"By all means," French said.

The doctors went back to the Medical Unit, prepared enough sampling syringes to test the entire crew, and began taking samples that day.

Bennett called the ship's video camera specialist, Captain Voitinsky, and instructed him to install a hidden camera without calling attention to himself in the Medical Unit's pharmacy section.

Voitinsky installed the camera inside an empty box of bicarbonate of soda.

Two days after French began her testing, she called Bennett and Barnes to the Medical Unit.

"Commander," French said, "we have a problem getting one of our crewmembers to come in for a blood test. He's Telemetry Analyst, Lieutenant Adams. We called him three times to schedule, but he keeps making excuses. Dr. Mallard spoke to him the last time, and she agrees with me that he is exhibiting suspicious behavior. Even more worrisome, his roommate Lieutenant Kessler has been acting strange also. He's been observed wandering aimlessly about the ship."

"Did Kessler come in for his test?" Bennett asked.

"No, he said he had a virus," Mallard answered.

"Now Barnes, haven't we heard those names before?" Bennett asked furrowing his brow.

"Yes we have. Maybe you were right about them after all."

Armed with that information, Bennett decided to speak with Captain Tanaka, the section supervisor for the two men.

"Barnes, get Tanaka on the intercom right away."

"Yes sir, but you should know," Barnes said, "in all likelihood he's probably asleep at this time."

"I don't care if it's his wedding night," Bennett snapped back, "get him on the intercom, now!"

Barnes picked up the intercom. "Captain Tanaka?"

"Tanaka here."

"Captain. I'm sorry I had to wake you..."

"Hold it! Hold it! Barnes, give me that thing!" Bennett barked. "Tanaka, this is the Commander—what's going on with Adams and Kessler?"

French and Mallard stood dazed waiting for Bennett to end his tirade.

"Sir, I haven't seen them since their reassignment."

Bennett lost control. "What reassignment?" he yelled. "You stupid fool—I would've had to sign off on any reassignments first! Get your *hide* to the bridge on the double."

"Yes Sir, on the double," Tanaka said.

"Sir, there must be an explanation as to why Tanaka believed the two men received transfers." Barnes said, in an obvious effort to calm Bennett down.

"Barnes, are you addle-brained? Can't you see these two drug addicts went off the deep end? I want to know from Tanaka what made him believe they had official transfers. Next, we're going to visit Adams and Kessler with Captain Millette and two armed guards to find their stash one way or another."

"Commander," French interrupted, "let me warn you they more than likely ingested enough of that drug to be quite irrational."

"Doctor," Bennett said. "What do *you* suggest? Should I send them a polite, written request for permission to enter their quarters? Get this people—this ship is *my* responsibility and I am not going to let a couple of *fiends* jeopardize our entire mission and the lives of everyone aboard. Barnes!"

"Yes Sir?"

"Call Captain Millette and tell him I want him and two of his burliest men to meet us at the bridge in five minutes. And tell him to bring two stun guns."

"Stun guns, sir?"

"You heard me Barnes—stun guns."

Barnes made a prompt call to Millette.

"Sir," Barnes said, "Millette is on his way to the bridge with Kimbaba and Benoit."

Bennett and Barnes returned to the bridge. When they arrived at the entry, they found Captain Tanaka waiting.

"Go in," Bennett ordered Tanaka.

"Captain Tanaka, tell me about Adams and Kessler," Bennett said. "What was it that made you believe they had official transfers?"

Tanaka handed Bennett the transfer papers, which had Bennett's signature. Bennett looked at them, shook his head in disbelief and handed them to Barnes.

"Barnes, tell me what's wrong with this picture?" he asked with bitter sarcasm.

"Sir, it looks somewhat like your writing style, but since when do you spell your name with only one T?"

"Captain, don't you know how to spell my name?" Bennett asked looking straight into Tanaka's eyes. "Weren't you supposed to verify any transfers with me before executing them? For God's sake, Tanaka, that's standard transfer procedure."

"Yes Sir, I made the mistake of trusting the transfer form was official. I'm sorry, Sir."

"Sorry my butt. Now go back to your quarters, and find your procedures manual. I want you to memorize section seven regarding transfers of personnel. When you think you are able to recite it to me verbatim call me, because I want you to quote it to me word for word. Now, get off my bridge before I think of something worse."

"Yes, sir," Tanaka said, happy to have escaped with his skin intact.

After Tanaka left the bridge, Millette reported with guards carrying stun guns. Bennett briefed Millette and the guards and ordered them to go to Adams and Kessler's quarters.

"When you find them," Bennett ordered, "take both to empty cargo bay two and lock them in. Then switch the cargo bay controls to the bridge. After you have done that, go back to their quarters and tear the place apart from top to bottom for drugs or anything else unusual. Then call me."

"As you ordered, Commander," Millette said.

Millette and the guards went to Adams's and Kessler's quarters, knocked twice, but got no answer. The door was locked so they used a security override password. When they entered, no one was there. Captain Millette posted Benoit outside the entry as he and Kimbaba searched their unkempt room.

When they finished, they had found several large bottles of medication tucked away into the bottom of a sleeping pouch. While sifting through papers stashed under a clothes compartment, they found an envelope marked for Commander Bennett with the word *Confidential* written on it.

Millette called Bennett at the bridge to report their discoveries. Bennett instructed them to bring the items to the bridge.

Meanwhile, Barnes viewed the closed circuit cameras and spotted Adams and Kessler riding in a carrier car. He informed Bennett, who then placed the entire E-Train under bridge control. Adams and Kessler had no way of stopping or exiting the carrier car unless Bennett allowed it.

When Millette arrived, he showed Bennett the bottles labeled Alprazolam. "What about the envelope you found?" Bennett asked.

"Sir, here it is." Millette said. "It was buried under a heap of clothes."

Bennett took the envelope. "Good job. That will be all for now."

"Commander, what about Adams and Kessler?" Millette asked.

"Look," Bennett said, pointing to an overhead monitor. "I have them locked on the E—Train."

"Where did they think they were going?" Millette asked.

"From the direction of the car," Bennett said, "my guess is they were headed for the aft airlock nearest Scout One. Maybe they thought they could jump ship with the Scout. It's unfortunate for them though—they won't make it."

"Commander, are you sure you don't need us any longer?" Millette said.

"Yes, I'm sure, thanks. I have the carrier system under Bridge Control. All of the other cars have been taken off-line and Adams and Kessler are getting the ride of their lives. Good job men, return to your regular duties."

Bennett had Adams and Kessler trapped aboard the carrier car. They pressed stop buttons for every location to no avail. They could be heard on the intercom begging to be let off. But Bennett was not finished with them yet.

He opened communications to the carrier car.

"Are you men willing to come clean about the drugs?"

"What drugs?" Adams said looking around with furtive glances, sweat rolling down his entire body.

"Okay men, tighten your safety belts a notch. Let me speed you up a little."

Bennett set the carrier car to go beyond its maximum speed, sending Adams and Kessler into wild gut wrenching turns.

"Stop the car! Let us off!" Bennett heard them screaming.

During hairpin turns, the carrier car's speed set it swaying outward, scraping the sides of its tubular enclosure. Sparks flew and loud eerie grinding noises could be heard throughout the ship.

In minutes, Adams and Kessler began vomiting into their space helmets, leaving them no choice but to remove them.

"How's the ride?" Bennett asked.

"Commander, please! Stop the car. Please!"

But Bennett remained determined to get to the truth.

The car continued racing around the ship with the two men holding on for dear life.

At one point, Bennett brought the car to a screeching halt, but the ride had not ended yet. He reversed the carrier car sending it backwards for a while.

Eden-459

Meanwhile, in a calm casual manner, he opened the envelope addressed to him marked *Confidential*. After reading the note, he gave it to Barnes.

"Had they made off with the Scout they would've escaped with a lot more than a piece of machinery," Bennett said.

Barnes read the note. "My God...and all this time we believed Lieutenant Collings's death was a suicide."

"Call Lieutenant Staeb right now," Bennett said. "I want him here for this."

"Very well, sir."

Collings's letter stated she overheard Adams and Kessler speaking about getting high on prescription drugs and their plan to take a Scout back to Earth.

"Commander," Barnes said, "I think we better check with Captain Tanaka to see how Collings managed to work with Adams and Kessler on the payload release."

"What do you mean?" Bennett asked.

"If she didn't know who was in the space suits when she went on the detail..."

"That must be it, Barnes," Bennett said. "She wouldn't have known who the other workers were because Adams and Kessler would've already had their helmets on. And if they didn't speak..."

"That's right, Commander."

"Get Tanaka on the horn and ask him if Collings got to the cargo bay before, during, or after Adams and Kessler."

Barnes called Tanaka and relayed Bennett's question.

Tanaka distinctly remembered Collings got there late.

"Now we have a different problem to solve, Barnes."

"What's that, Commander?"

"Getting them to admit they cut Collings's line."

"How?"

"Suppose I get the two of them to slip up under surveillance?"

"My God," Barnes said, "that would mean we have murderers on our hands, Commander."

"Yes, Barnes, that's right. Now all I have to do is squeeze it out of them."

"Again...how?" Barnes said.

"Watch me. May God forgive me for what I'm about to do," Bennett said.

"Commander, hold on a minute," Barnes said. "What are you thinking?"

"Adams and Kessler are now worthless entities on this mission," Bennett said looking straight at Barnes. "Their drug problem and the letter from Collings proved that. They had a *motive* to kill her. Now I'm going to find out if they took the *opportunity* as well."

Bennett switched on the voice intercom to the carrier car.

"Men, do you hear me?"

"Yes, we hear you Sir," Adams moaned. "We're sorry for taking the drugs. We were just stressed out over this whole voyage-of-no-return thing."

"Yes, I know how you feel," Bennett said with deep sarcasm. "Tell me, is that how Lieutenant Collings felt? But if she did, why didn't she say that in her *letter*? I think you had better put your helmets back on men. And then start talking."

Adams and Kessler froze, and began punching each other and blaming one another for cutting her tether line, forgetting Bennett was still listening. In a fit of temper, Adams pointed a laser weapon at Kessler.

"Go ahead Adams," Bennett said, "pull the trigger. It doesn't matter anymore."

"Why...? Commander!" Adams screamed. "What are you going to do?"

Bennett opened the cargo bay hatch. Adams and Kessler felt the sudden rush of air being sucked out of the carrier car's enclosure. They put their helmets on, gasping and trying to hold their breath, but soon found themselves in a vacuum.

"I'm glad you men put your helmets back on," Bennett said. "You're going to need them."

"Sir, don't do this to us," Kessler and Adams screamed. Please...no, no, no."

The carrier car raced along the final straightaway toward cargo bay two. Bennett knew what he was doing. When it arrived, the hatch was wide open. The speeding carrier car careened through the cargo bay and jettisoned out into open space.

The hatch was closed and quiet ensued.

Bennett called Lieutenant Kowalsky in the maintenance section.

"Lieutenant," Bennett said, "inspect cargo bay two for any damage and get the other carrier cars back on line."

Barnes stood in disbelief while he watched his monitor.

"Sir," he said, "the cargo bay is now empty."

"I know, Barnes, I know. Problem solved."

Bennett called Corbin at Earth Base.

"Henry," said Bennett, "we solved the question regarding Collings's apparent suicide. She was murdered by Lieutenants Adams and Kessler."

"Murdered?"

"Yes, that's what I said. Murdered."

"What do you plan to do about them?" Corbin asked.

A brief silence followed.

"It's been done," Bennett said.

Corbin grew quiet as he thought about what Bennett meant.

The next thing he heard was the Commander clicking off his communication line.

Chapter 36

After the Mars orbiting operation had been completed, the E-One set its course for Pluto, the most distant planet from Earth in the solar system. Over three billion miles from Earth's Sun, it took more than a year traveling at five hundred thousand miles-per-hour to pass the planet.

On New Year's Day, after traveling another nine billion miles, the ship left the Sun's Heliosphere: The spherical region around the Sun, beyond which interstellar space begins.

The ship experienced a heavy jolt and a surge of speed as it left all effects of the Sun's gravitation.

The crew observed galactic scenes never witnessed before. They needed protective visors to shield their eyes from the brightness of the star Altair. Multicolored nebulae were astonishing as well. The entire panorama of the galaxy appeared surrealistic in its offerings of strange and beautiful vistas.

The visual clarity at that point became magnified by a factor of three and the E-One's time clocks slowed by five percent.

The most important effect of the time slowdown was an increase in human longevity and a pseudo increase in the relative rate of travel from one point in space to another.

The E-One had traveled more than thirteen billion miles from Earth.

Chapter 37

Colonel Butler's wife, Diana became pregnant with their first child.

Several other babies had been born with no abnormalities and all of them flourished. The new babies in the nursery seldom cried except when hungry. Dr. French believed they were comfortable in the weightless state, spending most of their time in small pouches resembling sleeping bags lined with a soft thermal-balanced material.

A total of eleven pregnancies were underway. All had accelerated.

Commander Bennett's son Paul, and Lauren Brown's daughter Elaine, progressed well in their academic schooling. While young Paul found mathematics fun, Elaine Brown seemed to have a special ability with languages. Her teacher Mrs. Berger even taught her Hebrew as easily as English and Spanish.

Dr. Mallard had no common explanation for their high level of comprehension, except perhaps their alien ancestry.

Mrs. Berger felt confident they would soon be able to master Algebra, Geometry, Trigonometry, and Calculus, and by the age of sixteen, Quantum Math and Advanced Physics. She theorized the reasons for their unique abilities hinged on their elevated IQ, the environment, their climate of aspiration and a long attention span.

Back on Earth, these children would have been classified as exceptional, gifted and talented. It also appeared they could glean knowledge from their teachers even in the absence of oral communication.

It became obvious they were special young people with rare abilities no children back on Earth had ever been known to possess.

Mallard and French grew convinced it had something to do with their alien ancestry coupled with their conception, birth and development in the weightless environment.

*　*　*

Paul and Elaine had grown into strikingly beautiful teenage children. Paul's incredible large blue eyes seemed to speak by themselves. Elaine with her large dark brown eyes did likewise. It was not unusual to find them alone staring at one another in what appeared to be a silent conversation. Nods and smiles evidenced the phenomenon.

They found books and CDs covering astrophysics, quantum math, and astronomy most stimulating.

Young Paul Bennett spent more and more time with his father on the bridge and Elaine was drawn to Dr. French's Medical Unit's activities.

Chapter 38

Year 2027
Scout Vehicle One deployed

Once launched from the E-One, Scout One led the ship's position by almost three million miles, providing ample time for the E-One to maneuver away from any pitfalls encountered. A valuable asset, it functioned as an early-warning detection system preventing possible collisions with meteors, small moons, black holes, plasma fields, and other dangerous space objects.

The Scout vehicles—nicknamed Snoop and Scoop— sent data back to the E-One about newly discovered planets they had scanned. The Scouts' sensors were capable of detecting atmospheric content, surface temperatures, radio wave signals, elements, radiation levels, and various gases.

Since they operated via remote commands they could also be diverted into an orbiting mode around a new planet for investigation of its make-up and send the data back to the E-One for further analysis and review. The unmanned Scouts explored and performed needed tasks without risking human life. Another positive attribute of the Scouts was the option to have one or both of them retrieved by the E-One, retrofitted, and used as vertical take-off and landing shuttle vehicles for transporting personnel and equipment to and from a planet's surface.

* * *

Year 2029

After two more years of travel, everything normalized for the officers and crew of the E-One as they went about their daily routines.

But, their calm and normal life came to an abrupt halt when a loud eerie alarm emitted at all three Command Bridges. Scout One had detected and warned of the approach of a large object.

Commander Bennett switched on the video surveillance monitor. He gasped at what he saw.

"I think you'd better take a look at this, Barnes," Bennett said. "My God, if the Scout hadn't seen it first we would've been finished."

Barnes looked at the screen, his eyes widening. He almost lost his breath.

"It's huge, Commander," said Barnes, "and it's headed straight for us."

It was an asteroid, traveling over one hundred thousand miles-per-hour. Scout One reported it to be twenty-two miles across with a high-density, solid-iron core.

Bennett sent an immediate command for Scout One to change its course thereby avoiding a collision. Once the Scout had been diverted with a two hundred-mile margin of safety, he readied the E-One to be repositioned ninety degrees to the asteroid. He ordered the crew to secure their areas, strap in and be prepared for an emergency course adjustment.

Averting an impending disaster, he powered up eight engines to thirty percent and within minutes, the ship veered to a safe position out of the asteroid's path.

When the asteroid passed by, all they observed was a streak of light, and popping noises could be heard as billions of minute fragments the size of ultra-fine grains of sand from a debris stream peppered the ship.

As they struck the lead edge surfaces, the alarm indicators started blaring adding to the crew's tension. If even a single fragment the size of a marble hit, it would have inflicted serious damage and perhaps place the ship and its crew in peril. Everyone aboard feared the worst, thinking his or her demise would come at the hands of the asteroid. All they could do was hope and pray.

Eden-459

After thirty minutes of heavy pelting, the fragment field passed and quiet resumed. Bennett ordered an exterior inspection of the E-One by two space-walking technicians.

They reported only minor damage, scrapes, and some pinhead-sized perforations in the nose section, but no serious damage. The E-One's entire outer surface had become bright and polished, its outer skin changing from a dull metal appearance to that of well-polished chrome.

Bennett gave an advisory report of the incident to Earth Base. His journal received its first 'close-call encounter with destruction' entry.

Out of danger, Bennett ordered the ship back on its course.

He thought about what might have happened if the Scout had not been there to give a warning. An object that size would definitely have obliterated the ship. With the danger passed, he relaxed.

But his rest was short-lived.

"Commander," said Barnes, "I've identified the object. It was part of the asteroid, Chiron. A large chunk, over twenty miles in diameter, broke away from its orbit around Saturn and Uranus. It might be the result of gravitational changes from an unusual planetary alignment or a collision with another asteroid. The giant fragment escaped its orbit between the planets and catapulted away."

"Barnes, is there anything else?" Bennett asked shaken, seeing the look of shear terror in Barnes's eyes.

"Yes, Commander," Barnes answered frightened. "I'm afraid there is. I plotted the asteroid's path and by my calculations, that monster is headed straight for Earth."

"What! My God, Barnes, are you certain? I want you to triple check your calculations and have Perkins and Corell verify your findings. Not a word of this gets out. Do you understand me?"

Bennett's thoughts led him on a downward emotional spiral. He closed his eyes and could almost see the devastation.

"No World War even came close. If this thing hit, billions of people would be gone in days. Earth itself burned to a cinder. And how—how could I tell them? I hope their asteroid defense systems work—they are the only chance they have."

"Sir...Commander, are you okay?" Barnes stammered. His usual calm demeanor disrupted.

"Yes, Barnes I'm fine. I want you, Corell, and Perkins to report your findings to me at the Center Bridge by 12:00 hours tomorrow."

"Yes Sir, will do," Barnes said.

"And Barnes, if any of this gets past the four of us without my consent, I don't want to think about what I'll do to the person who leaks it. Is that one hundred percent clear?"

"You may be sure of it, Sir. I'll inform Perkins and Corell this is Top Secret and ultra sensitive."

"Very well then Barnes—tomorrow at noon."

Alone on the bridge, Bennett could only imagine what chaos and misery would ensue if the asteroid hit the Earth. The thought of that information getting into the hands of the Press left him trembling in a cold sweat. Some answers holding a possible solution were paramount before the danger became public. *If*—it ever did.

Barnes, Perkins, and Corell calculated the asteroid's course for five exhaustive hours and reached the same conclusion. Earth's final destiny would be to suffer a catastrophic blow.

In turmoil caused by their findings, they could not sleep. At 06:00 hours, they decided to call Bennett in his quarters asking that the meeting be held at once.

Bennett had not slept either. He told them to be at the Center Bridge at 07:00 hours.

He began to think about the report he had sent to Earth Base regarding the near miss they experienced the day before and was glad they did not ask him for the asteroid's position and direction of travel. But he shuddered at the thought he would someday have to inform them of their peril.

At 07:00 hours Barnes, Perkins, and Corell reported to Bennett at the Center Bridge. Bennett asked Colonel Butler who was manning the bridge, to leave.

"Yes, Sir," Butler said.

"Go to the Forward Bridge until I get there," Bennett said.

Bennett hoped and prayed Barnes had miscalculated. He understood quite well the annihilation an object of that size could inflict on the Earth. He closed his eyes for a few moments in deep thought and prayer as they arrived. But Bennett, excellent at reading faces, did not like what he saw as they entered.

"From the look on your faces I guess Barnes's calculations were correct."

"Sir, we regret to tell you, he *was* correct," Corell said.

"The asteroid is on a direct collision course with the Earth," Perkins added.

"God...if only we could do something to prevent this from happening," Bennett said. "I see no way for *us* to stop it. Let's keep this to ourselves for now. I do not want them to know what is coming yet. Perkins, how long do they have?"

The three astronauts looked at each other, confused. Why keep this possible catastrophe a secret, they mused.

"We calculated the timeframe to be about twenty three years, or 2052 at its current rate of speed," said Corell.

"Can you imagine the worldwide panic and anarchy that would occur if the news media ever got wind of this?" Bennett said catching his breath. "We have to sit tight for awhile. In the meantime, we can hope they will discover the asteroid themselves in time to take action. If they do not, when it is about ten years out, we will warn them. We might be the only helpless surviving descendents of the end of the world."

Bennett code named the asteroid, Babylon, and dismissed the group, reminding them of the sensitivity of the knowledge.

"Just a minute, Commander," Barnes said.

"What is it, Barnes?"

"Sir, how long do you intend to sit on this information? Isn't every hour of advance warning for the Earth critical?"

"Barnes, you are one of my best people and I trust you, why are you questioning my judgment *now*?"

"Sir, I'm just concerned that they will have adequate time to prepare."

"Don't you think I'm just as concerned as you are?"

"Of course I do, but why not get them involved right away?" Barnes asked.

"This isn't the time, because they can't make a move on it until it gets a lot closer. You all should've known that."

"Sir," Perkins spoke up. "I think Barnes is right. We should tell them now so they have enough time to plan."

"Now there *you* go, Perkins. Just like Barnes, you want to rush into it. All of you get this straight. Babylon has a twenty-three year journey before it reaches Earth. I am not going to jump the gun and risk mass worldwide panic. Timing is the *key* to this problem and when I feel the time has come I will be the one to decide. I have had enough dissent for one day. Now trust me, and get back to your duties."

Day by day the senior officers became more perplexed and anxious over Bennett's logic in delaying giving Earth such vital and important information. They felt the more time Earth had to prepare an attack on the asteroid, the better.

Following their many attempts to change the Commander's mind, they decided to turn their request into a mandate. They understood his fear of the news getting out to the public and what it might turn the world into.

But his senior officers' overcame that fear as they insisted Bennett inform Earth right away to afford them as much time as possible to avert the inevitable lurking doom.

Their plea became strengthened when new facts surfaced after recalculating the asteroid's path. An error had been made when estimating its speed and angle of approach to Earth.

The asteroid's course estimate would bring it closer to the Sun than previously thought. As a result, the Sun's gravitational influence would cause an increase in the asteroid's speed to almost double, by whipping it away and toward Earth. The *slingshot* effect would shorten the time of impact. Worse yet was the fact that the asteroid's position behind the Sun would obscure it from the scanners and cause Earth to be blindsided.

Perkins, Barnes and Corell could not remain mute any longer. They reached a consensus that compelled them to insist Bennett act at once. They would stalwartly demand he warn WASA immediately of the danger. If he did not they would consider *mutiny*. Dawn Perkins acting as spokesperson, made a nervous call to Bennett.

"Sir, we have alarming news regarding Babylon."

"Alarming, Perkins?" Bennett asked. "Explain."

"Commander, Barnes and Corell are in agreement with me. We're coming to the bridge in ten minutes."

"Ten minutes? You make it sound as though I have no choice."

"That's right, Commander. We're not going to sit on this any longer. We're on our way."

"No you're not, Perkins," Bennett said. "I've closed the bridge to visitors."

"Closed the bridge, Commander?" Perkins said. "How could you do that?"

"That's simple, Perkins: I am the Commanding officer of this ship."

Barnes, having the distinction of being Bennett's right-hand man, chimed in.

"Dawn, let me speak to him. I think *I* might be able to persuade him to listen."

"Commander, this is Barnes," he said speaking into his communicator, "we understand your reasoning for holding back on warning Earth. Until now, you were right, but we have just discovered information you must be made aware of. Everything has changed, and they have a lot less time than we thought to prepare."

Barnes was patient as Bennett thought about what he just heard.

Corell looked at Barnes and held up his crossed fingers.

"All right people, come to the bridge," Bennett said after a long pause.

They boarded the E-Train to stop number One—the bridge.

They entered and found Bennett standing over his plotting board.

"Show me," said Bennett. "What's changed?"

"Babylon's speed, Sir," Perkins said.

"How could that be? I thought you figured all that out already," Bennett said.

"We thought so too, until..."

"Until what, Barnes?" Bennett's short fuse started heating up.

"Sir, we took the liberty of giving our best computer the task of building a model of the situation."

"And?" Bennett asked.

"The result is that the Sun's influence on Babylon's path turned out to be greater than we thought."

Bennett wondered how there could be any worse news about Babylon than what already existed.

He listened intently to their new estimates.

"I see. What is the revised date of impact?" he asked.

"14 July 2042, Sir," Perkins said, "just thirteen years from now."

Bennett gasped and looked at each face on the bridge.

"But wouldn't an increase in speed cause Babylon to miss the Earth?" he asked.

"That's a logical assumption to make Commander," Corell said, "but remember the Earth stays in a fixed orbital pattern."

"We all know that, Corell, but why wouldn't its change of speed cause it to miss?"

"Because instead of it striking on the twenty third orbital pass it will strike in the thirteenth."

Bennett studied his charts and drew a diagram of the Sun and Earth in their orbits. Using a slide rule, calculator, and compass he calculated Babylon's current speed, trajectory, and where the Earth would be in thirteen years.

Barnes, Corell, and Perkins looked over his shoulder as they checked every formula he used to make his calculation.

"Okay," Bennett said, "your estimate of Babylon's current speed was accurate. Now I'm going to calculate it again using your new speed estimate."

Fifteen minutes later Bennett slumped in his chair.

"The chances of a speed increase not causing a different crossing point in space in the thirteenth year are about ten billion to one," Bennett said. "But, in this instance, it does work out that way. Only heaven knows why, but it does. Gentlemen, you're correct."

"I'm glad we can now agree, Commander," Barnes said. "When are you going to make that call to WASA, Sir?"

"We can't hold back any longer," Bennett agreed. "I'll call WASA on the secure line today. We'll just have to hope they'll keep the information from leaking out too soon."

"Thank you, Commander," Barnes said. His relief was incalculable since he knew he would have had to take over the command if Bennett did not see the light.

Bennett knew that Director Corbin, although aged and ill, still refused retirement. Corbin was the only one at WASA Bennett had any confidence in to keep a secret. He put through the communication to Earth Base without any delay.

Barnes, Perkins, and Corell breathed a sigh of relief. They discovered firsthand that Bennett's tough and sometimes cynical way of thinking could be persuaded, but only with cold hard facts.

Corbin awoke at 03:00 hours to the sound of his phone ringing. He dropped the receiver, cursed, and picked it up.

"Corbin here."

Earth Base called. They had an emergency message from Bennett.

Corbin shot up. "Okay, patch him through."

"Henry, I have bad news for you," Bennett said.

"Phil, I didn't think you called me at this hour to ask about the weather," Corbin said. "What's wrong? Are you okay?"

"Fine Henry, everything's under control here," Bennett faltered.

Corbin, noticing the pause, gave Bennett his complete attention.

"Sounds to me like there's more Phil. Let me have it."

"Henry, here it is. We just survived a near miss with a large asteroid."

"Yes I heard—thank God for that," Corbin said. "Are there any injuries or damage? Base never filled me in. They just said everything worked out. Didn't want to put too much stress on these old bones, I guess."

"Just some minor scrapes and pinholes, nothing too serious. But Henry, you haven't heard the worst of it," Bennett heard a gasp at the other end.

"What do you mean?" Corbin asked. "If there are no personnel injuries to y'all or serious damage to the ship then what could be worse?"

Bennett bowed his head, his heart racing. He wiped the sweat from his hands on his legs.

"Henry," Bennett said. "I'm afraid the asteroid is headed straight for Earth."

Corbin sat speechless.

Bennett listened for a response, but none came. He wondered if the line disconnected.

"Henry, are you still on? Hello, Henry?"

"I'm here, Phil," said Corbin. "What the hell do you want me to say? What do we do now? What can anyone do?"

"I understand, Henry. I am sorry to be the one to have to tell you. I can't believe we are having this conversation. I just don't know..."

"Phil, we have to think positively, we have to make plans. Tell me, how big, how fast, and how much time do we have?"

"Bigger than you want to know. It is twenty-two miles in diameter and will be traveling at well over one hundred fifty

Eden-459

thousand miles-per-hour. We estimate the impact will occur in thirteen years."

"Why didn't our people see it?" an angry Corbin asked.

"Because the asteroid's path has been shielded by the Sun. Once it looped around you would have detected it, but by then you would've had just months to act."

"My Lord Jesus! Now what...? How do I tell the world it was just given its death sentence?" Corbin whispered. "Have you put a tight lid on this?"

"Yes I have. We know how sensitive this is."

"Thank God your ship was out there. We never would have had much warning without it. I'll get back to you later today," Corbin said.

"Ten four, oh...and Henry?"

"Yes, Phil?"

"Good luck."

"Thanks."

Corbin executed a high-level emergency notification procedure. The following morning, Washington, WASA and Pentagon heads joined in a teleconference to assess the situation and plan a defense strategy.

Meanwhile, Babylon sped toward its final destination: the Moon and Earth. The potential for mass destruction loomed. The only hope of avoiding the impact rested with WASA and the military's ability to alter the asteroid's course in some way.

The Earth's single chance would be to launch multiple rockets armed with nuclear warheads that could intercept the asteroid far from the Earth, and then detonate the weapons with the hope of altering its course. But, since Babylon's errant orbit had brought it streaking toward the Earth's solar system at over one hundred fifty thousand miles-per-hour, the difficulty in achieving the desired result would be equivalent to hitting a bullet with a bullet.

In addition, the asteroid's size and density rendered the attempt to change its course futile at best.

Martin J. Stab

Another possible solution entertained was to land a rocket on the asteroid in the hopes of steering it into a different path. But the discovery that it was spinning rapidly red—lined that plan.

Corbin would never have to face the decision-making process or the failures, if any occurred—he made his calls to the Pentagon, hung up his phone and suffered a fatal coronary.

Chapter 39

In October 2040, a secret emergency conference of over one hundred world leaders, including the Vatican, took place at the International Convention Center in New York City, on Governors Island, to discuss the asteroid and its imminent threat to the Earth.

Media coverage was prohibited. The agenda covered defensive actions and worst-case scenarios if the Babylon asteroid struck. Special speakers included scientists, military personnel, and experts in the fields of astrophysics, astronomy, geology, geophysics, and other related fields.

At the request of the chairperson Dr. Leon Stabinski, Director of the World Health Organization based in Geneva, a panel of experts built a computer module depicting the sequence of events.

A heavy cloak of security enshrouded the Convention Center. It was imperative that information as to the nature of the conference did not leak out. To fend off media interest, they dubbed it *The International Security Review Regarding Terrorism*.

As a precaution, Armed United States Marine security guards with K-9 units patrolled the small island as Coast Guard vessels and helicopters encircled the offshore waters.

To ensure only those authorized to participate would be in attendance, all access by ferryboats and private watercraft had been prohibited. Only restricted, pre-arranged helicopter transports would be given landing privileges.

At 08:00 hours, the guest speaker panel began setting up their maps, charts and oceanic and topographical displays to be used in explaining the effects and after-effects of the asteroid strike.

By 08:50 hours, everything was ready. The attendees took their seats. Most knew the information to come might be hopeless, and as a result, their mood was grim at best.

The conference opened with a subdued "Good morning" from Dr. Robert Crowley, Astrophysicist from NASA. Dr. Crowley had been analyzing the asteroid's path ever since the E-One reported it.

The scant crowd of one hundred attendees sat in rigid attention.

"We know why we are here today. In all sincerity, I wish I had better news to impart, but I regret—I do not.

"Here are the facts. We have calculated the path of the Babylon asteroid with much care and precision, and estimated it will soon be traveling at one hundred sixty-five thousand miles-per-hour on a collision course with our planet."

Sighs of disbelief filled the meeting hall. One attendee stood up and declared, "It's the end of the world." Others began to weep and moan.

Crowley asked for calm and began his peroration.

"The asteroid will first graze the Moon's surface at an angle of seven degrees. The Moon will suffer severe damage and its orbit will alter, as billions of tons of its surface will be blasted outward into space. Though it will appear a quite beautiful and colorful event to objective eyes, this disturbance will soon have a profound effect on the Ocean tides and deliver debris toward us in the form of heavy meteor showers.

"About one hour later, the night skies will illuminate for about thirty minutes as streaking rocks and debris enter our atmosphere and disintegrate.

"Afterwards, a one-hour calm will ensue, but for those living near river deltas and harbors in the Northern Hemisphere, an incredible phenomenon will occur. When the Moon's orbit alters, it will have a devastating effect on the ocean tides. In the areas above the equator, they will begin a drastic recession. Major harbors and rivers up and down the coastlines of North America, Western Europe, and those countries bordering the Mediterranean Sea and parts of the West Coast of Northern Africa and Asia will empty.

"The drop in the ocean water level will be seventy-five to one hundred feet. New York, San Francisco, Boston, Baltimore, Port Everglades, Miami, as well as Liverpool, Hamburg, Tokyo, Hong Kong and other harbors in the Northern Hemisphere, including those throughout the Mediterranean Sea, will see ships aground on muddy bottoms."

Several of the attendees became ill or fainted and received assistance from the medical staff.

Dr. Crowley shaken and pale turned the microphone over to Professor Hans Schmidt, Geophysicist from the Berlin Conservatory of Sciences, who wasted no time with introductions.

"Ladies and gentlemen, our study unit has been involved in forecasting the point of impact of the asteroid or—*Ground Zero*. We have determined it will strike in the middle of the Atlantic Ocean at the Abyssal Plains, which is located approximately mid way between the U.S. and French coastlines. The area was formed one hundred fifty million years ago when the continents of Europe and North America divided. The location is a hotbed of volcanic activity at depths of four to five thousand feet.

"If a small asteroid struck in an ocean it would be to our advantage. But—it is not a small asteroid. It is monstrous, having a diameter of over twenty-two miles."

Some attendees stood shouting, nearing hysteria.

"It's the end of the world!" one woman screamed.

"We should go home to our families," another person shouted. "There's nothing for us to do."

Dr. Stabinski interrupted the speaker. "Everyone please—please be calm. I know this is terrifying information, but we must remain calm. I think you will feel better after hearing what our military planners have to say."

"Thank you Dr. Stabinski," Professor Schmidt continued. "The first view of the asteroid following its glancing blow to the Moon will be of a bright object as it nears Earth. Within seconds, it will impact in the North Atlantic.

"The force of the impact will be equivalent to that of one hundred fifty thousand, one thousand megaton hydrogen bombs detonating at the same point. A blinding flash of light in the sky will be visible by at least half the Earth. The impact will be of such a severity, that a jolting shock wave will be felt over the entire globe, toppling many structures.

The cities of New York, Philadelphia, Boston, Washington, Paris, and London will be heavily damaged, reducing older structures to piles of debris. The loss of life will be heavy in the extreme—but it will not be over yet.

"The ocean will be split into a seventy-five mile wide abyss, after which a firestorm of super heated gases traveling over seven hundred miles-per-hour will radiate in every direction racing across the ocean toward landmasses. The firestorm will scorch and burn everything in sight. Anyone exposed to it will be cremated on the spot and others will die from burns, shock and toxic gases."

Oswald Kirchgesner, the representative from Germany stood up and started to speak when, without warning, he suddenly swooned and collapsed to the floor. Medical aids determining he had suffered a heart attack, performed CPR, put him on oxygen, and rushed him to a local hospital.

After the interruption, Professor Schmidt hung his head for a moment and looked ready to collapse and a fellow panel member went to his aid with a glass of water. He took a drink, wiped his forehead with a handkerchief and continued.

"Please bear with me as I conclude and then turn it over to my colleagues for further elaboration.

"The asteroid is immense and will penetrate the Earth's crust at a depth causing a major volcanic eruption in the middle of the ocean the likes of which the planet has never seen. It will spawn a new volcano taller than Mount Everest and spew enough of the inner Earth's molten materials to almost join Europe with North America."

Professor Schmidt choked up and was unable to speak. He excused himself and was relieved by Dr. David Ng, from the Chinese Institute of Technology and Science at Hefei, China.

Dr. Ng nodded his head toward the audience, indicating he agreed with the scenarios given.

Eden-459

"Ladies and gentlemen," he said with a noticeable accent, "the fact is—this has happened before, but not of this magnitude. The Yucatan we believe was struck by a large asteroid millions of years ago. The resulting firestorm traveled across North America at a speed of five hundred miles-per-hour and caused the end of the dinosaurs. Finally a cosmic winter occurred.

"Our estimates of damage to the Earth from the coming asteroid is of more concern than what you've just learned from Dr. Crowley and Professor Schmidt." Dr. Ng took a deep breath. "Most of you have seen a computer model of what a tidal wave would be like if an asteroid with a diameter of six miles hit near New York City, Hong Kong or Tokyo.

"It would be taller than the former World Trade Center Towers—over two thousand feet in height. That is frightening, I know, but now we are facing an even more monstrous wave. If our calculations are accurate, this wave will be much larger than two thousand feet."

The audience gasped, mumbling among themselves in disbelief.

"To start with," Dr. Ng continued, "we will face the swift mass destruction of most of Eastern North America and Western Europe."

The assemblage stood and began milling around in shock as the realities of impending doom sank in. Dr. Ng asked for calm as members of the audience started talking to those around them.

"Let him finish, please sit down," many voices implored.

"I'll summarize what we may expect when this phenomenon has subsided. The entire Earth will have been rocked on its axis. Hundreds of devastating earthquakes will likely erupt, sending heavy plumes of ash and gases high up into the atmosphere. That is when the final blow to our planet will be realized. The Sun's warmth will be blocked by the clouds of ash for such a long duration that the Earth will once again be forced into a Cosmic Ice Age lasting for thousands of years."

"Why are we here then?" someone shouted. "Isn't there anything we can do? My God, all you're giving us is a doomsday outlook!"

"I am sorry to be one of those asked to give you this information, but..."

The Chairperson Dr. Stabinski took the microphone and thanked Dr. Ng.

"This is an horrific situation, I know. But let me share with you a glimmer of hope we have of avoiding the Earth's destruction."

The assemblage stilled in a heartbeat, as they glued their eyes, desperate for hope, to Dr. Stabinski.

"We have here with us United States Air Force General Rodney Fairchild, Secretary of the Joint Chiefs of Staff in Washington, who will share our defensive plan with you.

The audience sat alert in their chairs.

"Take heart," General Fairchild said, "we're not done for yet. We have developed a plan we think will give us a chance of diverting the asteroid. Named the *'Dolphin Project'*, on January 20, 2041, we will simultaneously launch missiles from the United States, Russia, China, Great Britain, France and India designed to detonate seventeen powerful H-bomb warheads in the face of the asteroid. By any means, it is not a surefire strategy, but it is a plan we must execute to stand any chance of averting the Earth's destruction. If we hit it just right we might alter its course enough to miss our planet."

The group began to buzz at the news there was, at least, a chance.

"I said it was some hope," Fairchild continued with a warning. "Let's not think we are home free yet. It is a difficult target and our chances of pulling it off are about one in a thousand."

He then handed the microphone back to Stabinski.

"We have to hope and pray we will succeed in this mission," Stabinski said. He then concluded the meeting with a message for all the attendees to take home with them. "Not many people get the opportunity to discuss how or when they will die, we should all make the best of it."

Several people in the audience could be heard sobbing as he ended his address.

"Please remember everyone, what was discussed here today is sensitive and confidential and must not be leaked out to the general public. Let us all hope our missiles find their target."

The stunned and emotional audience vacated the meeting hall praying for a miracle.

20 January 2041

Military Commanders from the on-board nuclear-capable countries stood by, nerves on edge, watching the countdown on their launch clocks. At 09:20 hours GMT, the missile command centers received a "go" for the Dolphin Project from launch control at WASA Headquarters, Houston. The unannounced launches sent people on all sides of the globe scurrying to their phones and televisions, but nothing could be reported except the standard explanation—the military was conducting routine tests of their missile systems.

Nine months later, on October 29, at 20:00:20 hours the missiles would intercept the asteroid. With just minutes until the detonation, the space station's telescopes were fixed on the target.

Then, it appeared—it looked like the birth of a star. A massive brilliant lingering explosion flashed in the heavens. The detonations were executed as planned.

As the crew aboard the space station observed the awesome mammoth blast, they felt certain that such a huge amount of concentrated explosive nuclear power would be effective in altering the asteroid's vector. It would take at least one hour to determine whether any change of Babylon's course had been accomplished.

A communications link established between the Pentagon and the orbiting space station carried their answer at 21:00 hours Eastern Standard Time.

President Grooms of the United States, in constant communication with world powers, sat hopefully near a cryptographic printer in an underground Situation Room with his Secretary of Defense Cary Newman at his side. When it started to print, it would spell out the Earth's fate.

The president suffering from alternate bouts of sweats and chills, sat silent, tapping his fingers on his desk. So far, just a full page of alphanumeric test characters could be seen on a sheet of paper dangling from the printer.

He agonized in heavy anticipation over the results of the Dolphin Project, knowing full well its implications—success or doom.

The printer advanced paper and began to print out Earth's fate. He started to rise when his Secretary of Defense said he would get the printout for him.

With care, Newman tore the sheet from the printer, and folded it without reading it. He carried it to President Grooms and placed it into his extended hand.

Sweat rolled down the President's face. He swallowed hard, unfolded the paper, and read it. He paled, dropped the paper to the floor, and started to walk out of the room.

"Mr. President...the message?" Newman called out.

"The Dolphin Project failed...we missed."

"Where are you going Mr. President?" Newman asked.

"I don't know," President Grooms said, obviously choked up. "I just don't know. Get busy on the International Hot Lines and call Andrews. Tell them to have Air Force One ready."

The Earth had been destined for destruction. The crew of the E-One listened in horror to Earth Base's description of the events that would take place in July of the following year.

Eden-459

Knowing they would be the only humans alive in the entire universe, they began asking themselves, "S*uppose we never do find a suitable place to land? What then?*"

Chapter 40

July 2042

It had been a warm and balmy evening along the Breezy Point shore of Queens, New York.

At the small private beach community, the residents enjoyed a cooling light on-shore breeze. Many sat on their decks sipping drinks as they gazed at a beautiful full Moon.

Just prior to 10:00 p.m., the sound of oohs and ahs could be heard from up and down the row of beachside homes when the inhabitants observed what appeared to be spectacular fireworks high in the heavens.

After a few moments of watching the celestial light show, the realization hit that the display in the heavens in fact came from the Moon.

Nearby, crowded Coney Island was having a busy evening as thousands of fun seekers enjoyed rides and games. What a pleasant night it was. Young children could be heard laughing with delight. The air rifle booth elicited the familiar pop, pop, pop, and the scent of popcorn and the feel of sticky cotton candy filled their senses.

People stopped in their tracks looking up at the sky to watch the show. Seeing the ominous display of orange, white, and green rays streaking far out and away from the Moon, their feeling of well being changed to one of trepidation.

Helplessness and fear soon turned to horror as the colorful display of burning debris being blasted from the Moon went out of control and headed for Earth. A mass exodus began as everyone started to run for safety.

An announcer, heard on a portable radio issued a bulletin:

"Many calls have been coming in regarding the spectacular fireworks-like show in the heavens. Do not be alarmed, it was just a meteor striking the Moon."

But, those words could not be farther from the truth.

After twenty minutes the *fireworks* subsided. Most people on the East Coast of the United States simply carried on, having no idea a deadly and devastating chain of events had begun on the oceans of the Northern Hemisphere.

The change in the Moon's orbital position in relationship to the Earth had shifted due to the giant asteroid's hard glancing blow. One hour after the Moon event, Earth's gravitational forces altered. The tides of all the oceans north of the Equator began a drastic ebbing.

As predicted, harbors in the Northern Hemisphere began emptying with rapidity, stranding ships everywhere. Smaller watercraft worldwide got caught up in the hyper-currents of the giant southward tidal swing. Helpless and doomed vessels radioed *May Day* calls, swamping Coastguard stations. The entire maritime system north of the equator was interrupted and in peril. Fishing boats on both sides of the Atlantic failed to respond to radio calls.

Meanwhile, south of the equator the opposite effect took place. Ocean water quickly began to rise along the shores, harbors, and lowlands. With swift abandon, and without any warning, entire coastal cities and their populations were engulfed and wiped out by rising water levels. Many cargo and cruise ships on the high seas were capsized or sunk by the force of giant waves, whirlpools, and gargantuan swells.

Still, most of the world's populations had not yet learned what was happening. When word of an asteroid strike had spread to the masses, panic erupted on all parts of the globe.

Demands for calm over radio and television stations went unnoticed or ignored. Many were struck with fear in the face of the major catastrophic event.

After two hours of tidal flooding and the draining of every harbor in the Northern Hemisphere, another preemptive sign of the asteroid's visit made itself known. Heavy meteor showers began to rain down all over the world.

The night skies lit up like daylight, as thousands upon thousands of small and medium-sized meteors entered the Earth's atmosphere and burned up. Little did anyone realize that he was seeing debris from the Moon strike.

People on the daylight side of the Earth, not witnessing the *fireworks* display, received alerts from radio and television bulletins that major oceanic disturbances had been wreaking havoc in the harbors and on the seas.

By the millions, they began to scurry home from their jobs to be with their families.

Earth Base suddenly lost communication with the space station. Its on-board personnel became some of the first casualties as they suffered a fatal blow from Moon debris strikes.

People the world over began to panic and migrate by the millions away from the cities. Most were unable to move along the grid locked roads and choked-up highways. Cars, trucks, vans, buses, and bicycles could be seen stranded everywhere. Many left their vehicles and started walking or running. That too proved useless. Hoards of people began pushing, shoving, and stampeding one another. The streets and walkways had become strangled with humanity. The old and sick were either left behind or trampled on by the panicking throngs.

On the Caribbean Islands, waters receded everywhere, exposing coral reefs never revealed before.

One hour before impact, official warnings went out to the public via radio and television bulletins that a large asteroid would soon be striking the Earth. The bulletin advised everyone to take shelter and stay indoors.

Terrified—people were at a total loss as to where to go or what to do. Some committed suicide in their homes or jumped out of skyscraper windows. Others began to pray in repentance.

Families tried to reach each other, but were stymied by the worst traffic jams imaginable. Communications systems were severely overloaded, making frantic phone calls impossible.

Those people still at their jobs up and ran when they got word. Their futile efforts to get home, blocked by hordes of confused and dazed people taking flight from the business centers. Mobs looted stores, and banks were robbed. No one stopped them

Eden-459

or even noticed, since most businesses had already been abandoned.

Police too, gave up trying to control the wild and unruly pedestrians. Prison inmates found temporary freedom as guards ran away, leaving cells and gates open. Caretakers abandoned city zoos allowing animals of all kinds to run free in the streets.

Many ranking government and military officials hurried to secure underground bunkers for safety, as others boarded planes hoping to find an escape via air routes.

Churches, synagogues, mosques, temples, shrines, and all other houses of worship swelled with followers. Many of those who could not get to their places of worship simply knelt down at home and prayed for mercy. Great numbers of people read their Bibles and other religious works...many, for the first time.

Hospital workers abandoned sick and dying patients in their beds and on operating tables.

Doctors and maternity personnel fled leaving women in labor to fend for themselves.

Thousands of newborn babies were left hungry, crying, and alone in nursery wards.

As rumors spread, school children the world over left their classrooms screaming toward home.

Seconds before the cataclysmic impact, a bright luminous object could be seen descending from the sky. It became larger and larger and soon illuminated half the planet.

Traveling at one hundred sixty-five thousand miles-per-hour, Babylon struck exactly where predicted: In the middle of the North Atlantic Ocean.

A pilot flying a commercial airliner from Rome to New York at forty thousand feet, radioed in he had just witnessed an unbelievably blinding blast on the ocean's surface. His description was cut short when an enormous shock wave ripped his plane to pieces along with two hundred eighty passengers. Thousands of commercial aircraft pilots found themselves trapped in the sky with nowhere to land.

Commercial shipping vessels near Ground Zero called in to report horrific ocean disturbances when in an instant, communications were lost. May Day radio calls came in by the hundreds from planes and ships that were damaged and going down. Few if any received an answer.

In the middle of the North Atlantic the intensity of the impact created an enormous abyss over one hundred miles in diameter. The force of the impact displaced many trillions of cubic yards of seawater. It penetrated the ocean and sliced downward with such force that it caused the Earth's *mantle* to fracture. As a result, the contents of the Earth's outer core—liquid iron and nickel—were released upwards through the fracture and set in motion the creation of the largest volcano ever fathomed. Liquid magma surged with enormous violent force upwards through the fractured mantle. It began to build and build upon itself until it rose above sea level.

As the volcano erupted, the asteroid strike's devastating shock wave radiated out from ground zero at seven hundred fifty miles-per-hour in all directions. It first struck at Greenland, Iceland, and then Great Britain, where the early-morning jolt added to the misery of panicking populations. The shock wave's intensity caused people to lose their breath—and their lives.

Many older and weaker buildings, churches, bridges, homes, tunnels, railways, and other structures cracked, twisted, and crumbled.

Europe and North Africa's turn came minutes later as the majority of their populations were also slammed into mass bedlam and overran the countryside. From Norway south to the mouth of the Mediterranean, Morocco, and Liberia, the massive shock wave struck. In those places too, the populations received a shattering blow as everything standing fell into ruin. Crossing all of Western Europe, the shock wave struck Italy, ravaging its art treasures, slamming the remaining ancient Roman and Greek ruins to the ground. In North Africa, the continuing shock wave hit the ancient pyramids of Egypt, reducing them to rubble.

Eden-459

North America's turn came. Though some heard warnings from sparse communications that got through from Europe, the 01:00 hour's jolt found most of that continent's population too busy to listen as they scrambled to flee their cities toward the country by the millions. There, the effects were the same.

In Toronto, the shock wave caused extensive damage to city structures, including the CN Tower, rendering it useless when its foundation failed and it began to tilt toward Toronto's harbor.

Upstate New York's Niagara Falls suffered severe fissures at its base, sending torrents of water down below the falls. A giant wall of water crashed over the automobile-clogged Rainbow Bridge connecting the American and Canadian borders. All disappeared within seconds.

The stunned people of New York City feeling the effects of the strike, also found themselves trapped. No escape was possible from Manhattan, Staten Island, and the Bronx since every bridge, tunnel, and highway had been damaged or destroyed. The city's subway system had shut down as severe flooding and loss of electrical power disabled it. The entire darkened skyline of Manhattan became re-contoured into giant mounds of broken buildings and smoking rubble, as major gas lines ruptured and burst everywhere in the city. Numerous fires burned.

Road rage gave way to *people rage* when those who could travel tried to scramble toward Long Island and Connecticut in a futile effort to escape the wild unruly throngs of people, but got nowhere.

When the people of Queens and Brooklyn looked out of their homes, they felt awestruck and bewildered: How could all those giant skyscrapers be gone? The Empire State Building lost half of its top as many of the city's financial-district towers leaned—one against the other. Most of the mid-town buildings no longer stood. The majestic bridges over the East River vanished.

On the Hudson, the George Washington Bridge lay broken in pieces and the Statue of Liberty leaned facing Bayonne, New Jersey instead of New York Harbor. The tunnels under the Hudson and East Rivers fractured and filled with water.

To the west of New York City, along the industrial sections of Central New Jersey, hundreds of oil refinery tanks filled with crude oil, heating oil, and gasoline ruptured and burst into infernos of flame, sending heavy billowing clouds of black smoke high into the sky. Eleven million people in the New York Metropolitan area lost electrical power, water, communications, transportation, and emergency service. They had nowhere to go.

Every major city along the East Coast felt the devastating shock: Boston, Newark, Trenton, Atlantic City, and Philadelphia, Baltimore, Washington, D.C., and cities and towns all along the Southeastern Seaboard as far south as Ft. Lauderdale and Miami, suffered similar effects.

Nuclear power stations sustained severe damage to their containment structures releasing high amounts of deadly radiation, precipitating catastrophic meltdowns.

The worldwide estimate of lives lost from the shock wave leapt into the tens of millions. Many more incurred injuries and needed medical care, which would never arrive. The devastating psychological effects became overwhelming to the world's entire population. Death, confusion, pain, and horror in those areas hit hardest by the shock wave left millions of people numb and in physical shock.

Mass anarchy ensued, which only added to the rampant confusion and human misery.

After the shock wave weakened as it crossed the European and North American continents—the newborn volcano in the North Atlantic continued to grow to immense proportions. In just one hour it had risen higher than the six thousand foot Mount Mitchell in the Black Hills of North Carolina.

No one knew how high it would grow, but at the rate it climbed, it would dwarf Mt. Everest's twenty-nine thousand foot summit.

Besides the birth of the new volcano, many of the old volcanoes worldwide erupted. Those spared from the immediate effects of the shock wave would soon have even something worse to deal with.

Eden-459

In California the San Andreas Fault, part of the 'Pacific Ring of Fire' stretching through much of the state, shifted with such force it caused the feared *Big One*. The Pacific Coast population rushed to the east to seek refuge in the mountains, but there too the grid locked roads and expressways became strangled with vehicles of every kind and people on foot.

Major earthquakes causing widespread destruction and loss of life, rocked most of California. The entire city of Los Angeles disappeared in seconds as it plummeted into the Pacific Ocean, leaving the Hollywood Hills perched at the edge of a new coastline.

Resulting from strong earthquakes in the northwest, Washington State's stratovolcanoes, Mount Rainier and Mount St. Helens, along with Oregon's, Mount Hood awoke. Seattle's Space Needle toppled to the ground, as did many of the city's tallest buildings.

Every part of the world suffered devastation from cataclysmic eruptions of long-dormant volcanoes. Japan's Mount Fuji, a fourteen thousand foot volcano near Tokyo, exploded in violent fury sending heavy plumes of hot pyroclastic gases and ash billowing down onto the city. Only a few of Tokyo's populace had any chance escaping its fury.

In Mexico, too, Popocatepetl, a semi-dormant volcano with a seventeen thousand eight hundred foot summit, exploded with a vengeance sending deadly sheets of ash and hot lava raining down upon Mexico City. It left nothing and no one untouched.

The number of reawakened volcanoes reached into the thousands. Those not affected by either the shock wave or the earthquakes and volcanoes would not escape the asteroid's wrath. When the shock waves abated and the Earth was shaken and burned, another effect of the asteroid strike arose.

From Ground Zero radiating outward, a firestorm of superheated toxic gases and ash followed the shock wave. The parts of the world that were struck earlier by the shock wave met the next harbinger of death. Traveling at over six hundred miles-per-hour, the firestorm raced outward from the impact zone and engulfed the same areas the shock wave had struck. When it reached the European and North American continents, the blast of its burning and scorching heat incinerated every living person, plant, and animal.

It blackened and blistered everything in its path and left homes and industrial buildings aflame.

In other parts of the world hurricanes and typhoons born from the atmospheric changes of the firestorm, caused even more destruction.

Typhoons of wicked proportions also ravaged parts of the Pacific. The firestorm did not last long, but it brought forth the second tier of destruction and death. Most forested areas on the two continents were set ablaze and all wildlife perished.

When the firestorm and its effects abated, a sickening thick and murky fog sealed in a choking acrid stench, wafting in from the ocean over the western half of Europe and the eastern half of North America. For the few survivors left, even breathing became a laborious task.

As most of the world suffered the effects of the asteroid's powerful plunge, the few remaining survivors began to think they might have been spared.

But behind the multi—layered curtains of smoke, fog, and burning debris was another juggernaut of even more horrifying proportions: Tidal waves. Though by far the slowest of the forces unleashed by the asteroid, it would be the most powerful for anyone or anything in its path.

Radiating in an outward circle from Ground Zero at more than six hundred fifty miles-per-hour, it was early morning on the East Coast of North America and mid-day in Europe when it reached the shorelines.

The wave grew to over six thousand feet in height as it reached land. The ground rumbled and shook as it neared. Just the sight of it caused heart-stopping fright. It swallowed up all of the lower regions of Greenland, Iceland, and Great Britain. London's entire landscape was scoured free of any hint of civilization.

Eden-459

The entire western half of Europe received its final demise at the hands of the wave. In North America too, the eastern seaboard fell prey to obliteration beyond recognition.

The wave crashed over the entire Eastern Seaboard of the United States wiping the landscape clean of people, structures and anything else it touched.

The wave then crested over the Pocono Mountains of Pennsylvania and onward along the Appalachian Trail southward to Tennessee.

By the time the waves diminished, the geography of the West Coast of Europe down to Western Africa and the eastern parts of Canada down to Key West, Florida had been eradicated of any semblance of humanity.

The total number of dead reached into scores of millions.

The E-One received hundreds of reports from Earth Base in Houston about the asteroid and its effects. The final voice communication from WASA stated the entire Earth was a ball of flame. Words could not describe the crew's emotions as they listened in horror to the fate of their fellow human beings. Commander Bennett ordered a three-day period of mourning for the lost world. After losing all communications with Earth Base, he went to the ship's chapel and offered private prayers for the dead planet and its inhabitants.

Following the immediate effects of the asteroid, the remaining unscathed parts of the Earth would face their final ending. With each passing day, the Earth's atmosphere became filled with heavy clouds of volcanic ash and toxic gases from vaporized matter and smoke, rendering the Earth dark.

Meanwhile, the volcano born in the middle of the Atlantic reached a height of thirty two thousand feet. It became a major contributor to the thickening of the Earth's atmosphere as it continued to spew trillions of tons of ash and volcanic gases into the air. Its ash and smoke-laden billowing clouds also entered the Earth's atmosphere encircling the entire globe, blocking out sunlight, causing the Earth's temperatures to plummet. Black snow began falling where snow had never been seen before.

Day by day, the scant pockets of populations still alive succumbed to the final cruel blow of the asteroid: The arrival of another Cosmic Ice Age, which covered all the landmasses on Earth for thousands of years.

Gripped with the fear of death and unbearable cold temperatures, the misery, anguish, and pain of those still barely clinging on to life in remote areas of the world including Australia, Indonesia and other Southern Pacific regions did not last long.

Armageddon had come to pass.

Chapter 41

The shock of Babylon still fresh in the minds of the E-One's crew, they continued on their brave voyage. They, along with four of alien ancestry, had become the last remnants of humanity. Onward they pressed toward their final hope and destination, the Planet Xeron.

*　*　*

Twelve more children had now reached school age. The ship's teachers, Mrs. Berger along with Captain Epstein an Educational Specialist, held class early every day. The children studied all the basics. Though not quite near the level of intelligence of Paul and Elaine, almost all of them were in the gifted range. One obvious attribute seen in the children was their long attention span. Most days, they did not want to stop their lessons.

They were like sponges, soaking up every bit of knowledge imparted to them. Science, Math and Astrophysics were their favorite subjects.

The study of Earth fascinated them. They wondered what it was like living in a world with gravity and virtually unlimited freedom of movement.

Mrs. Berger always left time at the end of class to answer any questions they had about the Earth, its solar system, and the possibility of finding a similar planet they could call home.

"Children, the regular school session is over," Mrs. Berger said one day, "does anyone have a question?"

Tyler Smith raised his hand.

"When I use the encyclopedia," Tyler said, "I like to see the pictures of Earth. But some scare me."

"Me too, Tyler," Mrs. Berger said, "but just what pictures frightened *you* the most?"

"The pictures of what they call *war*, where I see people hurt or dead and there is a lot of destruction. Will we have to see those things when we find a new planet?"

Mrs. Berger thought what various possibilities a New World might offer. Did the fates see these pioneers reliving their forefathers' experiences, or, enveloped in a peaceful respite from former human chaos and conflict?

"Tyler," said Mrs. Berger, "we all have a special opportunity to make our new world a wonderful place to live. That is, of course, if we learn to love and treat others with respect."

* * *

The E-One's educational successes thrilled Commander Bennett and the children's parents, but something had been lacking which all the education in the universe could not replace—good social order.

A new generation aboard the E—One had developed with a different set of social and environmental stimuli. These influences began to take on symptoms that only the Earth-born aboard the ship could recognize as being problematic.

Bennett brought in the ship's doctors, teachers, and parents to assess the youngsters' behavior. A number of serious issues became evident during the meeting.

The youths' attitudes toward peers, parents, and authority figures could be described as cold and indifferent at best. Though their communicative skills were adequate, a certain *new* language seemed to have evolved. The children made up words only they could understand. Anyone overhearing their conversations had trouble deciphering what they were saying.

Discipline enforced by teachers and parents usually resulted in retaliation of some kind. Common courtesies learned by Earth-born crewmembers were almost non-existent in this *first generation of space children.*

After listening to the panel's concerns, Bennett decided to look into the situation himself. He formed a special committee, which would write a strict *Code of Ethics and Conduct*, to be enforced in every classroom and by the parents as well.

He stipulated—unless an improvement could be measured, he would devise a system whereby problem children would lose their freedom of movement, be constantly monitored and assigned daily tasks in addition to their normal routines. He placed the onus on parents and teachers to affect a solution.

"We have borne many hardships and given up our entire lives for this mission," Bennett said. "The last thing I'm going to tolerate is a cadre of delinquents thinking they will walk all over me, their parents, teachers, and the other crewmembers. From this day on, I am holding everyone responsible for the behavior of our young generation. I cannot imagine, when we get to our destination, finding an advanced, intelligent society willing to cope with problematic people. We must deal with this problem right now."

The panel wrote the Code of Ethics and Conduct and presented it to the Commander. He reviewed it with his senior officer staff and found it acceptable. Every crewmember received a copy. They read it aloud at the beginning of each school session. The children were expected to answer questions regarding the code at any time from any officer encountered.

Bennett demanded the children learn strict military-style protocol. Young children at the age of five would learn the rudiments of proper behavior. He realized it would be the only way a successful mission could come to fruition.

*　*　*

The E—One continued at its maximum speed of five hundred thousand miles-per-hour.

Paul Bennett spent many hours on the bridge with his father and the other officers often assuming the role of pilot, affording him valuable experience. Commander Bennett did not object since he foresaw the time when Paul would officially step into the position of Commander.

The other six children born on the voyage, now seven years of age, showed superior intelligence and abilities for their ages, and happily evidenced a dramatic improvement in discipline and behavior.

Doctors French and Mallard had documented and charted all the children's progress, but they could not explain Paul and Elaine's ability to communicate by eye contact alone.

They were, however, encouraged by everything these two part-aliens had displayed. The medical team felt that when Paul and Elaine found a world in which to live and multiply, they would advance their kind at a pace never before imagined on Earth.

At age thirty-one, Paul and Elaine continued to amaze their graduate level educators and the E-One's crew. Paul's interests drew him increasingly to the bridge and his father's work.

Elaine had already earned her designation as an MD. Since there were no formal colleges aboard the E-One, she mentored under the close supervision of Doctors French, Mallard and Karley. At the rate she progressed, she would easily become their replacements as they became too old, disabled or died.

***

So far, Commander Bennett had performed twenty-three marriages. For some unknown reason, married life aboard the craft brought the couples a high degree of contentment and happiness. Not one divorce had been requested and the number of pregnant women increased to nineteen.

Chapter 42

Working solo on the bridge, Bennett opened sealed and time-dated orders from Earth Base that had been stored in the E-One's computers.

The message revealed a special code word the Pentagon had previously determined regarding the transfer of a nuclear weapons payload to an alien ship. For some strange reason, it also stated that Colonel Anderson be briefed regarding the transfer.

He summoned Anderson to the bridge. On arrival, he explained the plan in every detail and instructed him to make ready for the transfer.

Anderson went to the weapons bay, per Bennett's order, and moved the specified payload onto a flatbed carrier car. He then took it to cargo bay one. Once there, he called Bennett for further instructions.

"Stand by," Bennett said. "When I give you the order, open the bay doors and release the payload. Then secure the hatch and come to the bridge."

After Bennett learned the code word *Amber-eight*, he awaited the arrival of the alien craft.

A short time later, the E-One's scanners detected the alien ship. After closing to within one thousand yards, Bennett sent out an ultra-high-frequency encrypted message, requesting a response to the code.

In seconds he received the return transmission of 'Amber—eight' from the approaching alien ship.

Though tempted to begin a dialog with the aliens, Bennett followed the standing directive given by Earth Base, prohibiting him from doing so, as any unnecessary transmissions could compromise the security of the weapons transfer.

Bennett ordered Anderson to release the payload from the cargo bay, and observed it drifting away from the E—One.

Once it had reached a safe distance, he saw the alien ship's cargo port begin to open. A small robotic device exited and latched onto the payload ferrying it inside.

But Paul, having been his father's eyes since Bennett had only partial sight, caught something on the monitor that Bennett did not.

"Father, why did Anderson go with the payload into the alien ship?"

"What? Are you sure?" Bennett asked, alarmed.

"Yes, I'm sure," Paul said. "He rode the payload all the way and went in with it."

"Paul, Quick!" Bennett said, "Rewind and play the external video monitor tape on drive four."

Paul entered a command into the bridge's external video monitoring system to replay the last ten minutes of the weapons transfer. After reviewing it, Bennett too realized that Anderson entered the alien ship.

Bennett called out to Barnes on his communicator.

"Barnes, report to the bridge on the double."

"Yes sir," Barnes answered, "on my way."

"What's going on?" Paul asked.

"Paul, Major Anderson must have abandoned ship!"

"How could he do that when his own daughter is here with us?"

"I'll tell you how. His father Antar was not from Xeron. He went to Xeron from an enemy planet disguised as a defector. I've had my suspicions about Anderson ever since I realized he and McManus were a little too chummy."

"Who's McManus?" Paul asked, confused.

"Never mind about him," Bennett said. "For all we know *he* could be on that alien ship too."

"Barnes, we have a problem," Bennett said when Barnes arrived at the bridge. "Anderson defected to the alien ship positioned off our stern."

"Defected?" Barnes asked, his eyebrows rising in disbelief.

"Yes," Bennett said, "and now I'm beginning to think that McManus might be on that ship too. The government, NASA, the Pentagon and WASA were all duped into a scheme to steal our nuclear weapons." Bennett's face flushed.

"Commander," said Barnes, "are you telling me we made the mistake of giving an enemy alien ship nuclear weapons?"

"Yes Barnes," Bennett said. "That's what the Pentagon ordered as part of a secret effort to help a friendly planet. But that ship must be an imposter. We will discuss it later, but now go to the weapons storage section and inspect what is left. It's possible that Anderson may have played a few more tricks on us."

"Yes sir," Barnes said, "I'll get back to you after I check it out."

"Good, Barnes, and one more thing."

"Yes, Commander?"

"Be careful, Anderson may have set a trap."

"I'll be careful, Sir."

"What are we going to do?" Paul asked.

"We have to assume they'll try to attack and destroy our ship the first chance they get. We'll play their game for now by staying as close as possible to them."

"Why?" Paul asked.

"They can't strike while we're close," Bennett said. "They know we have powerful weapons and if they attacked, the detonation of our ship would destroy them also. I want you to break the news to Elaine about her father. It will be hard on her, but she has to know what he did. We'll keep our ship close to theirs while I meet with our senior officers."

"I'll go to her now," Paul said, "what should I say to her mother if I see her?"

"Nothing, I'll talk to her later. Just go," Bennett ordered.

Bennett sent out an emergency message to every crewmember.

"Attention, this is your Commander. Every man, woman, and child must put on his or her spacesuit and proceed on the double to the Deck Two Auditorium for further instructions."

Barnes reached the weapons section and called Bennett.

"Commander, it looks like Anderson knew what he was doing here."

"Why, what did you find?" Bennett asked.

"It appears he has armed one of the warheads."

"Damn!" Bennett yelled, "are you sure of that, Barnes? Exactly what did you find?"

"At first everything looked normal," Barnes said, "but when I went to the last missile, I discovered a cable running from its detonator control module to a black box."

"Whatever you do," Bennett said, "don't touch the box. Just tell me what it looks like."

"It's about twelve inches square and two inches thick," Barnes said. "There's a small pulsing red indicator on its top."

"What else do you see?" Bennett asked.

"Hold it," Barnes said tensely, "there's also a small digital display panel on the back of it. It's changing its value every second."

"Hurry up Barnes, read the number to me."

"It reads two-zero-four-zero-point-eight-seven-three one, Sir."

"Copy. Barnes, do not touch it! Just get out of there and return to the bridge."

Bennett sent a Code Ten to his senior staff. When they responded via communicator, they were ordered to report to the Bridge on the double. Only moments later Perkins, Corell, Butler and Staeb, joined Barnes and Bennett at the bridge. Bennett ran through the situation emphasizing either defusing or jettisoning the armed nuclear device in the weapons storage bay.

He briefed them on Anderson's defection and sabotage, but before he allowed amazement to set in, he ordered them to offer recommendations.

After deliberating, they concurred that the display represented the number of hours, minutes and seconds left until detonation. To a man, they decided defusing was the best avenue to take.

Bennett and Butler agreed and went to the weapons section. They had no choice—Bennett said a prayer and nervously disconnected the cable between the nuclear missile and the black box. Miraculously—nothing happened.

When he returned to the bridge, he briefed his officers. Following two hours of deliberation they came to the consensus their situation was dire indeed. A move away from the alien ship was imperative.

Meanwhile the E-One's laser pulse weapons had been aimed and readied. Even the slightest hint of a hostile move on the aliens' part would be their last.

His patience paid off when after ten hours of parallel travel the alien ship vanished ahead of them.

Having had no sighting of the alien ship for over a week, Bennett ordered a reduction in their alert status. An air of normalcy returned, but as a prudent extra precaution Bennett ordered their second Scout vehicle armed with nuclear missiles and deployed behind Scout One.

The tactical defensive maneuver proved to be one of Bennett's best since his decision to join the astronaut team and the mission.

After three months without any contacts, Scout One detected the presence of an approaching alien ship traveling on a direct intercept course toward the E-One. It became obvious that they intended to attack. By then, Anderson and his alien crew realized the nuclear device Anderson rigged to destroy the E-One failed. Their only mission would be to go back to the E-One for the kill.

Because of Scout One's early warning, Bennett was able to devise a brilliant defensive plan. He used Scout One to shield Scout Two. The alien ship's systems never detected Scout Two had been deployed.

Anderson without realizing it, gave the E-One crew the best advantage it could ever want by telling his alien superiors Scout One had no armaments. Unknown to Anderson, however, Bennett had Scout Two armed and deployed in a defensive move behind Scout One.

Bennett used Scout One as a decoy to get the alien ship into Scout Two's range by broadcasting garbage frequency radio beams toward their ship. He wanted to fight the battle as far away from the E-One as possible, even if he lost a Scout.

The E-One's senior officers joined Bennett at the bridge to observe the action. If the trap succeeded the aliens would detect Scout One's radio frequency transmissions blended with the targeting transmissions from Scout Two. In effect, the aliens would not even realize there were two Scouts.

After two hours of intense monitoring, the E-One's crew received confirmation that the aliens had closed in on Scout One. Better yet, once they realized it was a Scout and not the E-One, they veered off and headed straight for the E-One.

As hoped, the aliens never detected Scout Two, which had locked them on as a target.

Bennett looked at his fellow officers. They returned a confident grin as he held his finger over the fire control button.

"Commander..." Barnes started to say.

But before he could get another word out, Bennett pushed the button, sending Scout Two's four nuclear-tipped missiles toward the enemy. The time it took to strike their target seemed an agonizing eternity. Bennett ordered the E-One to full red alert with every weapon at its disposal prepared to make one final stand in case they missed.

The alien ship never saw what was coming and thirty minutes later, a huge fireball lit up the dark of space. Scouts One and Two both confirmed an intense nuclear blast had occurred. Moments later the Scouts reported—*no more contacts.*

By the time the cheers of the E-One's officers had subsided, the spent Commander Bennett had quietly left the bridge. He took his Journal with him to record the incident.

As he transcribed the blow-by-blow account of the battle, he came across a sheet of computer printout tucked in the front pocket of his Journal, which had only faint print indentations. Obviously, the printer's ribbon had broken. Curious, he held it up to a lamp and read the almost invisible message which had been sent directly after the first security code message regarding the weapons transfer:

ORIGINATION: The Pentagon, Washington D.C. 4 February, 2015

METHOD: Cryptographic Encode.

CLASSIFICATION: TOP SECRET EXTREMELY URGENT

DESTINATION: Commander Bennett E-One Mission

AUTHOR: LIEUTENANT GENERAL WILLIAMS Active, USAF

TO: COMMANDER PHILLIP BENNETT:

Disregard previous security-code assigned by former Colonel McManus/RE: *Amber eight* when it appears on your ship's computer. The replacement code = *EDEN-459*.

WARNING: Honor no other codes.

Bennett could not believe it. A broken printer ribbon had played a crucial part in the survival of an alien attack. If the message had been received as intended, the E-One without a doubt would have been destroyed for refusing the transfer.

"A broken printer ribbon," Bennett thought to himself.

"How lucky can you get?"

Chapter 43

Commander Bennett's communicator sounded. It was Dr. French.

"Go ahead doctor," Bennett responded.

"Commander," French said. "I'm sorry, but we just lost Barnes. He had a stroke."

"My God," Bennett said in shock. "He was one of my best astronauts, not to mention my best friend."

Too full of emotion to speak any longer, he ended the communication, just staring at Barnes's bridge station reflecting on their past decades together. He had lost his right-hand man.

* * *

Year 2043

Paul and Elaine continued to astound the elders with their intelligence, attractiveness, and hard work. A new dimension had expressed itself in their lives, which surprised neither their parents nor the rest of the crew. They were often seen spending time together, alone.

Their relationship seemed to be built on a mature intellectual level. Paul showed no outward affection toward her when others were around, but his actions in private, were another matter. Though discreet, it was obvious he took extra efforts to be close to her. She responded in kind and on several occasions, they were observed in each other's arms.

Elaine's mother noticed the attraction, and accepted it happily, as she had a high regard for Paul as well.

"Do you think you may marry Paul some day?" she asked Elaine.

Elaine looked into her mother's eyes and Lauren knew from that moment on she would indeed marry him. Elaine had communicated her answer without uttering a word.

In the year 2044, Bennett announced the marriage of his son, Paul, to Elaine Brown. He informed the crew the wedding day would be a holiday for all non-essential crewmembers.

On their wedding day, everyone gathered at the flower-adorned auditorium.

The bride looked radiant and beautiful as she approached the altar carrying a bouquet of white roses.

The ship's chaplain, Rev. Colonel John Conlon, greeted the couple at the altar. Both had been raised as Christians.

Rev. Conlon began with an opening prayer.

They were no ordinary couple. Paul and Elaine were the first children born outside the Earth's atmosphere and their talents and abilities were astounding. From now on, they were one, together. A perfect blend of human and alien bloodlines.

The rings they exchanged belonged to Paul's parents. Phil Bennett wanted the children to have them and they wore them with pride and love. The bride and groom beamed with joy after exchanging their vows and received a blessing from Reverend Conlon.

At the reception their friends offered brief anecdotes about the couple and wished them health, happiness, and a long life together, giving them gifts they had made to adorn their new private living quarters.

The newlyweds went on their honeymoon, which consisted of a ten-day leave. They spent their days as they wished. It became a custom for newlyweds aboard the ship to visit with all the other families and friends.

Paul's father gave the newlyweds a special wedding gift by commissioning both of them as First Lieutenants, thus making them officers of the E-One's crew.

One year later Elaine gave birth to a son, Christopher. Her pregnancy had accelerated at the same rate as her mother's, and the neural paths from Elaine to her unborn child were the same as those observed earlier before *her* birth.

They celebrated the birth of a girl, Lexa the following year. The infant's physical characteristics mirrored those of her brother.

By now, there had been seventeen births since the mission began. All of the newborns had done well, with one exception.

Fetal complications had developed for Lieutenant Rafaela Marino, an unmarried mother, during her first birth. The pregnancy became a borderline Caesarian delivery when the baby's movement through the birth canal had stalled.

Despite the recommendation of Dr. Bennett, Rafy as she was known, refused to take labor-inducing medication. Elaine had prescribed it, because her natural contractions had been weak even though the baby was well positioned for delivery. Elaine checked the baby's fetal heartbeat and found it acceptable.

Following five hours of labor, Jasmine Singh, an OB GYN resident, observed a sudden drop in the fetal heart rate and alerted Dr. Bennett who explained to Rafy it had become imperative for her to deliver the baby one way or the other.

But it was too late. The fetal heart rate dropped to a critical level. They performed an emergency Caesarian delivery. The child's reflexes and color were abnormal. However, he was breathing on his own, but the doctors feared he might have suffered brain damage from prolonged oxygen deprivation.

After six weeks, Dr. Bennett determined little Jonathan Marino indeed had suffered a degree of neurological impairment.

Rafaela contemplated terminating Johnny's life rather than burden the crew with a retarded child, but Commander Bennett's approval was tantamount. She requested an immediate meeting with the Commander along with Doctors Bennett, Mallard and Singh.

They met at the bridge at 09:00 hrs as planned.

"Doctors, do you certify we have a child with retardation?" Bennett asked.

"Yes Sir, I do," said Dr. Singh.

"And you, Dr. Bennett?" Commander Bennett asked.

Eden-459

"Yes, I concur," said Dr. Bennett.

"Dr. Mallard?"

"Yes."

"Lieutenant Marino," said Bennett, "I understand how you must feel and I'm truly sorry for what happened. It is hard for a mother to make this kind of decision alone. If you will allow, I'd be happy to give you as much guidance and support as you need."

"Commander," Marino said, "I am a single parent...but Jonathan's father wants very much to be part of his life and is willing to stand by me."

"I understand," Bennett said, "but why don't we listen to what the doctors have to say first? Maybe they will help us make a rational decision. Elaine, what do you think?"

"We have determined Johnny is moderately retarded." Elaine Bennett said. "Dr. Singh and I believe there's adequate support and expertise necessary to ensure he has a good quality of life."

"Commander," Dr. Mallard said. "I agree with Dr. Bennett. If Lieutenant Marino will accept the difficult challenge, and love her child, we stand to have a happy and welcome addition to our team. I am not in favor of terminating Jonathan's life."

Commander Bennett faced Rafaela.

"Do you have any questions or comments before I render my opinion?"

"Commander, after listening to the doctors—I want my baby," Marino said.

"Somehow I knew in your heart that's what you wanted," Bennett said.

"Commander, I was under the impression you wouldn't want the crew encumbered with the problems of a retarded child."

"There's one thing I value more than all else on this mission," said Bennett.

"And, father...that is?" Elaine asked her father-in-law.

"In a word—Life," he said. "By the way Rafy may I ask who Jonathan's father is?"

"I thought you knew, Commander. He's Captain Staeb."

Chapter 44

Year 2050

Bennett announced a general briefing for all senior officers, section heads and crew. At 08:00 hours, he and his senior officers, First Officer Colonel Paul Bennett, Colonel Anton Butler, Colonel Brian Black, and Doctors Mallard and Elaine Bennett arrived first and had taken their positions at the front of the auditorium. The other attendees filed in and took their places.

* * *

"I've assembled you here," Commander Bennett began, "to share the latest events concerning our ship-board family. As you are aware, we have had four more deaths in the past year. Colonel Barnes from a massive stroke, Colonel Corell of heart failure, Dr. French of cancer, and Elaine's dear mother Lauren Brown of pneumonia following a surgical procedure.

"They were all dedicated astronauts who gave their entire lives to our mission and served us with honor. Each of them will be missed, but must always be remembered as significant contributors toward our final objective: Finding a new home.

"Please let us all bow our heads for a moment of prayer for our beloved fallen astronauts."

After a moment of silent reflection, Bennett regained his composure.

"It gives me great pleasure to inform you our new Co-Commander will be my son Colonel Paul Bennett, who will follow in Colonel Barnes's footsteps with the same level of dedication I am sure."

The crew agreed to a person with Paul's appointment, offered their congratulations expressing their full support. He had been the one chosen to complete his father's dream. The one and

Eden-459

only person with the knowledge, experience, energy, strength and drive to get them safely to a New World.

"I have another personnel announcement of equal importance to make. From today forward, Dr. Elaine Bennett has the helm as the ship's chief physician."

She too received unanimous approval and respect for her years of hard work and study in the field of medicine.

"I congratulate Paul and Elaine for their outstanding achievements and wish them well in their new roles."

Bennett went to Paul and Elaine and embraced them. He felt proud of his son and Elaine's accomplishments and knew he had made the right choices for the mission.

He thought to himself what a humble experience for WASA's medical team it would have been had they known of Elaine's abilities, and in particular for Dr. Hunt, since he had ordered her termination.

"I've decided to share some exciting information about our mission with all of you," Bennett said. He then paused, attempting to overcome a dizzy spell. Not wanting to draw attention to himself, he pulled himself together and continued.

"We have long suspected the pyramids of Earth were more than just burial sites. From an astronomical viewpoint, we felt they held far greater implications.

"Our course has been set to follow the exact heading indicated by the former Giant Pyramid at Giza in Egypt. Before the Earth's destruction, radio signals were received from that same location, specifically from Planet Xeron. The planet holds exciting potential for us." Bennett downplayed the positives concerning Xeron. He knew the real reason for traveling to that particular planet. It was friendly and habitable. Even more exciting—it was his ancestral home.

In the 1950's, a covert Pentagon program was instituted. Its charter was to accomplish the human colonization of Xeron. The only aspect in question would be the timeframe. But now, it was only a matter of years away, not decades.

"But before we get our hopes up, we must be sure Xeron holds all we think it does. Imagine the letdown and disappointment if we were wrong? Are there any questions?"

"Commander, if Xeron fails to meet our expectations, what will we do?" Elaine Bennett asked.

"That area of the galaxy is a hot bed of solar systems and planets similar to Earth," Bennett explained. "There are numerous possibilities for us to explore. In addition, we have all the resources needed and are capable of stretching our alternate planet search program for another fifty years if necessary."

"Commander, our ETA is the year 2110," Colonel Black said. "It is obvious that the majority of our crew will die before we get there. Will we have an adequate number of personnel to continue, assuming we find Xeron habitable?"

"We have estimated our ship's population will be in the neighborhood of one hundred sixty. We also have an ideal mix of couples who have been providing us with an excellent birth rate."

"Are there any other reasons for our course toward Xeron?" Paul Bennett asked.

"Somehow I knew *you* would ask that question," Bennett replied.

"Why shouldn't I ask?"

"It's okay, I don't have a problem with it. The answer is yes. But I regret to say, to elaborate further at this time isn't prudent."

Bennett knew Paul would learn every cogent detail from his Journal when the time was right.

"So please have patience, in time everyone will hear all I know about the planet. Let me add, I believe we *are* headed to a world which stands an excellent chance not only of being hospitable, but also of holding intelligent life forms."

The group thirsted for more, but trusted Bennett had his reasons for not divulging everything he knew.

After the briefing, Colonel Black spoke to Commander Bennett.

"Sir, may I have some time with you later today at the bridge?"

"Of course, Black. Is there something I can do for you now?"

"Sir, it's better if I speak with you about it later."

"Fine colonel...15:00 hours?"

"Yes, Sir. Oh, one more thing."

"Yes? What is it?"

"I think it's advisable that Paul, Elaine, Butler, and Perkins be there also."

"Very well, they'll be there."

"Thank you, Commander."

Colonel Black, age thirty-three, and the youngest of the senior officers, was born aboard the E-One in 2017 and spent his entire life since age ten studying physics, mathematics, astrophysics, astronomy, and cosmology. Everyone aboard the ship viewed him as a social misfit, albeit a nice one, but when they required assistance with difficult scientific and mathematical questions, it was Black they sought out.

Colonel Black considered Albert Einstein his idol. He even skipped meals and sleep allowing him more time to concentrate on formulae, especially when it involved light, time warps, and their effects and counter-effects. He was one of fewer than twelve people who ever comprehended The Einstein Theory of Relativity.

Because of his extraordinary abilities, he proved himself valuable to the mission in many ways. When the effects of unknown objects needed analysis, Black answered the call. No matter what—a star, black hole or other strange gravitational anomaly, he rose to the occasion. His expertise proved vital in keeping the E-One on a safe course.

Whenever he moved about the ship, his computer went with him. It had been known to almost everyone that he even slept with it, in particular when he started a lengthy and complicated mathematical formula, which took billions of computer cycles to complete. When he awoke, his answer awaited him. He had a red light installed on the outside of his living compartment entry hatch to warn any visitors he was busy and did not wish to be disturbed.

Because of his incredible knowledge and dedication to his field, he received early promotions. He may not have been the greatest conversationalist, but everyone thought he was equal to Einstein when it came to intelligence.

* * *

Black went to his computer and prepared all the necessary charts and graphs to make his presentation to Bennett.

At 15:00 hours, he arrived at the bridge. From the look on his face, Commander Bennett knew he had something vital to share with the group.

Black mounted a dozen charts and graphs on a plotting board and started his computer. He remained silent until he was fully prepared for his presentation.

"Are you ready *now* colonel?" Commander Bennett said, becoming impatient with the delay.

"Yes," Black said, "thank you. I have made quite a surprising discovery. Watch..."

Black suspended a small steel sphere over Commander Bennett's plotting board. He asked Paul to nudge it to his left. As Paul did so, the sphere moved the distance of the plotting board.

"What's the point, colonel?" Paul asked.

"Didn't you see what happened?" Black asked. "It began to slow down somewhat before it reached the end of the board. Do it again, but this time everyone watch closely."

Paul repeated what he had done. Again, he nudged the sphere to the left. As the sphere moved across the board it did indeed slow down.

"Yes Brian," Paul said. "I saw it slow down."

"Black, what does that mean?" asked Commander Bennett.

"Okay Paul, do it again. Only this time move it to your right."

Paul nudged it to his right.

Eden-459

"That's strange Brian," Perkins said, "the sphere began to speed up. Am I correct?"

"Exactly. And that's why I'm here."

"Brian," Bennett said, "without a doubt your demonstration shows something unusual. "The sphere behaved in an unexpected way. But, what does that mean?"

"It's quite simple: In order to understand it in technical and mathematical terms we need to spend a number of hours calculating and crunching numbers. Is that what you want, Commander?"

"No, Brian. That would not help us. Please explain it in simple terms?" Bennett said sighing.

"Of course," Brian said. "The bottom line is that we are accelerating."

"Accelerating, colonel?" Perkins asked.

"I don't want to frighten you," said Black, "but we are approaching a *black hole*."

"A black hole?" Bennett shouted. "Perkins why haven't *you* determined we were headed for disaster?"

"Sir," Black interrupted, "it's not her fault. Sometimes these things are encountered with little or no warning. They cannot be detected easily unless you notice their effects. If we had not seen the change in speed at this time, by the time it was noticed it might have been too late. The rate of our acceleration seems small *now*, but when we get closer, it will become much more noticeable."

"Okay Colonel Black," Bennett said, "how will the ship be impacted? Are we in serious trouble?"

"Only if we don't take proper actions," Black responded.

"Please explain," a jittery Perkins asked. "I don't like the sound of any of this at all. Could we perish?"

"Let's keep calm," Paul said, "and listen to what Black has to say."

"Our situation involves The Einstein Theory of Special Relativity," Black continued. "To put it in simple terms: We are physically being drawn toward a black hole and accelerating at a steady rate. Also, there is no difference between what we feel as gravity and what we feel as acceleration. The two forces seem the same. Now here is where things get technical. There are three main factors we are going to encounter and must consider as we continue toward the black hole.

"First," Black went on, "when we get closer we will be traveling at over half the speed of light. That means we are going to be subject to the effects of Time Intervals.

"Second, the E-One will approach the hole's quadrants in an off-center attitude, which means we will be doing what's called, Frame Dragging.

"Third, The Einstein Special Theory of Relativity takes over. In short, when a space ship gets closer to large areas of dense matter, time slows. Conversely, when a ship leaves the dense area, time accelerates."

"How will that affect us?" Paul Bennett asked. "And how can we deal with it?"

"If we prepare for it now—we'll be okay," Black explained, "and we will have a good chance of getting to our target planet in one piece. But I must warn you—if we fail to do what is needed we *will* be in peril."

"Can you please get to the bottom line?" Commander Bennett asked. "Exactly what may we expect if we do everything right? And when do we have to start making preparations?"

"First we must retrieve our Scout vehicle," Black said, "then calculate where the exact center of the black hole is located. After we have accomplished that we must position our ship to enter its Time Frames at a ninety-degree angle within the quadrant we want to exit. Just prior to our ship becoming a pure energy mass at the speed of light, we must bring our engines to a full burn, which will allow us to slow down enough to remain atomically stable. Assuming we are successful we will gain back the time we lost while inside the hole's quadrant."

"Black," Perkins asked, "how can we possibly slow the ship down by bringing our engines to full power?"

"Dawn," Black said, "remember we are not dealing with real time here. In fact, without even realizing it we'll have lost eighty years of time inside the edge of the black hole."

"I can't say I understand everything you're saying, but are you telling us we will be in a time warp?" Paul Bennett asked.

"Aha! See? We do have someone who is catching on to what I am saying. Paul is one hundred percent correct. We are going to lose eighty years of atomic time to the black hole, but what will happen next is impressive."

"Let me take a wild guess," Bennett said, "we get the time back when we escape?"

"Very good, Commander. But you are only half correct."

"How so?"

"We are going to gain back only forty years of the eighty we will have lost."

"If that's true," Perkins said, "what happens to us during the forty years?"

"Great question, Dawn," Black said. "That's where we gain the advantage I mentioned. What will happen is that we will never miss the forty years. In actuality, we will have traveled eighty years in atomic time in a matter of forty. The net *theoretical* effect will be that we traveled closer to our destination at nearly twice the speed of light. We will give up only forty years of real-time at the expense of eighty years of atomic time. Thanks to the black hole, we will have had our first-ever time warp."

"All of this is getting pretty *fuzzy*," Bennett said. "Brian, tell me, what will the crew experience during this so-called time warp?"

"That's the nice thing about it, Commander," Black said. "Nobody will even know it happened, except us of course."

"Colonel," Paul said, "do you suppose other intelligent travelers have been using time warps to their advantage for millennia?"

"I see no other way—I believe they have," Black said.

"*Fantastic*, Colonel," Commander Bennett said scratching his head. "It sounds to me as though we are going to be in atomic hibernation."

"You could call it that. In fact, I think I will give you credit for coining that phrase. I see two more questions I am surprised no one has asked.

"What?" Perkins asked, in a slight state of shock.

"The year we will be in when we get back to real-time and how many more years we must travel to get to our destination?" Black said.

"*I'm* interested in knowing that," Commander Bennett said.

"We will return to real-time in the year 2090 and will need to travel another twenty years to get to our target."

Bennett shook his head and said to everyone with a chuckle, "I think we'd better go pack!"

From then on, just as Colonel Black had calculated, the E-One continued to accelerate. The crew felt the increasing pseudo-gravity as the ship went faster and faster. Once the ship had accelerated to almost half the speed of light,—it happened.

In what seemed like just a heartbeat, the E-One went from the year 2050 to 2090. Commander Bennett called his officers to the bridge.

"Brian, why don't we feel gravitation any longer?"

"Commander," Black said, "because we have just completed eighty years of travel in forty years."

Are you telling me that it's over?" Bennett asked, "We've warped toward our destination?"

"Yes, Commander. It is done and we are fine. We have not only survived a black hole, but we have used it to our advantage."

"Wait a minute...wait just a minute...what?" Bennett said, befuddled.

Black could not suppress his laughter. He tried to speak in between gasps of air.

"Commander, let me try to make it simple. We traveled the equivalent of eighty years in a moment. The Black Hole consumed eighty years of atomic time, and when we escaped its effects, we gained back half of that time, or forty years."

"Yeah, and I'm a chimpanzee!" Bennett said. "That's simple? I don't know what the hell you just said."

"In the end," Black said, "there's one more phenomenon that we'll all be subjected to." Black hesitated while the others cocked their ears.

"Black," said Bennett, "stop taunting us and spit it out."

"All right Sir," Black said with a grin, "every person on the ship will experience an age reversal of about forty years."

Dead silence prevailed—no one even dared to ask how.

"Let me give you a brief explanation," Black said. "Because we've been traveling at five hundred thousand miles—per—hour for all these years, our internal biological clocks have slowed. That is why you, Commander, appear to be only about sixty years of age instead of your actual eighty.

The group began to look at one another, studying their age wrinkles and hair color.

"We have gained another twenty-year biological clock advantage from the time warp we experienced—thanks to the black hole."

"Go on Black," said Paul Bennett. "What's the bottom line in all this?"

"It simply means that if Commander Bennett lived long enough to see Xeron, he would be at the ripe old age of about one hundred forty in Earth years. But, his physical age would appear to be that of a person of one hundred."

"That's still not young enough for me," Commander Bennett said, "What about Paul and Elaine?"

"They will be about one hundred years of age in Earth terms, but will have the physical characteristics of people nearing sixty. Also, their children will look like thirty year olds, when in actuality they'll be nearing seventy."

"All right Black," Commander Bennett said, "I'm getting depressed. Are you through now?"

"I'm through Commander, unless there's something else you would like explained."

"No Black," Bennett said, "thank you, but we've heard *quite* enough for one day."

Black picked up his computer and charts nearly passing out from laughter.

"Commander," Black asked, "then may I be excused, sir?"

"Please, please—yes, by *all* means, go," Bennett said. He looked at his control panel and shook his head.

Colonel Perkins was still sitting in a corner of the bridge with her eyes wide opened. She did not know whether to laugh, cry, or scream. Shaking, she got up and in silence and left the bridge.

Bennett ordered Scout One re-deployed.

Chapter 45

Year 2090
　　Planet Xeron—a New Hope for the human race.
　　With twenty more years to go before reaching Xeron, Commander Bennett would not live long enough to see it. His son Paul would assume command of the mission.
　　The aging Commander Bennett began to lose his strength and his reasoning abilities. At times, Colonel Black had to wake him to give him updates. The Commander also experienced shortness of breath and dizziness.
　　He visited his daughter-in-law, Elaine at the Medical Unit for an evaluation. After a battery of tests her diagnosis was clear: He suffered from severe coronary artery disease.
　　Following an angiogram, she determined that Bennett's condition was serious. Because of his enlarged heart and the severity of the damage to his arteries, the treatment of choice was cholesterol reducing, blood pressure and blood thinning medications.
　　To avoid stress, Elaine suggested he consider stepping down from command.
　　Bennett trusted Elaine and asked a favor of her.
　　"Please don't tell Paul how ill I am. I don't want him worrying about me."
　　"Fine father, I won't say anything."
　　"Thanks Elaine," he said and slowly left sickbay.

* * *

　　One fateful day on the bridge, Commander Bennett, Paul at his side, checked routine object scanner reports received from the Scout.
　　"Paul," asked Bennett, "would you please take the bridge for awhile?"

"Are you okay, father?"

"I just need some rest."

Bennett's voice sounded raspy as he began telling his son something he had never revealed before.

"I want you to hear these things from me before you read them in my Journal after I'm gone."

"Of course, father," said Paul, "what is it?"

Bennett sighed as he straightened up in his seat. He gathered his strength, leaned over to Paul, looked into his eyes, and tried to speak, but instead, lost consciousness his head slumping.

"Father! Father!" Paul called. But, there was no response. Paul placed his forefingers onto his father's wrist. There was no pulse, his eyes were rolled back into their sockets, and he was not breathing.

Sure his father had suffered a heart attack, he made a frantic call to Elaine. She arrived within moments. Paul sat helpless while Elaine made several desperate attempts to resuscitate him. It was not to be.

Elaine closed Commander Bennett's eyes, went to Paul and embraced him.

"Dear, your father's heart had been seriously impaired for several years. He never wanted you to know—he wanted to spare you any worry."

For a moment, Paul sat gazing out at the stars contemplating the future without his father.

When their children entered the bridge, they all stood by the fallen Commander until Reverend Juan Castillo arrived to give him Last Rights. Paul embraced his children and reflected on his father's life.

"He is in God's care now," Reverend Castillo said, placing a crucifix over the Commander's heart and praying. Turning to leave, Rev. Castillo handed Paul Commander Bennett's onyx ring.

"Your father gave this to me when I took my final vows and was ordained by Reverend Conlon some time ago," Castillo said. "He instructed me to give it to you when he died. He said it has special abilities that would help you in finding your alien roots when you reach planet Xeron."

Paul recalled his father saying the ring had been passed down from his grandfather Luxor who gave it to him when he completed his astronaut training.

Paul placed the ring on his finger.

That afternoon Reverend Castillo made an announcement to the rest of the crew.

"I regret to inform you our Skipper, Commander Bennett, has died. A funeral service will commence tomorrow at 12:00 hours."

Paul had his father's cremated remains placed into the same urn with his mother's. He knew that was what they would have wanted. Being together for eternity.

* * *

The last of Earth's progeny continued on its voyage to Xeron.

Paul read his father's Journal for the first time. He discovered what his father sought to tell him with his last breath. It explained in full the circumstances of his grandfather's origin. It revealed why his father and Anderson had scars on the sides of their hands. It told of a place called Roswell, where his grandfather landed on Earth and began a new life. It cited every trial and tribulation the crew of the E-One faced from the day it departed Earth.

The Journal detailed the building of an International Space Station. How each piece had been systematically lifted into orbit and assembled. It told of numerous experiments that yielded many key results for the success of the E-One's mission.

It exposed his father's love for his beloved mother, Eva. She was his heart and soul.

Reading on, he began to see an image of his father depicting his true nature. Bennett was half alien, but truly embraced human emotions, especially *love*.

He always fought for what was right and fair. When he saw injustice, it pained him deep within his heart. This was the reason he confronted and challenged Henry Corbin over the years. He viewed Corbin as a weak and chronic *yes man* for the Pentagon. Had Phil Bennett been in charge, the alien insiders would never have achieved any of their destructive goals.

Sadly, it told about his father-in-law, Bill Anderson who was the second alien assigned to the mission. Anderson, Dr. Hunt and McManus had all deceived WASA, the Pentagon, and Commander Bennett, but in the end—failed.

Anderson and Dr. Hunt conspired to terminate the first child born aboard the space station simply because it was female. A girl did not fit into their plans. Paul read about his father's gallant fight with Director Corbin to save the child. How he, French and Mallard put their jobs on the line.

The Journal explained Anderson's evil destructive plan to cause the mission to fail in its attempt to reach Xeron. Not even the fact that his own daughter Elaine was aboard stopped him from attempting to destroy the E-One space ship.

He read about his father's true reasons for joining the E-One's mission, which was much more than just scientific achievement. He had a hidden sincere personal charter—to blend Earth's people with the people of Xeron.

What Paul read helped him to understand why Xeron had been targeted as their destination. The Xeronians indeed had the technology to travel about the galaxy, but were under possible siege and unable to defend their world against a hostile force from the planet Sadarem. They were not warriors and found the need to build and store defensive weapons repugnant, but necessary.

Paul discovered many facts about the Xeronian people. The Journal described their way of life in detail. The information he gleaned from the Journal strengthened his resolve to get there.

To help protect them from planet Sadarem's attempts to take them over, the E-One held a hidden charter. It carried a cargo of nuclear weapons, which were to be transferred to a Xeronian ship many years before. But shrewd evil aliens infiltrated the

Pentagon and tricked them into ordering the E-One to share its nuclear weaponry with *their* ship instead. Later they attempted to destroy the E-One. However, Bennett's ingenious battle strategy proved successful and the alien ship was destroyed.

Commander Paul Bennett carried the onerous responsibility for transporting the last human offspring to a New World. The possibility that Paul might still have living alien ancestry on Xeron sustained his energies to succeed.

The haunting thought of Xeron having been taken over by an evil civilization persisted, however. The only way for Paul Bennett and his crew to find out for sure was to visit the planet.

He began to orchestrate an operational plan of approach. His first directive was to send the Scouts into orbit around the planet to scan its surface and monitor it for intelligent activity. From there, a *Chess game* began.

Only after he was convinced no threats existed could he consider sending a landing party to the surface. After devising his plan, he consulted with his senior officers to improve it and fill in any details he might have overlooked.

Paul sensed there were other hidden pieces of information as to why the Xeronians needed help from Earth. He went through the rest of his father's personal files and made a discovery that led to more questions than answers. It was a file labeled 'UNITED STATES ARMY the PENTAGON, WASHINGTON, DC—TOP SECRET—A-51-USAF-001947.'

The file contained a report that explained why the Xeronians traveled to Earth soon after realizing the atomic bomb had been tested. Planet Xeron had none of the elements needed to build defensive nuclear weapons.

The report further told of how the United States Government communicated on a regular basis with Xeronian visitors and even brought Luxor and Antar to the Pentagon from time to time.

Paul thought the time was right to share his father's words with his crew, and met with his senior officers to inform them of his findings.

Martin J. Stab

They decided the E-One should be put on high alert until they reached Xeron. Though no intelligent signals were detected coming from the planet, the possibility Xeron had been taken over by a hostile enemy was real.

* * *

By now, only four of the original astronauts from Earth survived. None of them were expected to live more than a few months and would never see Xeron.

The population aboard the E-One had increased to one hundred sixty-six. The average age of the astronauts was about sixty years. Though they were content with their life aboard the ship, they all eagerly desired to find a habitable planet on which to live and flourish.

Chapter 46

The long, arduous journey neared its end as the year 2110 arrived. The E-One reversed its position and at thirty percent power began to slow its speed as it bore down on Xeron.

After slowing to half their maximum speed, Commander Paul Bennett and his crew calculated they had to keep the ship in the reverse position and increase thrust to forty percent. They did not want to overshoot their destination. If they did, it would require months of backtracking.

Bennett knew the slowdown maneuver would make life aboard the ship difficult for a while, but it had to be done. Moving at two hundred fifty thousand miles-per-hour, the E-One's engines' thrust had been increased to forty five percent. They kept this power setting active for two days, and at a speed of twenty five thousand miles-per-hour, Bennett ordered thrust reduced to twenty percent.

Traveling fifteen thousand miles-per-hour, the engines were shut down. The E-One maintained itself in orbit one hundred twenty miles above the surface of Xeron.

Maintaining a stable orbit while the crew rested, the Scout vehicle Snoop traveled in a lower orbit scanning more and more of the planet's surface. There were no signs of life and no intelligent incoming signals.

Bennett did not rule out his hope that this was an intentional silence.

* * *

Bennett made his final entries into the ship's log. He reread his father's Journal to refresh his recollections.

He gave great credit to the many dedicated personnel who helped carry the last remnants of Earth's civilization to a New World. He had no problem with documenting the continued voyage, but he was frustrated he could not yet tell whether life still existed on Xeron.

His first edict originated from his father's request to honor the first casualty of the mission. He ordered that the previously mapped and named Samaritan Plateau would be called the *Richard Greaves Plateau.*

In his heart, he had always wished to find a planet with an intelligent civilization. He held his father's Journal dear. He hoped he had the key to the connection between his father, his alien grandfather's origin, and the planet. Once there, he planned to make the search for life forms a high priority.

The crew became more and more enthusiastic as the images of the planet began to reveal details of its surface. Oceans with indigo blue water, green vegetation, forests, lakes, rivers, and snow-capped mountains were evident. Infrared scanners found no active volcanoes.

Bennett's curiosity got the better of him when one of the images sent back to the E-One from Snoop showed a large object on the planet's surface. He ordered a closer look using Snoop's high definition telescopic lens camera. The image baffled him.

"Black, come to the Forward Bridge," he said pressing his communications button. "I think you'll find this interesting."

"Ten-four, Commander, on my way." Black arrived at the Bridge to find Bennett staring at his display.

"Yes, Commander, what do we have?"

"I can't say for sure, but doesn't that look like a pyramid?" Bennett asked.

Black studied the screen for a moment.

"Commander, I don't think the object *looks* like a pyramid. It *is* a pyramid. Let's send Snoop down lower for a better look."

"Ten four Black, on the next pass we'll get it down to one hundred ten miles. The zoom option should be able to confirm it for sure."

"I agree. Why do you think the Pyramid is here?" Black asked.

"I guess we'll have to find out from whoever built it."

On the next pass over the area, Scout One assumed an altitude of one hundred ten miles. This time Bennett and Black watched the real-time image being sent by Scout One's camera.

Black pointed at something.

"There it is, Commander...dead center. Let's zoom in for a better look."

Without a doubt, the object was a pyramid. In fact, it could be a twin to the Great Pyramid that once existed in Egypt, only three times larger.

The bells went off in Bennett's head.

"Of course Black," Bennett said, "the pyramid back on Earth must have been used for communications with this planet for thousands of years. Now we'll have to ask the Xeronians why."

"If there are any Xeronians," Black said.

"Yes, if," said Bennett.

After several weeks of studying the images received from the Scout vehicles and those from their on-board scanners, Commander Bennett scheduled a planning session with his senior officers. The purpose: To evaluate the viability of a manned landing.

Bennett knew the dangers of visiting an unknown planet were real and many things could go wrong. If they did not build a thorough plan, it could mean trouble when they got to the surface.

Bennett enlisted his senior scientist Dr. Luk, and a dozen of his best-qualified crewmembers to build a list of logistical needs before landing on Xeron. From there, he had a solid agenda of essentials to be verified by Scoop for landing an exploration party.

Bennett ordered Scoop to be sent to the surface to gather the necessary samples for analysis. Still, no findings were made for alien presence, intelligence, radio waves, or structures, except for the pyramid. All other tests showed no apparent reason why they should not attempt a landing.

There were vast amounts of vegetation in the form of fruits, grains, and vegetables.

On the final Scoop survey, two jeep-type rover vehicles were delivered to the proposed landing site for use during exploration.

"Black, from what we can see of Xeron's environment," Bennett said, "it's a land of plenty."

Bennett scheduled a surface landing the next day and a five-man exploration team readied for the trip aboard Scoop. Heavy with gear, food supplies for one week, medical kits, cameras, tents, sleeping bags, communications devices, compasses, and maps, made from Snoop's radar imaging systems—they boarded the Scout, which had been retrofitted into a shuttle vehicle.

In just one hour and fifteen minutes, the life-long journey from Earth would be over.

The shuttle made a soft landing on the surface raising a cloud of dust. When the landing party set foot on the planet, they felt something they never felt before: Gravity. Though during the voyage everyone had been exposed to some semblance of gravity in a centrifuge-type exerciser, the real thing proved exasperating, difficult and burdensome.

The landing party had to crawl like toddlers to travel just a few hundred yards to the shelter of trees and natural canopy. They needed to learn something all humans had taken for granted back on Earth: How to walk.

* * *

Colonel Black exited the shuttle first. It was now or never as he inhaled the first breath of pure and warm Xeronian air.

"Follow me men, the air is good," he said turning to his team.

Crawling on the Xeronian surface on their hands and knees, they discovered something far beyond anything they could have imagined. The rich dark soil gave off a sweet aroma, and the entire plateau looked like a tropical paradise.

Bouquets of colorful wild flowers were everywhere offering up their beauty and pleasing scents. Streams of crystal clear mountain water cascaded over rocks from high snow-covered peaks above the plateau.

Varieties of bright colored birds sang, and fish jumped out of small ponds catching insects.

The natural canopy bordering the plateau held dozens of beautiful, blossoming fruit trees. What looked like banana trees held fruit almost two feet long. The entire area was purely inviting.

"This place is incredible," Black said. "I know the Commander and the crew will be excited hearing what we've found."

After setting up a temporary base camp near a stream, Black radioed Commander Bennett.

"Xeron Base to E-One. Come in. Xeron Base to E-One. Come in, please."

"This is E-One," Bennett acknowledged, "go ahead, Xeron Base."

"Commander," Black spoke with great emotion, "it's Eden here. I think we're home!"

"Thank God!" Bennett said. "Stay close to your base and keep alert. I will get the rest of the crew ready for the shuttle trip to join you at first light. Get the tents up and ready. Until then, I want a radio report every hour on the hour."

"Ten-four," Black said.

Back on the E-One, Bennett prepared the remaining crew and families for their transition from a lifetime of uncertainty and danger to their beginning in a New World. He asked everyone to thank God for a safe arrival.

He made his final entries into his journal and reflected on everything that had occurred during the long voyage. He gave great credit to all the astronauts and families who sacrificed so much, not least of which their lives, for the success of the mission.

The E-One had performed well. Its new and permanent function—a space station. The ship's nuclear and laser weaponry would be left aboard intact, but disarmed in the hope they would never be needed. Through the night, shuttle after shuttle carried all the necessary equipment and supplies to the surface of Xeron.

The next morning Paul Bennett, Elaine and their children stood near the ship's exit port watching the last groups of twenty travelers board the shuttles for their trip to the planet's surface.

"Where are the Xeronians?" Elaine asked.

"So far," Paul said, "we haven't detected a single shred of evidence that there *are* any Xeronians."

"But Paul, you told me your father clearly said in his Journal that his ancestors lived on Xeron. And how your grandfather Luxor traveled to Earth from here over a hundred years ago."

"Yes, he did," Paul said. "But he also wrote about a great pending battle the Xeronians faced with another planet in this solar system. The purpose for the weapons we carried on our ship all these years was to help them defeat their aggressors, but you see how long it took us to deliver them. We may have arrived too late."

"Could they have survived the attack without them?" Elaine asked.

"I don't know. I'm sure we'll find out what happened once we investigate."

By nightfall, he and his family were the last ones to depart the E-One. For them, it was a bittersweet moment as he carried all the memories of the past and hopes for the future into an Eden-like New World.

"What's that noise?" Paul asked.

"I don't know," Elaine answered, "but it came from your onyx ring."

Printed in the United States
1068400003B/176